Grand Mal Press

Published by:
Grand Mal Press
Harvard Building
280 B Route 130
Suite 2, Office 176
Sandwich, MA 02644 USA

ISBN: 978-0-9829459-0-2
Library of Congress Cataloging-in-Publication Data:

Campbell, Zoot/Zombie Bitches from Hell
p.   cm.

Cover art by Michael Lindsey

First Edition

ZOMBIE BITCHES FROM HELL

CHAPTER 1

I'm keeping this journal in long hand since all the power has gone off—yesterday in this area, anyway. Heard the shut-downs started back East and spread like a wave toward the West. Took three weeks at least but nothing could be done to stop it. Just too many dead men at the switches.

I'm Kent Zimmer, anchor newsman for KWAK out of Denver, Colorado. Whatever I may have recorded into my camcorder may never be accessible again. Frankly, this hand-writing may never be accessible again. But maybe I should begin at the beginning or at least at the beginning of the end. It sounds cheesy—is cheesy—but it's the goddamn cheesy truth.

We were all real proud eight months ago when Charlotte Smith became the first woman president of these United States. I suppose it was going to be a foregone conclusion that women would win a majority in both houses of Congress, too. Women from both parties and one or two that no one ever heard of until a year or so ago won big. Guess it was long overdue. But it was the year of the woman. And why not? They couldn't even vote a hundred years ago. Not in this country anyway. And now they not only got the vote but everything that goes along with it, I guess. I remember broad-casting the network tallies just after the polls closed on the West Coast. Actually, I bet Jennifer that George Fulbright would win. It just seemed more natural and he was as natural a TV generation candidate could be. Jen is my fiancée and while she lives on Cape Cod, we met at a medical convention she was attending here in Denver. I was covering it for the station and she was a medical researcher talking about a new anti-viral concoction that was developed in NYC along with her team at Harvard Medical. It was a breakthrough, alright. Based on human genome transference or some such process that was too complicated for me to understand when she told me about it, let alone my trying to remember it now three years later.

If you're hoping I'm going to tell you what Jen looked like and smelled like and talked like and fucked like, think again. You're not going to wack off with visions of Jen in your head. I know that self-abuse has become the national pastime since the "GaGa," but you'll have to remember somebody else or conjure up some vision of a chick before she began to rot. This is no easy trick. Once you've seen one of them up close and personal, it's hard to go back.

Maybe you're a lucky one and your wife or daughter or mom is still near you and you're waiting for the GaGa to hit her, hoping it won't happen. I'm thinking Jen is one of the lucky ones and I'm going to bet my life on it because it isn't life anymore without her. I'm going to get to her no matter what or how long it takes.

I've got this idea; it's more than an idea. It's my only hope and I think the best shot at getting across this country. I'll be using the prevailing winds, west to east. Taking a hot air balloon. Not just any balloon, either. I ran one of my feature stories, not long ago, on a man that used a mylar-oleate bonding process to create a high altitude balloon that was impervious to the weather and held the heat in longer than anything previously known. There is not much of a chance to get across with one tank of propane, but I am going to try. With luck and a shove from the El Niňo transfer, it could work. Food's another matter. I'll have to land at some point for provisions. But anything worth having is worth . . . well, maybe your life.

I need to travel light. I got a pistol but I'm not much of a marksman. I also got MG my mutt with me; he's too good a pal and has helped me get through some tough times. I can't leave him behind and I can't kill him. No way. He's fifty pounds of muscle and grit with a heart bigger than a Volkswagen. Jen and me picked him up at the pound. She said she thought he had a face like Mel Gibson, the geezer version not the young dude chasing wackos in Mad Max. So I named him MG—and not for that old Brit car you sometimes see riding around with bailing wire holding it together, so if you don't know what that is, you won't get confused anyway in case you're a dumbass reading this and maybe all the books have been eaten up too. But no matter. He's coming with me.

And I think my camcraman, Tim, will be going along for the ride. Known him since I started out at the station as a features reporter. You know, the idiot that interviews those skinny assholes that just ran the Denver Marathon. Or some knucklehead that grew the world's largest tomato in his bathtub by pissing on it three times a day. Or a woman who got hauled off for having 127 cats in her house. You should have seen her after she caught the disease. No, maybe you shouldn't have. You'd be losing sleep for a month the same way I did.

Now Tim, he's got a story but I'm going to have to tell it. He barely talks much these days, and definitely not about that, not after his wife ate their newborn son. He's kind of a hippy, or he was, but he's still good with a camera and as good a shot with a 30.06 as you'll ever meet. And he knows how to fly the balloon. Used to work one at the County Fair before he got his break into show biz. Some break. His dad taught him everything he knows. One of those survivalist types that we used to laugh at. Nobody's laughing anymore. They're the men that are mostly still alive—in outposts and caves and shit. Tim's dad was teaching him some new skills to meet the new reality, like to reload his shell casings with materials on hand like fat from a dead animal, at least until Tim's mother ate most of the man's face off while he was sleeping. And even worse, but I'm not going to get into that yet. Don't like dwelling on the negative. Ha! That's a laugh. Anyway, that's the way the disease works, it seems. You fuck them one time and the next thing you know, you're the blue plate special.

There's twelve of us holed up at the transmission station perched near the top of one of the Rocky Mountain foothills surrounding Denver. We started out with just four guys from the station, but a few days later, eight National Guardsmen showed up. With supplies and ammo. It was a blessing in a time when blessings are in short supply. The station has a gigantic tower, a concrete block electronics and works building and a few solid-built sheds, one of which houses a generator and sits with a 2000-gallon diesel oil tank to feed it. The compound is surrounded by a chain-link fence topped with razor wire. On a good day last year, the place looked like a prison for the terminally radio-obsessed. Today, it's heaven on Earth.

When reports started hitting the news desk about this new "disease" that was affecting women—and women only—we all thought that mostly it was a joke or some frigging blip on Mother Nature's radar. I mean, no one could believe that some strippers at a Boston club named Hot Foxes had attacked the patrons and killed and eaten most of them. One of the unlucky bastards had the smarts to pull the fire alarm. When the fire department got there they found his hand still attached to the pull box. That was all that was left of him. They found the ribcage and some bones in a heap by the back door along with the same bits from all the other patrons. And this was the pisser, the ever-loving pisser to end all pissers: mixed in with the bones and the intestines, the cops found nine plastic bags full of a gelatinous substance—actually turned out they were breast implants. Together with the vomit from the firemen, it was not a pretty scene. No, indeed. It was not a pretty scene. The strippers were gone and there was obviously no fire. The cops showed up and watched the security tapes. At the station, we got the full tape over the wire.

The lighting wasn't great. The club was just the way you might imagine it. Small tables in the dark perimeter, a wide bar that surrounded a u-shaped stage (stools at the bar), two shiny poles going from the stage up past the stage lighting into the ceiling. Two guys are sweeping, polishing the bar. A half hour later the stage lights go through their setting patterns. A DJ and a few thick types (obviously the bouncers) mill around. A guy in a suit and tie comes in and hangs one of those chintzy "Happy Birthday, Pete" signs between the two stripper poles. Another half hour and about twenty guys in suits and ties show up—I guess for Pete's party. They order a round and sit around ordering drinks and talking while the stage lights do slow fade-ins and outs. Another fifteen minutes and the jackets come off—now we got a whole bunch of guys in shirt-sleeves, ties dangling loose from open-collared shirts. They're yakking, then the birthday boy shows up—I can tell because they all give him the cheers and all that usual back-slapping, hand-shaking bullshit. Two girls sashay up on stage and start a slow strip dance, popping out their butts and shaking their tits. Look, I know this is nothing to write home about, but I'm not writing home and you got to understand the mood.

We got our junior execs whistling and tossing their one dollar bills at the broads, the lights are doing their thing and the music is pumping. Four more stripper types are working the guys, lap dances and feely-feelies and some not so pretty types are scooting around with trays loaded with long necks and mugs. The two on stage are down to g-strings and tits out, tits that barely move because they are faker than grandma's front teeth. These chiquitas are gyrating and slithering all over those poles and the stage and the bar. They're tight bodied and way fit considering they're just a bunch of whores trying to milk it for what it's worth. Ole Pete is getting a lap dance from a girl with tits bigger than volley balls—a good time is being had by all. And why not? I think. This is a great country, ain't it? We got a broad for president. Let the tits and ass begin!

Then the two girls on stage collapse and it can't be but a minute until the girls working the crowd and the waitresses drop where they stand or sit, as the case may be. The bouncers run in and start shouting and gesturing and pushing and shoving the shirt and tie guys and Ole Pete gets knocked off his chair right on top of the lap dance special. The lighting is terrible so I'm not sure what I'm seeing next is real. But it is real, my reader of the future. Too real.

The girls on stage sort of deflate, like the juice has gone out of them, like a pumpkin left on a Halloween porch until December filmed in time lapse. Excepting those fake tits of course. They stay full and flouncy in the name of modern medical cosmetic science. The girls' skin turns a grayish purply, black and blue fucked up mess like they each did ten rounds with a pissed off Mike Tyson. Me and the station crew watching this shit all think it's some, "Surprise, Pete!Happy fucking birthday!" But this is not part of any act. Each and every one of those girls turned into . . . we could not say. Even as I'm writing this, I cannot believe my own fucking eyes saw this go down.

While the bouncers are pushing, shoving and the shirts are fighting back, the girls get up! They are standing there looking like death warmed over, only it isn't death warmed over, turns out it is death period. And it isn't warm, turns out it's as cold as ice. I would have said colder than a witch's a tit, but if there were any witches in that room, they would've jumped on their goddamn broomsticks and got out of there, because those stripper bitches went nuts and eighteen light years beyond nuts. The one on the floor near Pete yanks his pants down to his ankles, grabs his junk and yanks it out by the root and then bites it off and eats it. Pete's's screaming like a banshee and then she goes for his neck, bites so hard that his head, in mid-scream, flops back like he was a puppet whose puppeteer took his hand out before the show was over.

One of the bouncers grabs the bitch and her tit comes away in his hand and the implant slides out and hits the floor. He's looking at his hand full of what used to be a glorious I'll-do-anything-to-lick-your-nipple and freezes in shock. Two of the girls pounce on him and go for his dick and balls and one, with a nut sack hanging from her teeth, goes for his face. In no time, the whole bunch of those guys are reduced to shirts, ties, pants and bones. It takes maybe a half hour. That was nearly a year ago. Seems like a century.

CHAPTER 2

I am watching TV with Jen, the North American Music Awards show live from Boston, and Lady GaGa comes on. She's singing her hit song, "Take Me to the Heights." She's using a stand-up mic and dressed liked a 1940s radio star. It's total crap but I'm waiting for the Rod Riders to come on. She's caterwauling away and I'm thinking, "Man, this is crap." Jen comes out of the kitchen.

"She is so cool, don't'cha think?"

"Yeah, well no. I mean, yeah, she's different."

"Kent, you have no taste in music. She is what it is all about."

I take a quick toke and think, Okay, I mean she's rich and tight-bodied. That's cool.

"Yeah, hon, you're right, sometimes I think only one-sided." I'm hoping this will get her off my back. It does.

We're watching, when all the fracas starts and neither of us is saying anything although I mutter, "what the fuck?"

In the middle of her hit song, the phrase, "Take me to the heights and put your tongue where . . . ." she collapses. The staff, all with headsets on and make-up people and security and her back-up dancers, rush to her. The camera cannot pick up her image because she is swarmed, understandably because she is this mega-star of fabulosity, right?

Then, like a bomb goes off, everyone pulls back and her hand and arm show up over the heads and shoulders in the foreground. It's the purply, black and blue, drained arm of the dead ones. There's a collective inhale. But that arm has grabbed the neck of a techie and is squeezing so tight he cannot scream although his mouth is wide open and his eyes look like moony hubcaps from a Hot Rod. She rises next to him and her eyes have the dry, bloodshot glazy look that we now know is one of the first signs of the disease; but we all

14

thought out in TV land that this was a part of her usually fucked up act.

"She is sooooo original," says Jen. Then the techie's throat collapses and blood starts pouring out like water from a fire hydrant in Harlem when the mercury hits 110. One of the security guys picks up the mic from the floor and smashes her head in. The brain is exposed and looks like a black cauliflower. She doesn't collapse, but stands there, oozing this purply stuff and her teeth are chittering and then she speaks and says, "Take me to the heights," but her voice is like two pieces of sandpaper being rubbed against each other. My reefer has dropped from my hand and landed on MG's back where it has burned a hole through the fur. He leaps up and both of us scream like girls, which is all right for Jen to do, but not so great for me. The TV goes off and a commercial for Tylenol comes on.

On the evening news, the talking heads tell us that Lady GaGa is dead from a disease of unknown origin and that it is likely not contagious. Jen says, "They got that wrong. Way wrong. Let me call the lab." Which she does. The next day, everyone is calling it the GaGa disease and that name has stuck, although subsequent investigations reveal that she was not patient zero but about third or fourth in a line of lesbian friends with whom she has worked and done other things that I won't bore you with. It's in my camcorder report if you ever get to see it.

Jennifer left the next day. I tried to avoid the boohoos at the airport but tryin' ain't doin', as they say. She grabbed a MidCoast flight nonstop into Boston. Little did I know that I might never see her again. People at the airport had that I'm-scared-shitless look on their faces. CNN was running that GaGa tape over and over and we led off with it until one day the station manager calls me in. Her name is Rhonda Fark and she is one of those tough-as-nails bitches that would deflate a boner on King Kong. She's married so I'm thinking somebody's getting her—Mr. Fark, right?—but I'm also thinking like most dumbasses that if she got laid real good, she'd be a whole lot nicer. Of course, I never thought that about Old Man Greenblatt, the former station manager who was the worst sonafabitch anybody could have as a boss. He got laid all the time. Got caught fucking the most fittest weather lady ever behind the green screen one day and that was the end of his job and the weather lady got a low seven figure sexual harassment award and married a fullback on the Broncos. I can tell you that weather bitch hounded Green-blatt—Harvey was his name—and if she was sexually ha-rassed, I'm a fairy princess—which I am definitely not.

Anyway, Mrs. Fark calls me in and says we need a new angle on this GaGa thing, that the station science reporter can't seem to get any information. Maybe I could get some-thing from Jen. "After all, Kent, she's been involved with that new AIDS vaccine, right? Right, Kent?"

"Well, yes. She is," I respond like a wimp. "But I don't know if there's a link and besides . . . "

"Of course there's a link! You know it damn well and if you don't get me the inside scoop from your fuck-buddy or cuntfriend or whatever you call each other nowadays, you'll be on unemployment. Try paying your rent on that fancy stud-muffin pad of yours in the Rocky House on that check. And if you think anyone, and I mean anyone, thinks you're a 're-porter' so you can get another job somewhere lickety-split, let me tell you that anyone in the news business knows that TV reporters are air-headed assholes that couldn't sniff out a story if it jumped up and bit them on the ass. Which, I might add, is where this GaGa thing is going. So, Mr. Reporter," she says this with her hand on her hip and her eyes drilling a hole into my now very much softened brain, "So Mr. Reporter, do some reporting and get me some material on this goddamned GaGa disease. Now get out of here and you better have something on my desk within 48 hours. It's Pulitzer time for me, honey, and while I am not working with any prizes, I intend to get one. Now go!"

She has made me a believer in the innate superiority of one who threatens and can act on the threat. I e-mail Jen and ask her for some background stuff on the research. I promise her name won't be brought up, but, and I really fucking said this in that e-mail, "the public has a right to know." Now, I must tell you that I personally think that the American public has the right to know jack-shit. But Mrs. Fark's words are rattling around in my brain and that off-handed comment on the rent has struck home, no pun intended. I know I call her Mrs. Fark. I cannot help it. You meet Hitler, you're gonna say "How's it hangin' Adolf?" I don't think so.

Like a true trooper, Jen FedExs a packet to me at the office. She told me before she sent it that it was copies of her material, notes and testing results right from the lab but the information and calculations were so complicated that she doubted anyone could make sense of it (especially at a TV station), but she was glad to help out with Miss Thing Bitch if she could. "Love, Jen." She had a way of telling me how she loved me in the most off-handed unrehearsed and natural way possible. Her nearly perfect body, her straight teeth and the smell of her would have been enough for most. Her ass and the way she wiggled it when she delivered head would be enough for everyone else to know she was the real deal. I was already convinced, as much as a self-absorbed twenty-something dickhead could be. But I will confess that thinking she really loved ME, me, made my world, brother. It made my world. And I have no reason to bullshit thee.

The minute the FedEx guy drops the package on my desk, I rush to Mrs. Fark's office. She's on the phone yelling at someone and I'm thinking, I'm next. Shit.

"Oh, Kent. Good, come in. I was hoping you'd pull through. You know the AP is running this AIDS vaccine story and the White House has gotten involved and...they're putting a gag order on the media. If we so much as say anything about this GaGa thing, our license is pulled. I was just on the phone with Ted Armstrong. He's the . . . well, of course you know who he is. He signs your check."

I'm relieved and not at the same time. A gag order on a free press is something I never heard of.

"This came in from my fiancée just a minute ago. It's supposed to be some important information that might explain . . . "

"Well, dearie, hand it over and let's have a look. Maybe there's something in here we can use when the order is lifted. That fucking President must think she got elected Empress or something. I think CNN and Fox News are in court right now looking for a restraining order. How's that for two total assholes suddenly deciding they might be on the same side of an issue. I never knew Fox to be anything but asswipes."

As she's talking, she uses her Tiffany silver sharp-as-a-razor letter opener on the packet, holds it up by a corner and jiggles it. About ten pages of stuff plop on her desk.

"Well, what have we here . . . ?"

She starts reading and I come around to her side of the desk getting closer than I think prudent but very anxious to see what my Jen has sent. Fark is reading and I suddenly see that the hand she is holding the pages with is shriveling from the finger tips up her fingers, past her hand to her arm and she starts inhaling like she's snorting coke. Quick deep snorts. I jump back just as she collapses.

"Mrs. Fark, Mrs. Fark? Are you all right? Hannah," I yell to her secretary. "Quick call 911!"

Hannah says, "Is everything OK?"

"Stay the fuck out of here. Call 911, I think she's got . . . "

Fark starts writhing on the floor like some kind of half woman-half octopus. Her saggy skin with the tell-tale purple blotches is splitting at the wrists and the folds at her neck. She opens her eyes and lunges up at me with her mouth open and her black tongue aimed right at my goddamned face. Her hand grabs my crotch but before she grips my balls, my expensive suit pants block her hand because I'm crouching and the seam is pulled taut. Mama always said to buy the best clothes I could afford because clothes make the man. And to always wear clean underwear because you never know when . . .

"Fuck me!" I yell as I leap up and grab her fancy chrome designer desk lamp and smash her face in, because I've seen this all before and I know where it's going. Her face caves like a giant prune, teeth drop like Chiclets to the floor and the deep dark ooze starts.

Now I'm standing there pissed off, annoyed, scared. I never liked her much anyway but knowing she literally wanted to kill me has me huffing mad, my adrenaline chugging like a train engine. "And it's fiancée, not fuck buddy, you goddamn bitch from hell," I yell as I give her another whack with the same lamp right into her chest. The ribs split open under those purple wounds and her lung flops out like a sack of raisins. Her heart is shriveled and dead, a dark musky brown. But she's still flopping around between her desk and the wall, grabbing at my ankles. I stomp her arms and crack them into pulp. Hannah is screaming in the background and Buddy, the copy boy comes running and grabs me, pulls me out the door and slams it shut. Hannah has passed out on top of her desk, her blouse buttons have popped and one very curious nipple is peeking out of her twisted bra.

Two security guys come running up. Too little, too late. But I'm OK even if Fark is floundering around on the floor oozing black crap like a giant slug on acid and knocking everything over; we're all watching through the plate glass panel. Speechless. Her bronze art nouveau coat tree topples down on her and two of the hooks penetrate her abdomen just below the navel. It's the coup de grace, as some French asshole would say. She is quite dead, I'm believing. Hoping.

"Everyone stay out of that office. That's an order," says

Patrick the security guard as he closes and locks the door. I know his name because he has a plastic tag on his Dacron shirt right near his tin badge. I guess he's in charge now. Good, I think. Let me tend to poor Hannah here.

I lean over being sure not to button anything up. I want to make sure she can breathe and gently slap her pale cheek.

"Hannah . . . Hannah wake up. It's Okay," I say. Yeah, Okay like it's Okay to picnic on a nuclear waste dump. I am covered in Fark's blood or whatever it is that used to be her blood. A drop gets on Hannah's ever so pert chin.

"Everybody back, everybody back," shouts one of the cops running down the hall toward us. We move to the walls as they get there, one of the cops smirking as he sees poor Hannah. I'm still leaning over her when her eyes flutter and glaze over to a milky white. From the spot on her chin, the creeping GaGa has started, sucking every drop of moisture as it works its way up her face and down her neck.

"What the fuck?" says Officer Krupke. I'm already across the room.

"What did you do to her, you little twerp?" says the sergeant turning to me like I was Jack the Ripper. "John, arrest that guy," he says pointing at me.

"He didn't do anything," says Buddy. I'm thinking Buddy is a well-chosen name for that kid. But it wouldn't have made a difference. Hannah has leaped up on to the sergeant's back and has gnawed through his hat into his skull. He's screaming about the Virgin Mary or his mother or somebody when she spits out a piece of bone and scalp and digs into his brain with both jaws chomping like a wood chipper. He's trying to run but topples over. The other cop fires right into the back of Hannah's head and one of her eyeballs flies out onto the rug. But she's still squirming and biting, eating her way through the sergeant's head like it was full of toasty-nut oatmeal. He fires two more shots into her chest, but she's still at it.

"Motherfucker," he mumbles taking point blank range at the back of her head again.

"Shoot her in the gut," I yell. "In the gut . . . right at the base of her back!"

He does and the chomping stops. Buddy vomits. I help him wash up in Fark's private bathroom as two guys with body bags haul her and Hannah off. I'm thinking she probably won't mind. Mrs. Fark, that is. About us using her private bathroom, I mean.

CHAPTER 3

A month ago my phone rings and it's Jen.

"Jen. My God. Are you all right?

"Kent, I am, I am. I'm not sure how but I am. I'm so glad you answered. I don't think the phones will be working much longer."

"Yeah, it came over the wire yesterday. Most of D.C. has the GaGa and the men are all dead or mostly but I think there's a bunch of military high honchos holed up in the Pentagon bomb shelter. They can last there for years but I don't know if that will—"

"Fuck them, Kent. Listen. Let me tell you what this fucking GaGa disease is all about. You need to prepare so you can come get me. You will, won't you?"

"Uh, yeah, of course. Sure. Where are you?"

"I'm in the basement in a house on the ass end of Cape Cod. In Provincetown. This place is mostly populated with gay men and so a bunch of them are in hiding and doing okay. But they're killing any women they find and so I've got no one. I'm alone here and living on peanut butter and tuna and bottled water."

"That is fucked up."

"Tell me about it, honey. But listen. This is the straight story on the GaGa. We were working on an AIDS vaccine and using a genome switch-on to trigger a natural immunity to the HIV virus. Everyone has an X chromosome and women have two. So the idea was to have one of the chromosome d-types on the X gene mutate to provide an immune response to the HIV bug. Are you with me?"

"Yepper. I think so."

"Only the gene mutated differently than it was supposed to. The mutated gene starts a chain reaction whenever there is more than one X chromosome which means only females get it. To the best of our knowledge, males do not."

"Wow. Now I see it."

"The mutated gene is in every cell in the victim's body. Every cell. But it travels in the skin cells from person to person. So you know we humans slough off hundreds of thousands of skin cells every day. Right?

"Yeah . . ."

"And those cells float around indefinitely. They're the primary component in house dust. You know how quickly dust settles on every surface at home, right?"

"Of course."

"If just one dust particle touches a female's skin, the transfer occurs. Remember that YouTube vid we saw where some geek put four thousand mousetraps in a room and threw a ball in the room?

"Yeah . . ."

"Well that's how the chain reaction works inside the victim's body. It takes less than a minute for the infected mutated skin cell to transmit the cellular information to every other cell. This immediately kills the female that is infected."

Now I know how Fark died. Some female skin dust must have made its way onto Jen's notes and into the FedEx. Shit, Jen killed Mrs. Fark. But how could Jen still be alive?

"Jen, remember those notes you sent me for Mrs. Fark? Remember I told you she died right when she opened it?"

"Yeah."

"How did it not kill you?"

"I didn't send those docs. Jerry Mackwell did. I haven't been to the lab since I got back. Director Faggione called and told me to stay home. Now I know why. He saved my life. God, he saved my life." I could hear her crying softly and did not want to go there.

"So, if an infected female is dead, how does she keep moving and killing?"

"We don't have that answer, but it seems that in the mutation process, the cells want to regenerate, like stem cells. So, this is the hard part."

"Go on, hon."

"The women who get infected are dead but still moving—ambulatory is the word and because their cells are reproducing so wildly they crave a huge amount of fresh protein nutrition."

"As in 'guys'?"

"That's it."

There was a silence louder than a cannon shot.

"Two more things," she says.

"What?"

"I love you."

Shit, I say to myself. I'm not going to answer this. It never worked and will never work. Once I say it, especially if I mean it which I fucking do, I am major Nobel-Prize-winning fucked.

"And I think I have the formula for a vaccine. It hasn't been tested, exactly, in ideal conditions but . . . "

Click.

"Hello? Hello?...Jen?" Gone. Dead air. I try again, but nothing. I text her. "Me too. C U when there. MayB 2 weeks, 3. I'll find U." Don't know if she'll get it. Don't care. I'm outta here.

CHAPTER 4

A week later I negotiated the sale of the balloon with its owner, Rick Calle. He was an intense sort, nothing like the complete nerd you'd think would spend time and money on the most impractical form of transportation ever devised by the walnut-sized mind of man. Until very recently, you went up in the fucking thing standing in a wicker basket—wicker as in straw. A huge propane tank fed a blazing flame six feet high that filled a silk balloon with hot air and then you trusted Mother Nature to push you along on her sweet air currents. Wherever she decided to blow you—and not the fun kind of blowing, either—you went. Where she stops, nobody knows. All I know is that having the balloon means avoiding traffic jams and being on the ground with those things. And not a lot of worry about plane or helicopter engine problems.

Rick had made some improvements; not many, but enough to reduce the chance factor of winds pushing you where you do not want to go. Actually with the help of little tanks of compressed air, you could sort of steer the thing away from hazards like high tension wires, mountain tops, etc. You were still stuck with the prevailing winds but you could nudge the craft along on a roughly predictable route. It was insulated, covered and had a 2-way radio and a GPS system along with enough room for supplies.

The story I covered for KWAK was Calle flying the thing from Virginia Beach, Virginia to Madrid, Spain. He actually made it, sort of. Landed the thing about twenty miles north of where he needed to land but no harm done. Not exactly Lucky Lindy, but good enough. The catch with my using the thing was that he was going along. So for my life savings which was not very much, I got the contraption and him to fly it. His wife was one of the early victims of the GaGa and he had only escaped being chow by locking her in their twenty

25

room mansion in DC. He drove to his hangar where the balloon was stored in a moving van along with his other treasured crap and he headed west. Got attacked just outside of Denver, got saved by some state troopers on patrol and ended up here—with his only acquaintance in the area, me. It had been a year since the interview, but it made him world famous for the requisite 15 minutes and he was grateful for it.

I suppose it's my good luck that Tim can also fly the balloon. These days good luck is in short supply. We've hauled the thing onto the grounds of the radio tower and are getting it ready for the relatively easy-seeming flight from here to Massachusetts. I know Jen will wait for me. I mean really, what choice does she have?

We still get signals from all over the country and we've heard from the Pentagon that Europe and Asia are in worse shape that we are. Mostly that's because they are more tightly packed. A lot of families headed out for Siberia. How is that for a mind-fuck? For generations that place was the hell on earth. Like one person per fifty square miles. Now, it's that same isolation that makes it the safest place. Get your women to Siberia, blow up the bridges behind you, wreck the rail lines. Mine the two or three roads into the place and you might all survive. The Kremlin types, a bunch of Russian mafia and some Eastern European big-wigs all got out. They are smart. Spread out and even if the infection starts, it's easy to contain.

Look, I really don't give a rat's ass about the rest of the world. I can't do anything about it. Right? And if I could . . . ah, fuck them all. There's a voice in my head that tells me Jen is one of the ones responsible for this mess. Scientists. It's always those fuckers messing with this and fucking with that. Opening doors that should stay shut. Who the fuck knows? I mean, it could have saved lives, I guess.

Anybody tells me they love me, I say nothing. This way nothing is hanging out there waiting to be shot down. Sometimes you got to accept the status quo. Why get involved? You fuck with things, they're gonna blow up in your face. Like telling some chick you love her. Maybe you get lucky one time and something good comes of it. But you know in the end that every time science comes up with something new and nifty, some motherfucker turns it into a weapon. It's what we do. Sounds crazy but it's true if you think about it. But I stopped thinking about it. Yeah, Jen was one of the ones who brought the world to its knees. Just a little while ago she was on her knees giving me a blow job. Who'da thought? And if I did, would I do anything about it? I think not. Maybe I should've knocked her brains out or pushed her out a window or backed my Jeep over her. But I didn't. So we're all fucked.

The day before we're scheduled to leave, another vid comes over the national security wire. We are told to broadcast it as soon as possible. This is what we see in the control room editing station:

It's the feast of Ramadan, which is the Muslim holy month. You may know it as a time when all the faithful crowd to Mecca in Saudi Arabia and they walk around this humongous black cube that looks like a special effect from *War of the Worlds*. I don't pretend to know why they are marching in a circle over and over but I know its only men and they are in the thousands. Apparently, women are not allowed and personally, I don't give a rat's ass whether they are allowed or not. I only know these bastards were rooting for the cocksuckers that knocked over the Trade Center and I'm thinking, fuck 'em all. Usually wishin' ain't getting'—another of Mom's enigmatic precepts which is truer than anything you'll find in the Bible. But I digress.

So these dudes are doing their marching in a circle routine when off-camera we can hear shouts and screams and the signs of minor mayhem. But it is most definitely not minor. From the left we see a swarm of about five thousand black-cloaked broads running in to where this cube thing is. Now be sure that the cube is blocked in all around by walls—looks like a gigantic courtyard bigger than two football fields. In other words, getting in may be an orderly event through a gate or something but getting out is not going to be so simple if everybody is in a hurry. These women are in their burkas like I said before—you know the black-hooded bathrobe looking thing that the men force the women to wear so other men cannot lust over these ugly fucking broads that only a blind dude would lust over anyway. I mean, even some computer hacker geek who wacks it five or six times a day would still marry his palm rather than go near the pussy of one of these stank factories. Well, maybe not every geek, but a big majority.

We're all thinking that the broads have had enough and it's probably the end of their world too like the dumbass Christians have been bally-hooing about for maybe a thousand years and maybe all these assholes on both sides of the aisle finally got it right. I mean you put your bet on number ten on the roulette wheel long enough—like a hundred years, every day, ten times a day—it's bound to come in, right? But we're watching the vid and some of the burkas have fallen off and underneath each one is a broad with the GaGa. They all got it, as a matter of fact, and now also keep in mind that these dudes always have guns on them—you know every time they celebrate some stupid shit thing, they fire a rifle in the air—even their fucked up leaders. But in this fucking "holy" place, you got to check your gun at the door like in Abilene when Wyatt Earp tells every dead-eye sheep-fucking cowboy they can't come into the saloon with a weapon; except him of course.

These GaGa bitches are berserking in a style we have not to this point witnessed: It is mess en masse. They are jumping the guys and biting and tearing, rending meat from the bones, dicks and balls being the main prize and then all the other goodies. Some cop types eventually show up and start shooting but everybody is covered head to toe in more black cloth than losers at a Goth Halloween party, so it's hard to tell male from female so they just shoot everyone they can. Everybody knows these cocksuckers don't give a hoot in Muslim hell who they kill, as long as it someone. But the GaGa bitches do not go down easily and if a man gets shot it just makes it that much easier for the hungry ones to chow down. In less than a half hour, mostly everyone is dead or dying. One of the cops takes out a pistol and blows his own head off but collapses near a bitch who is wounded and pinned under some other bitches. She still attacks his good parts the way you'd think grandma would eat some turkey on Thanksgiving.

Eventually, an armored troop carrier shows up and flame-throws the whole kit and kaboodle bunch of them. I like that about these countries. They don't think, "Maybe they have some constitutional rights that we need to consider." Nope, they shoot first and have fun later. They turn this fire hose on the bastards that is filled with Sterno or some shit like that and there is a barbecue the likes of which no one has ever seen. Thick black smoke goes billowing up into the sky and a good number of the pricks being burned are not quite dead so they are running around, screaming and trying to get help while the bitches are still eating even though they, too, are burning. One guy falls into a group of about six of the burning broads and as they are eating him from the belly up and he's shouting, their heads are on fire and the only thing anyone can see is the slashing white teeth glaring out from the blackened flaming heads. It doesn't take long for the entire crowd to be burned worse than a side of beef at a drunken Texas bar-b-cue.

More soldiers show up and pot-shoot at a few stragglers. It seems contained but unbeknownst to anyone at the scene, the smoke is carrying the human ash up and out where it is settling like tiny bits of soot everywhere in the region. One of the American scientists with a wry smile that he sorta hides like he's pretending to be the Mona Lisa, says that the population of the Middle East has been reduced by almost ninety-five percent. What the idiot didn't take into account was the fact that there are a whole lot of our guys in uniform over there and what has happened to them cannot be guessed but we all know it's not good. We're hoping they've safely holed up but Jack Larson, one of the interns, says, "Hey, guys, don't forget that there are a lot of women in the military. They got guns and ammo and know how to use it. Wonder if the GaGa makes them forget their training." No one answers but we all hope that the disease makes the bitches lose their human nature and just makes them mad with the hunger. What if they do get organized, I think. Crap, I sure hope I don't ever see that day arrive.

CHAPTER 5

I'll admit I could not sleep the night before we were going to leave. I went outside and sat next to a rock and looked up at the sky. There was no moon and every star you could imagine was shining and little meteorites shot past like bottle rockets I had set off when I was a kid. I could see the red tips of the guards cigarettes, hear them shuffling over the gravel as they made their rounds. The transmission tower that I was so impressed with when I got this job loomed up, black steel against the blue velvet sky. Sometimes I still think this is all a dream, a nightmare that perked in my brain because I saw too many horror flicks when I was a kid. Maybe this is a dream and I'll wake up or maybe this whole world is a computer game in someone's CPU, someone who's alive in the year 2500. And he's fucking with us. Makes us go through shit just to see what we'll do and knows that he can hit a key and we're all erased along with the seven seas, the seven continents, the eight planets, the milky way and the universe—that's it all in some supernerd's new game that he got for Christmas and he dreamed up the GaGa because he's bored with all the usual wars and cancer and AIDs and heart attacks and ragheads blowing shit up. "Hey," he says, "I'll turn all the females into flesh-eating raving lunatic monsters. Maybe that will be fun to watch. Those concentration camps were cool and I loved Hiroshima. But this is going to beat all. Hey, Fred, come here. You gotta see this. Check it out." Well, fuck him and his mother and his father and Fred and anyone who knows the prick. Fuck them all to hell.

So you see I'm not into wondering anymore and I'm not going to philosophize. No point and it isn't me. I'm biding my time until dawn when Rick and Tim and MG and yours truly get in that fucking balloon and head east to find Jen or whatever is left of her and if that doesn't work, maybe we'll just keep floating over the Atlantic or wherever to whatever.

I'm looking for the constellations and cannot pick them out easily because at this altitude and lack of humidity, there are so many stars that even the Big Dipper is buried in them. I look out over the valley and the purple glow of dawn is simmering on the horizon. I can see the city which is now just a bunch of dark cubes and rectangles like some kid's blocks left in a ditch overnight. No lights, no sounds, no cars, none of the reddish glow over the Mile High City that you could see from a hundred miles away just a year ago. I know there must be pockets of men hiding out in basements or attics or in the hundreds of mine shafts that pock the foothills. But I also know that most guys are going to bring their wives and daughters along, maybe a girlfriend. It only takes one and then they're all at it; the tearing, the biting, the gouging, the swallowing. The blood, the death. Just take one of them along and it's the end. My mom told me that the devil can't come in if you don't invite her. It's the most natural invitation any dick swinger could make.

I'm interrupted in my reverie. This guy named Alan opens the bunk door, steps out and lights a cigarette. Wearing a red and white striped shirt that looks like a barber pole. He starts walking to the perimeter and sees me, comes over.

"Hey, kiddo, how's it hangin'," he says. Alan is at most five years older than me but I guess he can call me "kiddo" if he wants. He was a copy editor—the guy that took the news from the wire service and translated it into the teleprompter.

"Beautiful night. Can't sleep much. We're leaving tomorrow."

"Yeah, I know. She must be something. That's a lonnnnng way through hostile territory for poontang. No offense. I'm sorry. Guess it's getting to me."

"No offense taken."

"But, ya know, maybe it's better than hiding up here, I guess. My wife went to Oklahoma City to help her mom recuperate from a fall. The old bag tripped on the cat and broke her hip. Haven't heard from her in weeks. Maybe she's hiding, maybe she's gone over to the other side. Not much I can do about it. I dream about her a lot. Sometimes she's a GaGa and I wake up sweating bullets; sometimes she's the beautiful girl I fell in love with and married. We honeymooned at the Grand Canyon. You know, that lodge that sits at the north quarter. We'd make love all night, wake up to hawks hooting the way they do and watch the sun rise over the eastern rim. When I wake up, I got tears in my eyes. I know you think I'm a sap or something. But I miss her. So I know what you're thinking and why you're doing it. I'd ask for a lift, but what would I do when I get there? I guess I'm just a coward." He took a long drag on his smoke and exhaled two perfect rings that floated up like magic donuts into the still night air.

"This whole shit thing no one could imagine. Whether I make it or not, don't think it matters. I'm taking it a day at a time," I say, making a good effort to not be judgmental.

"You think we can last up here?"

"I don't know a better place. At least it's out in the open. Not holed up like a rat in trap. Plenty of supplies. Communication with the outside world. Can't say."

Alan sat a while and stared up at the same starry sky. Didn't say another word. Got up, muttered something that sounded like "Good-night" and went back to the tech shed.

My cellphone rings and I jump up from a light sleep. It's Jen; not her voice but a text. Says: "Hurry. Need U. Vaccine."

Hurry? How the fuck can I hurry. Does she have the vaccine? Would it be too late? I text her back: "Coming ASAP. Hang in." Not exactly Romeo and Juliet, but this ain't Verona.

CHAPTER 6

The mountains are turning that dusty violet color when I see the surface of a foothill about a half mile out begin to move. I rub my bleary eyes thinking it's the dust and the sleepless-ness or maybe the updraft winds that own this valley are play-ing tricks. But no. It's none of these things. The skin on that hill is moving like a rug being pulled by a giant.

Then I realize it's people. Must be two or three thousand people moving in a slow swarm up from the city, up the foothills and inching toward us like lava in reverse.

I run to one of the guards—Jim, I think his name is. He looks and signals to the guy in the watchtower who uses his binoculars to verify what I just told them.

"Shit," he says. "It's a million of them. Movin' slow and steady up here. Don't make any noise. Alert the others. Maybe they'll just pass us by. No one knows we're up here." Right, I think. Pass us by. Sure. And maybe we'll sprout wings and fly to Hawaii for a fucking luau.

They do know. I'm up and running back to the shed where everyone is sleeping, shouting the alarm. I get Tim and Rick riled.

"Rick, get the balloon ready. Now."

He looks at me and knows this is not the plan of the slow rise into the wild blue yonder and the fond farewells. He also knows if we don't move quick, some of these guys are going to try to board the gondola, swamp it and we'll be fucked. For a moment, I think maybe better now than later. We're the dead men walking anyway. Then I remember Jen, tell Tim to get MG and get in the gondola pronto.

"Just do it quiet. No panicking or our asses are finished here," I say quite steadily considering I'm almost pissing my-self. As I head to the gondola, I remember that scene in the *Wizard of Oz* flick where they're all supposed to get in the

34

balloon with the phony wizard but Dorothy runs after her dog and misses getting in and the fucking thing takes off without her. But out back, I see Tim and MG already boarded.

Tim signals with his hand and has his rifle ready. Rick is firing up the burner. With a few quick steps and a hurdle jump, I'm in.

"Let's go," I loud whisper.

One of the guards—remember these are weekend warrior National Guardsmen who made it up here at the first sign of trouble—says, "Where the fuck do you think you're going? Get to the barricades."

"Captain," I say, knowing full well this is just an asshole in a uniform who worked at the local Ford dealer selling shit pick-up trucks to rednecks. "We're not going anywhere. Sir, we've already cleared the idea with the major. We're going to lift off fifty feet and do some reconnaissance. If it's trouble those bitches want, we'll rain down shock and awe on their asses. Permission sought, sir." Man, I am slinging it, hoping he doesn't realize there is no major here. I salute.

"Permission granted," he says saluting back. I'm thinking if we survive all this I'll carve this jerk-offs head next to Lincoln's on Mt Rushmore myself if I have to use a nail file to do it.

Tim grabs my shoulder and smiles at me with a nod as if to say, "Nice work." For someone who can't speak much, he can express himself.

The balloon rises about thirty feet off the ground and I'm watching the swarm approach. It is a massive horde of GaGa broads, some looking no more than seven or eight years old. There must be at least two thousand of them. They're moving at the same pace they'd move if they were at a mall looking for a bargain. The guys below are armed to the teeth and holed up in hidden spots all around the transmission tower. The perimeter fence is electrified but I don't know if it can handle that much resistance. It was designed to keep teenagers on a bender out. Maybe an itinerant drunk.

I was amazed that the guys could hold off firing until the bitches reached the sandbag barrier. They open fire on them. The barrier slows them down but the bullets do very little. It's still mostly dark so the flares from the muzzles looks like flashbulbs. Tim takes aim and I stop him.

"This battle is not ours anymore. Don't waste your ammo. We got a long way to go."

He looks at me and nods but still keeps the rifle at hand. MG is wagging his tale like he's expecting breakfast. I manage a smile at his dumb face.

"Release the line," says Rick.

I unhook the grillion from the loop guard and toss the rope to the ground. Rick hits full fire-up and the sound of that flame is like an atomic blast. Even the bitches stop in their tracks. The guys all turn and look up like maybe the Avenging Angels have descended from the heavens. But, no, it's just us running like rabbits for pastures unknown. One of the soldiers yells, "You traitors, motherfuckers!" and fires at us. We duck and he misses because the balloon is rising so fast and gets picked up by a mountain up-current so quickly that only an experienced hunter could hit us. We're all knocked to the sides of the gondola and even MG is flat on his ass quietly whimpering. I stand up and look over the edge with Tim. The sun has risen and the entire hilltop is illuminated in broad Rocky Mountain daylight.

The swarm is at the fence and the electricity is doing its thing. The bitches grab the fence and smoke streams out of their hands and their hair catches on fire. Large globs of the black ooze spill out as their faces burst open and the bullets fly through their dead flesh. (We learned much later on that the only way to kill a GaGa bitch is to shoot her ovaries. Either through the belly or through the back. I had seen Mrs. Fark and Hannah die in this way but I didn't know then why and can only guess now. Eggs? The source of the double X chromosome? My biology is probably fucked up so don't hold me to it.) And things change.

The moaning and screaming is filling the air. MG is huddled at my feet as we float over the scene below. The circle that was our "fortress" is completely surrounded by the swarm. At the northern end, where the fence has a slight break in it to accommodate a huge boulder sticking out of the rockface, the fence collapses and the bitches pour through. From the air it's a narrow breach but our guys just can't handle the flood. The shooting almost stops as the ammo gives out—I think—or the guys just instinctively start to run. But where can they run to? There is no cave, no shelter, not even a goddamned tree to climb. Some make it back to the generator shed which has smoke coming out of it but the bitches are on top of them. A new kind of screaming weaves its way through the desert air to us up in our balloon.

It's the sound of men being eaten alive. I can see the soldiers punching and swinging their rifles at the bitches but the sheer number of them is overwhelming. As the men fall, the bitches go first for the dick and balls, ripping off the pants with nails and teeth and pulling the meat out with a stretching yank. Red blood is lapped at like cats at a milk-filled saucer. The balls are fought over, dicks chewed from both ends, the bitches ending up face to face, lip to lip. Then the men's faces and necks when the screaming stops and finally the pulling open of the belly, intestines dragged out like rope uncoiling, the little girls fighting over the shit-filled tubes because the bigger bitches are getting the good parts. Two guys come running from the tech shed with machetes and they're hacking away as if they are in some deep part of the Amazon rain forest and are chopping their way through the undergrowth. But this is not vegetation; it is a swarm of mostly third stage GaGa bitches, ravenous as piranhas, numerous as flies on a buffalo carcass in the Sahara. The machete boys make a good go of it, bitches' heads flying off, tits being split open, guts oozing with the black coagulant that the bitches are full of. But in no time, the guys are down watching their balls being yanked off and fought over, dicks being devoured. One guy has his liver ripped out right through his belly. His head is being held down and gnawed by two old bitches and the young ones are squeezing the liver out like a sponge and blood is pouring into their mouths. He screams, but their teeth find his tongue and then his throat and all he is now is meat.

We're rising fast when I see the red and white striped shirt. It's Alan and he's firing point blank into some bitches who are getting ready to smother him. He's moving back and I can see he's moving too much in a panic. Trips over a dead guy's arm. The bitches are on him, chewing his face, reaching into his mouth for his tongue—maybe it's too far down to tell, but then his pants are ripped off and the tearing starts. He screams as he looks up at me as if to say, "Save me, kiddo, please." But I can't do anything; his mouth is wide and blood gushes as his empty pleas drift away in an updraft.

A thermal picks us up and carries us out over the Henderson Gorge to the east. The "fortress" is no longer visible. The echoing hollow sounds of the desert have returned. An eagle's shrill cry is the only scream. Turkey vultures like something out of the Jurassic period, huge, glide effortlessly by us in smooth sweeping circles drawn to the smell of blood and death. Cicadas begin to clack in the heat of the full sun. The valley below is full of boulders as big as elephants but from this height they look like gravel. The clouds are huddled below the horizon and we raise our hands to make a brim against the merciless sun from the east, a dismal salute to our fallen comrades. I'm thinking even God must be hiding his face.

Rick does his captain thing better than I could have hoped. He's teaching Tim the nuances and showing us the use of the GPS, the radio and the gauges, particularly the altimeter. By one in the afternoon, we've heard all we can stand from Rick and we use MG's excessive salivating as a hint to take a break and eat something.

"That dog looks starved," Tim says, looking at me with that secret code look. It's the first thing Tim has said in ages and I want to ask why but all I get out is:

"Me too."

"Let's break out the rations," says Rick like somehow he is charge. Frankly, I don't give a monkey's balls who's in charge. I just want to do the "Up, Up and Away in my beautiful balloon" thing and get to Jennifer. I start humming that tune, the Up, Up and Away song that made the Fifth Dimension a few mil back in the day. If you're thinking Superman, think again. The bitches would crack his testicles like walnuts.

"You know, pal, that if we make it and end up being some kind of heroes, that song may be the new national anthem. Wouldn't that be cool?" Tim says with a chuckle.

"Don't disrespect our country, dude," says Rick. "The rockets' red glare is good enough for me and it's good enough for you, right?"

Before Tim answers, I tear open a foil wrapped Q-Bar, the newest in earth-muffin technology. Nuts, seeds, molasses and enough calories to power Toledo, Ohio for a week. Taking a big chomp, I say, "Hey, guys, dig in. It's like Christmas dinner and Thanksgiving all rolled into one six ounce lump of rabbit food."

The stare-down between my two roomies is disrupted. I give a biscuit to MG.

"You're on a diet, too, my overfed man's best friend."

"That dog of yours may come in handy one day," says Rick. "Looks like he's got a good twenty five pounds of protein on him."

"Rick, sir, if you think anyone is going to eat this here canine eighth wonder of the modern fucking world, you can go fuck yourself. I'll eat you, you dumb fuck, before I'll let you touch one hair on . . . "

"Relax, relax . . . " he responds. "Can't you take a joke?"

"Not really. You may be joking, but I'm not. Remember I paid for this piece of shit contraption, whether you designed it, invented it or squeezed it out of your ass, I don't care. This is my trip in my rig. Like Aldous Huxley once said, 'All animals are created equal, but some are more equal than others.' I'm the more equal one on this tub. Ain't that so?"

Rick nods his head side to the side and lowers his eyes. I made my point, but the discomfort level on board the Good Ship Lollipop just got ratcheted up sixteen degrees. We're making the most of it by looking out the gondola at the scenery—ragged mountains unfurling beneath us, high thin clouds above, white cotton candy against the pale blue of high altitude sky. Little veins below are the only signs that humans ever existed here: veins that are the highways and small clusters of houses—capillaries. No cars are moving.

"Can't we bring this thing down a bit lower? I'd like to see what's going on," I say.

"Is that an order?" says Rick, with a pissy tone that reminds me of my first girlfriend, Sandy Grunski. Gruntin' Grunski everyone called her. Everyone but me. It is true that she could grunt like nobody's business when I was fucking her but I would have visited the Ninth Circle of Hell once a week for a year for one of her blowjobs. I guess listening to her opinions on pop music and sitcoms was the trade off. Now I'm thinking that the trip to hell might have been better.

"It is," I say. If he wants a master and commander, I'm it.

In a few hours we see Interstate 54 like a bright ribbon twisting here and there through cactus and mesquite and mugho pines. No cars, no busses, no trucks.

"Let's follow the road for a while. Maybe we can see if

anything's happening. It goes through some small towns. Gas stations. Truck stops. It can't all be gone. Can it?" I say.

"It sure can," says Rick. Turning to Tim, he says, "So what's with you, pal?"

"Tim ain't talking much this trip," I interject.

"Cat got his tongue?" Rick smirks.

"He's had some trouble, is all. How about watching where you're going, OK?"

"Aye, aye," he responds. "I'm going to take her down. There's an Exxon station up ahead. We can fill the propane tank and pick up some water. Maybe some chips and other good healthy shit."

"OK," I say. "Just be sure there's nothing around. I mean no bitches or anything."

Rick turns the gas jet off and we start cruising down. But at this altitude the wind does funny things. As I'm thinking this and about to tell Rick to bring it up a bit, a downdraft hits us like a giant's fist and we go freefall for I don't know how long. I'm holding on for dear life, MG is bounced on his ass while Rick grabs the burner control and yanks it too hard. We all bounce and Tim gets knocked over the gondola railing. As he goes over, I see one hand white-knuckled on the rail. I crawl over and, as the balloon steadies, I get up and reach over. Tim is wide-eyed and about to let go. He's kicking, trying to get his feet up and over but the wind is twisting him and the balloon. I grab his arm and reach over.

"Grab my hand" I shout. "Come on, Tim, grab it goddamn it!"

He reaches up and gets hold of my forearm while I grab his. But he starts slipping out of my grip.

"Man, don't let go," Tim shouts.

"I won't. Just steady yourself. And stop kicking. When I say three, I'm pulling you in. Three!" I yank on his arms as hard as I can and drop back, his stomach bent over the rail.

"Now get your feet over. I ain't lettin' go!"

"He topples into the gondola, sweating like he spent four hours in a sauna.

"Thanks," he says.

"Good to see you again," I say.

"I guess the cat let go of his tongue," says Rick. "Or is it pussy."

I can see that Rick is not going to make this trip any better, the asshole.

CHAPTER 7

It's late in the afternoon and as we descend the sun prematurely fades because we're in the shadows of the Rockies. At about a thousand feet, we see a bus making its way slowly through a winding local road that snakes gently through a section of foothills.

"That's a good sign," Tim says matter-of-factly. "There's still normalcy somewhere. Maybe it's been limited to a few urban areas. Who knows, maybe even they've stamped it out."

"A cure?" says Rick with a smirky tone. "They couldn't cure anything like this in so short a time. No way."

"I think he's right, Tim," I say. "But there's always hope. That bus is heading somewhere. And for a reason."

"Yeah, goin' west, right where we came from. They don't have a clue."

We watch the bus in a hover when Rick points to a rocky area about a quarter mile past where the bus is.

"Check it out," he says.

We pick out in the shadows a group of about twenty-five people in army green fatigues lying in ambush.

"Should we fire a warning shot?" asks Tim.

"We don't know who the good guys are. That bus could be crawling with bitches. Those could be bitches hiding up ahead. Looks like men but who can tell from up here?" says Rick. "Let it play out."

"Bring it down lower," I say. Rick looks at me as if he's finally had enough.

"Look," he says. "I don't mind your Horatio Hornblower, Captain Kirk bullshit when it's not dangerous. But we can't go lower than this and be safe. We need to go up. If those assholes on the ground feel like firing at us, it'll be a turkey shoot. We're lucky they're pre-occupied." As he says this and I'm about to agree, the bus makes its final curve into the ambush zone. We see boulders rolling down the hillsides from both directions. A few tumble across the road in front of the bus which seems to be careening all over the place, kicking up clouds of dust. But a few smash into the side and knock the thing for a loop. It hits a guard rail, jumps it, and the whole thing goes over the edge and slides down like a small steel avalanche, rocks, gravel, dirt and dust billowing behind it.

"They're fucked," says Tim. The balloon lifts gently up as Rick turns on the juice. We see a couple of the army ambushers look up as the roar of the propane echoes through the canyon. Small flashes of light pop out from behind boulders.

"Those cocksuckers are shooting at us," I yell.

Tim has shouldered the 30.06 and is firing at the men in green who are also chasing down the hill after the bus. A bunch of civilian types get out of the bus and are helping one another when the first group of men reach them.

CHAPTER 8

We had drifted all night following the arrow on the GPS uncertain as to whether or not it was accurate.

"Do these things need people on the ground to keep them up?" asked Tim.

"Geez, I don't know. Technology was never my thing. I'm thinking it's a satellite, right? And it spins along with the Earth, always at the same spot in the sky. Moving along because it's always technically falling but it falls at the same rate as the curvature of the Earth so it never crashes."

"Shit, man. I thought you said you're not a techie type. Was that a load of bullshit you just slung or is it true?"

"True. But I don't know if people are required. Probably after awhile. Who the fuck knows?"

"Good answer. Let's catch some shut-eye. No point in worrying."

Rick is standing there at the helm saying nothing. As they used to say just before the Indians attacked, "It's quiet, too quiet." He's definitely a too-quiet type. But who can read him? And who gives a pig in a poke anymore. I know he's got money, tons of it and he's a genius, if you consider inventor types to be geniuses. My own opinion is that there is barely a fine line between a genius and a complete asshole. But this asshole's balloon has saved my life. So, for now, he's a genius.

We are drifting smoothly at about three thousand feet. It's cold but our Mylar wraps do what they are supposed to do. It's a three dog night, but all I have is MG snuggled up close as he can and smelling as bad as he can. Someone once compared the smell of a dog to buttered toast. Some puppy-loving bitch who couldn't deal with a real man, I'm thinking. Then I realize how stupid I am. How stupid the whole world has turned. Three jerk-offs in a balloon cruising over this huge stupid country, pockets of dudes hiding from marauding undead bitches. Maybe stupid is putting it mildly. Maybe stupid would be good. I'm staring up at charcoal grey clouds, thicker than wool, heavy with the night, the weak glimmer of a weak moon trying to reflect some of the sun's rays through the thickness. Jen's face floats in the clouds and I drift off to sleep, hearing Tim's snoring, reassured that I'm not alone and confident, if that's the right word, that Rick will keep us on the right trajectory—his word, not mine.

At around 2 A.M., Rick wakes me up.

"I'm getting sleepy," he says. "Why don't you take over for a while? I've got the auto-pilot doing most of the work and the wind is co-operating. It's always easier at night, anyway. No thermals"

"OK," I answer. I mean what am I going to say. Fuck no, I want to sleep; you do it. This is a team thing, right? And I want everyone to do whatever he can. My turn.

I get up and Rick tells me how to operate things, how to keep my eye on the altimeter and the GPS and to be aware that we're in the Rocky Mountains and some of these peaks are high and come up real fast, sometimes faster than the altimeter can convey the information. We're not hooked in to radar like planes and it's sort of like a barometer which tells you the weather you are having, not going to have. In other words. keep your eyes open. "Will do," I say.

Rick leans up against the side of the gondola and tries to doze.

"I got a story for you," he says.

"That's okay, Rick," I answer. "Just go to sleep. Don't worry. I'm wide awake." You would be too, believe me.

"No, I gotta tell you this," he says.

I figure if he wants to talk, let him.

"I'm about nineteen and I just got kicked out of Duke for doing unauthorized work in their chem lab. I was hitchhiking, figuring I needed to put some distance between me and my old man. He lives in Atlanta with his third wife. I noticed that the asphalt is not black. It is a mucous gray, unyielding, lacking in sympathy. The road went out as far as I could see, rolling over the hip-like hills of West Texas. Noon or close to it, the spiteful sun was high, below loose gravel on the faded yellow lines at my feet. I kick the stones toward the sage and scrag weed, dry, clackety covering the landscape like hairy tumors on the back of a fat man. I despise fat men. That fat truck driver just dropped me off. He was fat, real fat and real lucky. Told me he had to drop me at that truck stop a hundred yards back. I was too slow to act, to edgy in my seat. Too much planning doth make failures of us all. Such plans. He kept looking at me out of the side of his eyes like that black cat wall clock, googly, humorous for idiots. Kent, I can tell you that that driver was really fat."

"Yeah, guess he was," I say.

"I watched him shift the big rig with his pudgy hand. His watch, too tight, too small and the fat on his wrist, he had no real wrist, he was so fat, the fat on his wrist rose up around the watch strap as if he was made of melted butter under his pink blotchy skin. I counted twelve small pimples on the side of his fat face, seven hairs that were long and brown on the same side of his fat face that he missed with his razor. I try not to count this stuff anymore. I used to do it all the time, counting, counting, counting, looking for special numbers but in the end, the number was always special. It was always up."

"I know what you mean," I say, thinking uh-oh. But I'm watching for mountain tops or crags or some shit thing that will tear a hole in this balloon.

"So he picked me up in San Angelo, Texas, a crap-hole of a town with no excuse to exist. I told him I was going to El Paso, which I was, but the lucky fat man let me out 300 miles shy. Go west young man, go west.

"Anyway, I'm thinking I'll just stand here in the white

light, the alum white of noon and watch the blue morning sky putrefy into milk. I have my uniform on: a Tulane University sky-blue t-shirt with milk-white letters, neat jeans, not the artificial ragged ones, white tennis shoes. They used to call them sneakers, but I guess no one likes to be thought of as a sneaker. I once saw a tennis match on TV. A tall lanky blond girl with a ridiculous Rusky name was grunting every time she hit the ball. Swing, grunt, bounce. Swing, grunt, bounce. Her hair glistened like the fillings in a cadaver."

"Yeah, I knew a guy who used to wack off to tennis players—I'm pretty sure they were girls. Now that I think about it, maybe not," I say, feeling edgier than I thought I should feel.

"I watched and watched, hypnotized by the stupid pointless game, reflexively squeezing my knife handle every time she grunted. Squeeze, grunt. Squeeze, grunt. I'm digressing, Kent, but it is regret that keeps me going now and even then, more so maybe. I mean my father was a real . . . anyway, I'm on the road, not like that drunk and sloppy Kerouac, but as cute, as clean-cut, as naïve, as collegian, as bright-eyed and bushy-tailed as I can be, which is very. It is the key to my success. I could make an info-mercial on my art; tell you to dial 1-800-slash, 1-800-bleed, 1-800-pity me for I have sinned. Free shipping and handling. My operator is standing by. He is always standing by."

Where is this going? I'm thinking.

"I made it from Duke in only two weeks. I arrived in a Volkswagen driven by a skinny girl. Girl? She was at least twenty-five. I despise skinny people. They show their bones to the world like a badge of honor. What honor is there in not eating or in having a too high metabolic rate that burns everything you feed it through a skinny mouth so fast that it does no good? It reminds me of an old Indian movie I saw while sitting on Dad's fat lap when the Indians mock the white men for building a fire that is too large. The fire of skinny people

48

is too large, too wasteful. They need their "Off" buttons pressed hard, real hard. This girl, I could see her ribs hiding under her tight t-shirt. Her little dried up skinny breasts, milk-less, useless, useless, useless, "like two fried eggs on a bread board," my mother used to say. My mother was fat."

"Yeah, I guess moms can get that way," I say trying to have something to agree with him about.

"I'm in New Orleans; it is gloriously in ruins. Drunken sots on every corner, whores, fags, dopey college kids, half the houses in spectacular decay, the smell of Katrina's blood everywhere, the smell of mold and mildew, the perfume of beautiful destruction. To have witnessed it, aye, there is a sight to behold. That smell of slime overhanging the city, the Big Mindless Easy, the smell of the mud of the Holy Ghost with wings out-stretched hovering over the aroma of humans' waste, of wasted humans. All cities should meet such ends, like New Orleans, in their own arrogance and idiocy, fighting against Mother Nature, her huge breasts the size of moun-tains, her feet bigger than Ohio, her farts the tornadoes that rip through cyclone alley and flatten everything, shred it, de-file it. I adore dying New Orleans. I had no trouble burying the body of that skinny girl right in the front mud lawn of a rotting church, algae and moss eating it from the ground up. The mud is clever, very clever, that mud in the church lawn in the Bayou section of town. Good bye, Bayou, good-bye. I left the skinny girl's jaw in the open guitar case of a blind min-strel singing "When the Saints Go Marchin' In." This way I could make sure her skinny metabolism would slow down in Heaven so she would not need to eat more clouds than her fair share. My mother and particularly my father ate more than their fair share. They were fat."

I'm suddenly aware that good old Rick is confessing to murder. Is this a good thing or a bad thing, I'm worrying. I'm not skinny but I'm not a fatty either. Just sorta middlin'. Never had a weight problem either way but should I be worrying about this now with what I'm certain is the end of the world going on below us a few thousand feet. I'm going to let him keep talking. Maybe he's just having some sort of schizoid reality break. Maybe an LSD flashback. Who wouldn't? People are eating people alive. That would be enough to make anyone a tad batty.

He looks at me to make sure I haven't dozed at the wheel. "A chubby guy in a white, short-sleeved shirt gave me a lift from New Orleans to Biloxi. He had a tie that said, 'No. 1 Dad.' His shirt had yellowish armpits that matched his eyebrows and the whites of his eyes that were not white at all. He was very friendly but the air conditioning in his car did not work so the wind, moist and putrid from the south swirled in the car like we were in a sleeping bag together. I could smell the lynched Black people ever so faintly. The odor of the dead, they say, never entirely leaves but rises and falls with the humidity like cat piss on the rug. It is always humid in the South.

"The driver was from the South. He sold repossessed printing equipment and he talked about this on and on until I went nearly crazy. Then he put his hand on my knee and kneaded it real gentle and told me he was lonely, so lonely, even though he was married and had children, so he said, and that he would pay me a few dollars, he did not have much. He said he would let me stay with him in the Motel Six just over the next state border. I said that would be nice because I had not been in a bed in nearly three weeks and I was tired of washing up in gas station men's rooms. A hot shower would be nice. He rubbed my thigh and I got relaxed. He was chubby like a guy that sits and watched TV all the time and eats jellybeans and Raisonettes. He said he would wash my back. My mother and my father did that. I said, OK, that sounds nice. It did."

"I wouldn't mind a bath myself right now," I say. Rick looks at me and then he looks at Tim who is still sound asleep.

I'm sending telepathic waves to Tim, telling him to wake up! We got a situation here! But Tim does not stir.

"Somewhere in Mississippi, on a long stretch of mossy-treed highway I asked him to stop by the roadside; I had to urinate. He said he did, too. We walked a ways into the woods. The trees were forlorn having had so many Black people hung on them the last century. The clouds were embarrassed to be over Mississippi. The shadows were deep and blue, lovely dark and deep, the gray moss like Father Time's beard hanging everywhere. He watched me urinate. On the way back to the car, I saw that he had three large sweat stains on his shirt and two small ones. That number five was his number. My blade went into his neck quite quickly, crunching in a way that reminded me of the sound of eating a potato chip in church. I left him there under the mossy trees. They were his mourners, more than he would have at a real funeral, I guess.

"Thinking all these things sometimes gets me confused but it doesn't matter. Maybe the skinny girl drove me to Biloxi and the chubby guy took me to San Angelo and so on and so forth. I never liked geography. My geography teacher was really fat and I paid her no mind, none at all but only daydreamed of what she would look like with those maps on the wall and her with no skin but only yellow globs of fat and all the other kids in the class laughing at her instead of at me.

"I drove myself to San Angelo, Texas where I parked the car in a bowling alley parking lot. I went in and bowled a game and half even though the lanes and gutters had crickets crawling or hopping or dead all over them. The skinny guy behind the counter near the cubby holes filled with old smelly bowling shoes told me that that every now and then the town gets a plague of crickets. It doesn't last long and then they just up and leave. So I had in my travels seen a flood and a plague and I'm beginning to think biblical. But I am no Bible boy. I'm not. I killed two people who were trying to convince me to spare them by reciting something out of the Bible. It didn't work for Jesus on the cross who started reciting scripture. It didn't work for these people either. When my mind is made up, it is made up. I guess that's the way God is. He makes up His mind, it's made up. Don't do this, don't do that. Don't do this, don't do that. Or else. I'm now believing that the GaGa is the Else."

Something is making me agree with him. Something is wishing I had never met this degenerate creep. Something is saying "Any port in a storm."

He goes on, "The trucker with the twelve pimples and seven hairs picked me up in San Angelo on the road to El Paso. He told me he was tired of seeing so many Mexicans hitching rides, he called them 'wetbacks,' and befouling the highways with their squat looks and greasiness. He actually used the word, 'befouling' so I was pretty certain he was a regular church-goer, like my father, fat like him, as well. I slept a lot of the way, the oily sun blasting in through the bug-smeared windshield as the day wore on. It felt like lying down in a tanning bed the size of a barn with the dial turned up to 'Extra High.' He turned the radio on and it was country music, Tammy Somebody and Billy Rae Whoever and Jim Bob Watchamacallit and so on and so forth. That racket bored its way into my brain like a cable guy's drill, the kind with the auger big enough to go through a wall. You know the kind of bit I'm talking about, don't you?"

"Sure. Those cable guys have great tools," I say, thinking I am the biggest idiot whoever drew breath.

"Well, friend, that caterwauling music and his index finger tapping on the steering well thirty-nine times made me tense up like when you think your pal, if you have one, may be hiding around the next corner to jump out and startle the Bejesus out of you. I don't usually blaspheme or take the Lord's name in vain but I tensed up real tight, real tight and I could feel the handle of my knife creeping out of my pocket toward my hand. What is this I see before me, a dagger with its handle toward my hand? That driver, fat as he was, saw me and asked me if I was all right. I said yes, I was, but he turned the radio off and commenced to telling me he was a father of twin boys and the sole support of his two elderly parents, one of them blind, like it would make a difference to me, which it would not. He saw a truck stop up ahead and pulled right in with barely enough roadway to slow down like he was relieved. He told me this was the end of the line and I needed to get out, which I did and thanked him. He was lucky, real lucky and real fat. Don't you agree? Don't you?"

"Well, sure. It's not easy hitchhiking and all. Sometimes you can spend all day . . . "

"Who gives a shit about your hitchhiking days, Kent?"

"I just thought you were asking, is all."

"I usually never have to stand by the roadside for more than an hour or so. My thumb is magic and charming and has never let me down. I'm hoping a nice girl will give me a lift, neither fat nor skinny, someone pleasant, someone understanding, someone my own age, someone that will not have parents, someone that will say nice things about me at my funeral because they are true and not because I am dead, someone who will carve a perfect epitaph for me on a granite headstone that might say, 'He was a good man, neither fat nor skinny, who tried to do right. He will be missed.' And she will remember to bury me with my knife in case I'm not really dead but in some sort of coma and I can dig my way out, get back on the road and try to continue to do right. Is that asking too much? And do I deserve to be stuck up here with you and . . . "

A shot rang out and hit Rick right between the eyes. It made a little hole like those Hindu ladies have only theirs is make-up, not a real hole at all. Rick's eyes focus for a millisecond on Tim who was not sleeping at all but had stealthily aimed his rifle right at Rick while he was blabbing his sick confession. Rick toppled to the floor like a way full laundry bag; collapsed more than fell.

"Fuck me," I yell. "Holy shit! Why'd you shoot him? Holy shit."

"Holy has nothing to do with it," says Tim. "That motherfucker is a serial killer who just confessed to you. Did you want to be next?"

"Well, shit, Tim . . . "

CHAPTER 9

"Hey, chief, check it out," says Tim pointing out and down.

"What is it?" I ask.

"Check it out."

I get up from where I'm sitting, every joint in my body feeling like someone super-glued them while I was resting. Stiff as pipe. I get up slowly, like an old dude. The sun is glinting off the balloon coloring it a morning orange. I look out over the brim of the gondola and as far as I can see is green, billowing waving, stippled green—yellow spots like a million stars.

"It's corn, man, more corn than I think I could ever see. Fucking look at it," says Tim.

I am speechless. What's to say? It's an ocean of corn spreading to the horizon. We're down to about a hundred feet.

"Why so low?" I ask. "Is it safe?"

"Safe? Fuck no, it's not safe but we need to scout out some grub."

"You're not thinking corn on the cob for the next twenty meals are you?" I ask.

"No. But look yonder," he says, pointing eastward into the rising sun. The clouds have all run away, like thieves in the night.

A half mile directly in front of us is the white steeple of a church, the sun catching the glint off of its honest to God bell, not one of those megaphone pre-recorded jobbers like you see nowadays. It's a real bell in a real steeple. Something out of Norman Rockwell. And don't ask me who that is. All I know, he paints cheese-ball paintings of happy people doing happy American shit like from the thirties and forties. You know, happy shit like eating dinner and talking at a town meeting and praying at a church that looks just like the one we're homing in on.

"Fuck, Tim. We're going to clear it, right?

"Yepper, Cap'n. Hard to up," he says as he fires the burner with a loud blast and sends us up another hundred feet. "I think we need to land near here. See that outbuilding near the church. It's the parson's house or some such thing. Might be good people holed up there. Look around. There's nothing for miles."

He's right. There is not a town anywhere as far as I can see and this flat field must go a good fifty miles in any direction. Could be the town is in a river valley and the low sun and waving corn is playing tricks with our eyes. The GPS says that Iowa state road 142 runs north and south about a mile ahead. So there is some civilization somewhere.

"Let's bring her down a few hundred yards past the church," I say, noticing at the same time that there is a full plank fence all the way around, making the church the center of a compound. I can make out what looks like a well house and, as the sun is no longer in our eyes, the skeleton frame of a windmill, spinning slowly in the morning breeze, the same breeze following us.

Tim steers the balloon like he's at the state fair, swinging wide around the steeple and dropping low, a sort of swoop that he has a way of doing that brings the gondola up and over and then down in a sort of hover outside the church, away from the yard where some asshole can't easily jump in it. Just before we land we see a sign, ST. TERESA OF AL-BICORN CONVENT with a pretty gold cross surrounded by a halo or some might say a wreath of corn still in the husk.

"Tim," I whisper. "This is a goddamned convent . . . a nunnery, dude. Bitches and nothing but."

"Now what?" he asks.

"How the fuck do I know. Maybe they're gone. Maybe they're holed up. Get the guns and don't fire till you see the pink of their nipples," I say, more a fool today than I was yesterday, less a fool than I'll be tomorrow. Tim jumps over the side of the gondola and does the tether thing, dimming the flame to an idle.

"I hope they have some butter and salt and a goddamned popper, because I'm not leaving until the show is over," he says as he starts walking toward the convent. "Forgive me Father, because I might have to sin. But I sure hope not."

I hate to do it, but I tie MG loosely to the inside of the balloon. It's hard enough for him to jump in and out and right now I don't want to have to carry him.

We approach cautiously and notice that the fancy wrought-iron gate in the middle of a ten foot high brick wall is not locked. I'm thinking this is like one of those lobster traps like where you put a piece of lobster food in the back of a cage and leave the door open. The stupid lobster thinks someone forgot his lunch and the next thing he knows he's bright red, covered with butter and deader than Abe Lincoln.

"I don't think this is safe," I say to Rick.

"Sure, boss, but what are we going to do about supplies? I think that MacDonalds is only serving breakfast and I'm hankering for some chicken Maccrappits."

"Well, let's be careful."

"Sounds like a plan, chief," says Tim. "Careful is one of my middle names. The other is 'Stupid.'"

The big oak door of the convent is locked tight and looks like it's been that way for a few centuries. A sign near the door says, DELIVERIES IN REAR. I wait for some inane comment from Tim, but he's looking more serious now.

We circle the building, crouching every time we go by a window. Around the back is an orchard and apples and are all over the place, stinking like mad and covered with a bazillion yellow jackets. The last window is slightly open and I hear a moan from inside.

"Tim . . . *shhhhh*," I whisper. "Someone's inside."

Tim circles a huge rose bush and gets low to the sill and

peeks over. I do the same. The room is dark except for some shafts of light streaming through a stained glass window about ten feet up. There are wooden chairs in neat rows and a crucifix against the wall. We watch for a while and see or hear nothing. Then, another groan.

I shade my eyes with my hand and scan the room. Nothing. Then I see the crucifix move and figure it's a trick of the light. We circle the building carefully crouching beneath each window. There is no one there, but there is a crucifix in every room. We circle again and still the same. There is moaning from one of the rooms. We look inside carefully and now realize that the crucifix has a live dude on it. It's just too dark and shadowy to see exactly what is going on.

"Let's go in," says Tim.

"What for?"

"He's alive."

"He's two minutes from death and even if he farts a prayer up to Heaven and manages to live we can't carry around a burden like that."

"Then let's get some supplies. And maybe there are other guys in here."

"What are you going to do with guys?"

"Save 'em. Just because the bitches are animals doesn't make us animals. Right?"

I just look at him and think that maybe the sun has baked his brain. I follow him to the back door and sneak in behind him as it creaks open. Flies are buzzing and it smells like garbage that hasn't been taken out in six weeks.

The kitchen is huge but nothing is used. It's as if everybody up and left in a hurry. There's a little cross over the door leading to the rest of the convent and a stitched sampler with the Lord's Prayer done in real neat threads and pictures of little girls and boys kneeling in prayer while an angel hovers over their heads.

We walk under the small cross into the dining hall. It's

huge with a table that could seat maybe twenty people. It's neat and tidy with a pewter bowl at each seat; no knives or forks. On the wall between the windows so that the glare from outside blurs our vision is a life-sized cross. There is a statue of Jesus lying on the floor next to it.

"Guess he thought it would be better to leave and didn't quite make it to his chariot," says Tim.

"But who the fuck is on the cross?" I ask.

"Help meeeee," a voice says. "For the love of God, help me." There is the man, naked, nailed to the cross in the place of the fake Jesus.

"Jesus," I say more like a dumbass than usual.

Tim heads over. "You okay?"

"Fuck no, man, do I look okay? The bitches have crucified me. Get me down before they come back. Please!"

"Before who comes back?" I ask.

"The nuns."

"Nuns?" I say.

"Yeah, they're zombies, man. Get me down."

"How?" asks Tim.

"There's tools in the drawer over there. In that chest of drawers. Get something to pull the nails out." Tim goes over and opens the draw pulling out a claw hammer. I stand next to the guy and see that he has ropes tied around both legs.

"Hurry. Please!" he says.

Tim pulls a chair over and stands on it and starts working the nail that's through the guy's wrists. Then I see that his feet are gone. And most of the flesh on his calves.

"Man, what did they do?" I ask.

"They cut my fucking feet off. To eat them. Drink the blood. Stop me from bleeding to death by tying tourniquets around the legs. There's more of us in here. Every room."

I can see he's delirious, going in and out of consciousness.

"Bless you my sons. This day you will be in heaven with

59

me," he says.

"That would be nice," Tim answers.

We bring him to a sofa and lie him down. He's bleeding and all his wounds are festering with puss and maggots. Flies buzz around us.

"How did he survive?" asks Tim.

"By the will of the almighty, my sons," he says.

"Can you tell us anything?"

"Help the others. I'll be OK."

"But are the bitches coming back?" I ask.

"Yesssssss. They will be here soon and you will become one with us and the Lord," he says.

"I don't think so, buddy. Can you tell us what's going on here?" asks Tim.

"They use our blood and flesh as part of a . . . ."

We hear the metal gate outside grinding open and the sounds of gravel crunching on the driveway. Tim runs over to the window.

"You ain't gonna believe this. Them nuns are driving. Did you know they could do that?"

"Shit no. How is that even possible?"

"Now what?"

"Put him in front of the cross like he fell off. Let's hide upstairs."

"Yes," he says. "Upstairs. They don't go upstairs. Never. But first do me a favor."

"Sure. What?"

"Kill me."

"What?"

"Please kill me. I can't go through this anymore."

"But . . . ."

Tim takes the claw hammer and smashes the guy's skull in with a solid thwack that spatters brain and blood all over. The family-friendly cameraman I once knew no longer resides in Tim's bones. The man has changed, but I am not complaining. Drastic times and all that.

"Come on. Drag him over here," he says. We drop him at the foot of the cross, toppled like he struggled, fell and crushed his own head.

"Let's get upstairs," I say.

"Aye, aye, Captain," says Tim as he runs for the stairway. "I hope that poor fucker was right."

CHAPTER 10

The second floor was a catacomb of small bedrooms. Really they were just cubicles with small cots with straw mattresses and a tiny bedside table with a lamp. The beds had not been slept in nor were they made. In the main corridor was a large grate in the floor which gave a view of the main living area below. I had seen this sort of thing in older houses where the heater was in the cellar and would generate heat in the upper stories simply by its rising through strategically placed vents in the floor. There were no blowers or any type of electrical assistance whatsoever; just convection.

Tim went into one of the cells and looked out a small window. He signaled to me to come over. In the courtyard below were a large van and a station wagon. The wagon had about six or eight nuns in it, all of whom stood by while two nuns unloaded the van. In the van were four guys in prison uniforms. It was obvious what had happened. The nuns were probably regular visitors at the state penitentiary to bring food and religious guidance to the bunch of miscreants within. When the GaGa hit, the bitches, formerly ladies of the cloth, took to using the prison as a stock yard, some part of their brain still latched onto their old daily routine. Those criminal fuckers could not get out and the nuns knew how to get in.

Here's what scared me the most. Those nuns were organized. Dead, yes, but somehow communicating and thinking. My only guess was either the virus had evolved in them, beyond something we'd ever seen before, or all of their prayers over the years had given them some kind of divine power.

The guys were in shackles and tied to each other chain gang style. One of the nuns had a gray outfit on, the others were in typical black and white. She was obviously the Mother Superior or whatever she was called because she was giving

silent orders to the others who said nothing but simply prodded the guys into the convent with pitch forks which they had
gathered from where they had been left along the side of the
building facing the orchard. I had seen them on our recon-
noiter but hadn't thought twice about it. I mean, nuns make
their own shit and grow their own food and such. I guess they
still do but it ain't corn, nor wheat, nor roses, my friends; it's
fucking creeps from the local pokie.

The guys' mouths were taped shut, but they were screaming anyway. Several of them had bloodied arms and legs and
unless my imagination had got the better of me, there were
tears in the clothing like they had been bitten by dogs. But
I'm sure it was the bitches putting the fear of God in these
bastards the best way they knew how: tooth and nail.

We watched with wide eyes and I kept thinking they were
going to see our balloon like a giant, swollen testicle in a field
of pubic corn husks, or hear MG's whimpering, but they were
too damned focused on their catch.

The next moments are still vivid.

Tim and I tiptoe over to the heat vent and watch the action. The door is kicked wide open and we can first hear the
men screaming through their muffled mouths. The bitches
are chittering with their teeth like squirrels that haven't eaten
in a year. There are six guys and they are all herded into the
room right below us. One of them tries to kick out at a nun
and she goes for the offending leg, biting through the tough
striped fabric and tearing away at the flesh of his shin. He
howls and is then smashed in the face with a right hook from
Mother Superior. He is knocked out colder than a wedge.

She motions to two of the nuns to untie him from the
pack and he is stripped naked. It is then that the bitches howl
because they have seen the guy that we tried to help. He's in
the other room but we hear the ruckus. He is dragged in and
laid out next to the new guy. The signal is given and he is devoured from the balls up through his gut. His face is stripped

of flesh and his nose is crunched in the jaws of a zombie bitch like a walnut in a nutcracker. She pulls it away with her teeth and what little blood the fucker still has in him pools around the floor where one of the bitches is lapping at it as it leaves a huge stain on the fancy Oriental rug. Nothing goes to waste and he is stripped bare to the bones, which are dragged out of the room and out of our line of sight.

Two nun bitches bring the empty cross that he had formerly occupied into the room and the new guy is nailed in place of the old one. He wakes up in the middle and screams through his duct tape gag until a reddish foam seeps out of his nostrils. I'm thinking that whatever this guy did that landed him in the hoosegow, I hope it was worth it. Then I think that if more of these fuckers knew that this might happen to them, people could throw their locks away, women could walk naked down the street and kids would never need to be afraid of strangers because no one, I mean no one, would want this as a punishment. Justice has a way of finding you, I think. It sure found these bastards. Tim looks at me like he knows what I'm thinking and gives me a thumbs up. That guy has got to have ESP or something, but then I realize that I can hear someone on the stairs coming up toward us and he's giving me the high sign to maybe get the fuck out of there. But to where?

We each slip into one of the cells. I can hear Tim slide under a cot. I do the same. We hold our breaths. A nun bitch ambles along the corridor. She enters one of the rooms and shuffles around. She comes into my room. I can see her face smeared with blood from the feast downstairs. She smells the air, raising her face like a hound on a scent. But the blood is masking my smell and she has some guts stuck near her nostrils. She leaves. I assume she does the same thing throughout the rooms, finding nothing. I hear her shuffling down the corridor, mumbling and gnashing her teeth until the sounds of her returning downstairs die away.

Tim opens the door to my room and says, "That was fun."

I climb out from under the cot. He signals to me to return to the grate with one hand, the other with his finger on his lips. Like I need to be reminded to be quiet, the dumb fuck.

The convict has been nailed to the cross and one of the bitches has jammed barbed wire onto his head like the crown of thorns. They drag the cross to the corner of the room and heave ho it up into the corner, the convict moaning and groaning, a puddle of urine on the floor where he was. The others have been pushed and shoved down the cellar steps and I can hear them grumbling and pleading through their gags with an occasional yelp that indicates the biting is still going on to keep control. The cellar door slams and the two nun bitches who got the convicts into the cellar join the rest around the current crucifixion.

The mother superior raises her arms and begins to chant some shit that sounds like Latin. I look at Tim and he shrugs as if to say, "This is the wackiest shit ever." Which it is. I can't make out a word but I see her take a large curved carving knife from under her robe and as she raises it, she speaks, actual fucking words, even if they're a guttural scraping from decaying vocal cords, "Take . . . . . . eat . . . for it is my body." Least that what I make of it. And she slices a slab off his calf as the other bitches kneel. The convict screams and moans and bleeds. The mother superior takes a bite of the meat and passes it around to the others who each take a slurpy chomp.

One of the nuns rises to her feet, goes into the kitchen and comes back with a water glass. She goes to the convict and catches the blood seeping from his wounded leg and catches it. In the glass, there is some milk probably left over from who knows where and the blood and milk mix like a strawberry malt.

The mother superior takes the glass and mumbles and moans, and through the guttural tones and scratchy nonsense I can decipher the words: "Drink this for it is my blood which is a covenant with you." She takes a big gulp and I can feel weeks of rations rise from my stomach into my mouth.

She passes the glass around and they each take a sip. Just when the last decomposing nun has drunk her fill, I let go with a barf the size of Cleveland and it drops through the grate and lands on a nun bitch's head kneeling there like Mother Teresa from Hell.

"We're fucked, good buddy," says Tim. I think he's right.

Two of the nuns start lapping at the vomit on the one's head. The rest begin their howling and start for the stairs. We head for the window.

It's locked and we can hear the shrieking, howling bull-shit and the clunking of the undead feet on the stairs, the Mother Superior shouting in some hideous garbled language.

Tim picks up the small nightstand and jams it through the window, knocking the glass, the mullions and the frame out like it was hit with dynamite.

"It's a long drop," I say.

Tim climbs out but I see him standing there beckoning me out. There's a ledge he's standing on. I climb out and we side walk our way along the ledge and rain gutter to a huge copper downspout. It's like a firepole. Tim shimmies down as I see the bitches climbing out after us. I fire a round from my pistol but the damn thing bucks and I blast a hole through the shingles above. Fuck it, I can't shoot well while trying to play Spider-Man. I follow Tim and we're on the ground as the first nun bitch reaches the downspout and goes flying down it like a sack of shit wrapped in white and black gift paper. Tim is in the station wagon and it looks like he's going to take off without me, but instead he turns the key and rams the nun bitch between the bumper and the side of the building and her eyes pop out of her head and hang there by the threads which ooze that tar-like black shit. He puts it in re-verse and she collapses, then puts it in gear again and floors it, hitting her so hard while she's crumbled that her ribs pop out through her habit and the downspout, which is what he was aiming at to begin with, comes down but with the Mother Superior hanging on to it. The others are on the ledge but start heading back through the window, which means they'll be pouring through the door in a few seconds.

"Time to go, buddy," I yell. But the Mother Superior bitch is on the hood of the car now and beating her head against the windshield to try to break it to get to Tim. He moves forward by flooring it again and jams on the brakes. She slides off but as she goes over the hood ornament, it slashes open her face, pulling some stringy arteries, veins and nerves along with it. She drops off the end of the hood but leaps up faster than you can say, "Hail Mary" and she's on the attack again.

Tim jumps out of the car and I figure he's going to run for it, but, no, he's on the offensive. I slide in to the driver's side while he pulls the bitch off the hood. She's snapping like a mad dog in fast motion, the grinding clacking teeth going a mile a second. He wrestles her off but she clamps down on the window of the open car door and crunches the safety glass into a billion little jewels. He punches her in the face where the gash is and her eye gets pushed back into her head.

"Get ready," Tim yells. But I'm seeing bitches staggering out of the door as if the condition of the Mother Superior has made them loopy. They're actually groping and bumbling around, arms outstretched like in a grade B movie.

"Better hurry," I yell.

He drags the Mother Superior to the ground while she kicks and screams and pieces of glass fly out of her mouth like popcorn in a popper and holds her head under the wheel of the car.

"Back it up slow," he shouts. I do and I can feel the crunch of something under the wheel which is, of course, her fucking head.

"Go, dude, go," he says. I gun it and I can feel the squash

of skull and brains.

Tim runs around and jumps in the back as the first nun bitches stumble over to us. We fly out of there and stop a hundred feet away. The undead nuns are gathered around the body of Mother Superior and trying to put the brain back in the head and one of them is holding the jaw and kissing it as she tries to fit it to where the bitch's mouth used to be.

"Man, look at that shit," Tim says.

As I'm about to drive away, I see the cellar window and there's a dude looking out with duct tape on his mouth and a please-don't-leave-us-here expression.

"Tim. Those prisoners. Whatdya think?," I say. It was his idea to look for any living men inside.

"Don't do the crime if you can't do the time," says Tim as he puts his foot on top of mine and jams the gas pedal to the floor, crashing us through the fence toward the balloon. "Appeal denied."

CHAPTER 11

The wind had finally tapered off and the moon's silver face shone through the clouds which scudded across the sky like rats following the Pied Piper of Hamlin. Tim was staring at the GPS and MG was asleep, curled up against the side of the basket out of our way, a position he learned worked best for his lazy self.

"It says we're in northern Ohio, near the border," said Tim.

"Shit. I guess we're lucky it's not worse. The fuel looks okay but we need to stop for water."

"Let's ride at three hundred feet and keep your eyes sharp for someplace we can get some . . . and land safe."

The balloon glided on a smooth breeze that followed us, the tops of tall pines aimed up like arrows in a huge quiver. The forest we were over spread in every direction and after an hour or so of moving slowly we saw the shimmer of a huge lake below, its silver edges like the scales of a fish.

"Lake Minooka," said Tim.

"Water, water fucking everywhere but not a drop to drink," I said. "We can't land anywhere."

"Where there's a lake there are lake houses. Where there are lake houses, there are roads and all we need is a two- lane with a straight stretch and we'll be all right. Keep looking for a roof or a dock or something that says, 'This is my fancy fucking cabin on this fancy fucking lake.'"

Staring down at the lake, I could see the lapping of small waves, edging white in the full moonlight as they lapped at a long dock stuck out into the water.

"There's one . . . a boat dock. Look . . . I can see the shine on the metal roof."

Tim peered over the edge of the basket right next to me with his arm extended down as he guided the balloon lower and lower, his finger pointing like a divining rod, mind-reading his way to a driveway, then a road. Like a flare, at least to me, I saw the glint of a double yellow line between the trees.

"There's a road. Check the GPS."

"Nothing here," said Tim. "The fucking thing is telling us we're 'off-road.'"

"Let's just follow the goddamned yellow line. There's got to be a break in these trees somewhere," I said. MG grunted in his sleep.

Within minutes, we were close enough to the tops of the pines to reach out and touch them.

"Take it easy, Timmyme boy. We don't want to get skewered on these things." There below us, the trees parted and a parking lot almost as big as a football field unrolled beneath us, its criss-cross grid of parking spaces illuminated by the moon.

"Damn. Finally. Bring 'er down . . . lean right . . . lean right . . . lean . . . " The basket bottom dragged on the loose gravel and ground the macadam, making us lurch forward where we came to a sudden stop, one of our lines wrapped around a "Parking By Permit Only" sign.

"Remind me to get a permit before we come here again," I said. MG had jumped up startled by the tipping of the basket. "It's okay, boy." I patted his grizzled head. Tim had his rifle out and I snapped the release on my holster. I never thought I'd be the type to find the handle of a pistol so comforting and so sub-consciously re-assuring. Tim powered down the jets.

"Let's sit a spell. Make sure no one spotted us," said Tim.

I let five minutes pass on my watch. No sound but the gentle breeze rustling the pines. Sounded like the beach, a distant surf breaking far away.

"Let's go," I said. "Looks fine."

MG was the first out by way of my hands on his hairy dog ass, nimbler than anyone would imagine. I climbed out carefully, holding the three gallon milk containers which had already saved our asses.

"Let's head back toward that house."

Tim had a worried look on his face. "You think that's a good idea?"

"Sure," I said. "There's nobody going to be up here."

"Dude, I think you're wrong. Look, it's only just turned September. There could be a whole family in that house that was here for summer vacation and they're holed up. Why not? That's what I'd be doing."

"Yeah, you're right. Let's circle it and case the joint. If it looks clear, we'll use the tap to refill and take whatever food we can carry. They might even have guns and ammo. I'm not big on drinking lake water and getting the runs at a thousand feet up." Tim looked at me as if to say, "Man, you are some pussy," but he thought better of it and just answered, "Come on. Let's do it."

CHAPTER 12

We followed the double yellow-lined road back toward the west, keeping to the trees that fringed it. It was no more than a mile back that we saw the hulking silhouette of the house which was actually a log cabin—not one like Lincoln lived in, but one of those fancy, machine made types with a metal roof and a wrap-around porch. There were four Adirondack chairs sitting on that porch empty and aimed at the lake. At this angle, the surface looked like it was covered with about a million silver dollars floating in the light of the moon. A few clouds passed by, covered the moon and threw everything into a dark so dark it was like the air had turned to ink. It was then that we saw a small flicker of light through one of the windows. It was a kerosene lamp. MG just settled into a bed of pine needles—these things were everywhere—and Tim and I did the Indian thing and crept over for a better look.

Peeping in as slyly as we can, we see a man, a woman, obviously his wife and two younger girls sitting around a table— looks like they're playing a board game or cards. Doesn't take a rocket scientist to see that the GaGa has not hit here. Frankly, in hindsight, it should've been obvious. This place is in the middle of nowhere. People that would have used that parking lot had to come from other places and my guess is they were—most of them—infected and then eaten. These guys got away with it through either good luck or good sense. The fact that the mother and kids are not making their way through the dude's intestine is a testament to the smarts as far as I'm concerned. This will never be known as "the time of the Lucky." The GaGa makes no allowance for luck. It is the end all be-all of a major Earth-Fuck.

"Check it out," Tim whispers. "He's got an arsenal on the wall."

I'm seeing at least ten rifles or shotguns and a bunch of

pistols laid out on a sideboard and a mountain of ammo that looks like the Cheops pyramid.

"Should we knock?" I say like a total dumbass.

"Are you a total dumbass or what?" replies Tim. At least I know where I stand, I think to myself.

"Well, we're on their side—we're guys and we must be okay?"

"Yeah, right, like those guys back in Kansas. We make a peep and one of us is gonna have a hole as big as the Holland Tunnel in his head. Listen. Back up into the undergrowth. I'll stand to the side of the door. Shout a greeting in your friendliest voice. If he comes out firing, I'll shoot his ass. If he comes out with a question on his lips, we'll try to make peace. Either way, we're getting provisions."

"When did you become chief of this operation?" I ask.

"I'm not. You can lead, friend, but I got to voice my opinion if I think you're going to get me killed for no good reason. Comprende?"

"I'll get in the bushes; signal me when you're ready."

I get out behind a tree and say loudly, "Er, excuse me, sir . . . I'm out here and I mean no harm. I'm a friend not a foe. Hello? Hello?"

Two shots in quick succession hit the tree I'm standing behind. Chips of bark fly off. I can see the flash points from inside the house. He's shooting at me through a partially opened window.

"Sir . . . are you fucking nuts?" I shout. "I'm a newsman trying to get east . . . "

Three more bullets hit that tree. I'm thinking this prick is going to saw this tree down with a rifle.

Tim has sidled up to the window, crouches down just below and grabs the barrel.

"Didn't you hear him, you stupid dickwad?" he shouts. "We're just passing through. Cut us a break. All we need is water."

73

"Got any females with you?" he asks.

"Fuck no," I answer. "We're clean. Been on the road for two weeks." I am not going to mention the balloon.

The guy waits, sizes us up. "There's a shower stall out back. Strip down, shower and scrub and cover up with towels. I got duds in here I can give you. I've got my wife and two daughters in here too and I don't want them contaminated. Go clean up. I'll explain later. And I got more than this rifle here and so does my wife. Check your bullshit at the door and you're welcome."

"Deal," I say. "Thank you."

We shower in ice cold water but without even realizing it, we haven't washed in over two weeks. No wonder MG sleeps most of the time as far away from us as he can. I guess we smell pretty ripe. I guess again that we're used to it.

An hour later we're past the introductions and sitting down to a duck dinner while MG rests in the leaves outside the door. He's got a few bits of duck meat he's wolfing down as well.

"I catch them on the lake. It's easy and makes no noise. Use a capture net. Ducks are pretty stupid. Dig in, fellas."

They're stupid? I think. They ain't being chased by a bunch of cannibal zombie bitches.

Turns out his name is Doctor Paul Walters. His wife is Agnes. He's got a twelve- year-old named Samantha and a ten-year-old named Hadley. We make some small talk but we know the spirit of the GaGa is in the room only no one wants to talk about it.

"Listen, guys," Doc says. "I'm in charge of an operation at the hospital in town. We're doing government research on the disease. Finster Teachers College is about ten miles north of town . . . mostly women students and they got infected when some books arrived from back east. That's the theory anyway. They killed and ate most of the male faculty and . . . "

"Paul . . . the children Must we talk about this over dinner?"

his wife says.

"Sorry, dear. Pass the salt will you, Tom?"

"It's Tim. Here's the salt."

Later, we sit around a small fire in the fireplace and things even seem slightly normal. Of course, they are most definitely not. Doc says he'll tell us more tomorrow. A picture is worth a thousand words and all that horse shit. But I'm not minding the peace and quiet and I can see Tim is looking chilled out and the way he might have been before all this started. I remember him then, but I never knew him. Funny, that's the way it is. You meet people, work with them, even, but you don't bother knowing them. You store them away in some file cabinet in your head and then don't ever bother adding anything or even remembering to check back. Then the shit hits the fan and all you've got in the world is a stranger you thought you knew. Now you need him to live. It and mostly everything else is fucked up. Isn't it?

CHAPTER 13

The hospital sits low and squat on a hillside just off of Main Street. It's got a walled-in parking lot, a great thing to have in place when your building is going to be used as a fort. At 40 foot intervals, soldiers with rifles are posted. A makeshift watch tower has been erected with a giant Klieg light and there's a row of sandbags as an inner barricade 50 feet beyond the fence. Very Afghanistan, I'm thinking.

Doc Walters pulls up to the gate.

"Hey, Jim," he says lowering the window. "I've got some recruits with me. Open up."

"Sure thing, Doc. Frank has been asking about you."

"Good. I like to keep him guessing."

"Say what?" the guard asks.

"Nothin'. Thanks for the heads up."

Of course the Doc has a special "reserved" space but it looks like there are not many other vehicles. But rank has its privileges. Just as we pull in, a large United Van Lines 18 wheeler pulls in and goes past where we're parking to an area at the back of the building. We get out and go over, led by the Doc who's very animated like he just won the lottery or something.

On signal a bunch of orderlies and guards come running out and they're holding cattle prods and steel rods with what looks like a large pin cushion on the end.

"Ready," yells one of the attending white coats. The driver opens the rear door, pulls the ramp out and runs for cover.

The GaGas start pouring out the back, stiff and disoriented, slow-moving and mostly naked. Many of them are wearing Denver U. t-shirts or hoodies.

"A wonderful batch, Carl. Wonderful. I knew those dorms would have a supply," says the Doc like its Christmas Eve under the tree.

There are about forty of these co-eds, all pale and pink, the white eyes blank as ice cubes. They immediately attempt to attack the men but these guys know what to expect and the bitches are prodded and poked and eventually led into the double back door of the hospital just to the right of the old Emergency Room entrance.

"Carl," says the Doc. "That blonde with no shirt and the warm up pants," he gestures. "Put her aside in the special room."

"Anything you say, Doc," and good old Carl throws a net over the blonde who sets up to howling and snarling trying to bite Carl and his helper as she's led into the E.R.

"Move it, you fucking whore," yells Carl. He stabs at her ass with the prod. "Get the fuck in there."

She screams, but obeys. Like a beef cow entering a slaughterhouse.

"We've been scouring the area for supplies of reproductively young victims for the important work we're doing here. It seems like an easy task, but Carl and I pour over municipal maps for hours thinking, 'where would we congregate if we were infected.' You see, they're a good deal like animals out of their natural habitat. Remember that scene in *King Kong* where the guy is trying to figure out where in New York City this giant ape will go. You see he's not in the jungle anymore. So Jack, I think his name is, sees the World Trade Center—obviously it was there when the movie was made—that was a tragedy, wasn't it, and notes that it resembles the two promontories that the ape called home back on his island. I think it was called 'Skull Island.' I love a good movie, you know. Miss them terribly. Now it's just me and the wife and the kids hitting the Parchesi board. It's not much, but it's all we've got. Oh, I'm boring you. Sorry. Yes, we try to figure out, as I was saying, where the bitches would congregate. You'll love this. We found almost a hundred of them in the designer section of Saks Fifth Avenue downtown. Now, mind you, they were not doing anything there other than eating the male sales help that had the misfortune of hiding in a department store. But no, they were simply milling about. Perhaps they thought it was familiarly comforting or something. I really have not devoted much time to the mindset of these creatures. Once I get past the physiological changes, I'll focus on their minds, such as they have minds."

Doc turned abruptly about and said, "Now, boys, follow me." Which we did. Tim nudged me and said, "This guy has more loose screws than a hardware store." The Doc smiled as in a world of his own. Don't know if he heard the remark or not. Don't care.

We're led up the main building steps. There's a statue of some dude in a toga holding an implement.

"Must be the God of Medicine," Tim says pointing. "That motherfucker is spinning in his grave."

We follow the Doc down a long corridor through three sets of double doors until we reach a place called "Outpatient Clinic." Doc calls it the "ward."

The ward was a large rectangular room with green tiles and milky white walls. Dead TV screens with their thick black cables stuck through the walls still watched blankly, their glassy reflections twisting the scene in kaleidoscope style. There were twenty beds, two rows of ten in the middle of the room. Along the periphery, rolling metal tables loaded with blipping beeping monitors and wires like the head of Medusa. The patients lay in the beds, all young women, all the victims of GaGa. The Doc was right. They looked almost normal. The third stage of the disease rejuvenated their bodies. They were flushed pink, maybe a little too pink, more like large babies than college co-eds. Their faces were blank and chalky but the beeping monitors clearly showed these were not dead people and they were not undead either. They were re-born dead people, revitalized dead people. We'd have plenty of time I hoped to come up with a fitting term that we could use to tell future generations what was born by our generation. Words would escape the most talkative morons who saw this.

The girls' eyes were milk white, the irises, just as the doc had said, were pure white, the pupil a tiny black hole, empty like a shark's eye. Many of them moaned, some made that rasping sound that became their signature voices. It was all a deep base sound like the sound of trucks passing over an elevated highway very far off. Rumblings, sputterings and an occasional minute squeal—was it a truck braking? No, it was the signal of pain as one of the orderlies changed an IV.

They were being fed through clear plastic tubes inserted into their tracheas—intubation I think they called it. The bottles that fed the tubes held a hideous concoction of what was clearly flesh and blood although from what animal, I would not find out.

"Fuck, Kent, they're feeding them ground-up people. These fuckers are crazy, man, crazy," Tim said under his breath. I could see his hands shaking.

"Listen, bear with it. It'll be okay. They're on our side, right?"

"Who the fuck knows."

The girls' arms and legs were tied down with thin leather straps and they were all uniformly spread eagle, a thin sheet covering them from toe to neck. From each bed, next to the traditional clipboard, hung a tube of KY jelly.

Doc Walters finally came over to us after checking some charts and conferring with a few of the orderlies.

"You see, we've discovered that roughly fourteen hours after the second phase begins, what we call the morbid phase, regeneration begins and the rapidly putrefying flesh of the dead victims of the GaGa re-invigorates. The heart and lungs resume their function and the rest follow, not unlike the newborn brought forth from his mother's womb on the delivery table. We call this third phase, 'regenerative' and the victims are called ReGens."

"Interesting," I say, sounding every bit the total moron I think I am.

"I think you'll find this more interesting," he continues. "We've failed miserably with artificial insemination. We don't know why it didn't work but it didn't. If we're going to turn the less than zero population growth problem around and follow the initiative from the Pentagon, this process has to succeed with at least a fifty percent success rate. Seems we're on the right track."

I looked at him and knew Tim was glued to the floor.

"These girls are all at the most fertile point of their cycles. We monitor them very carefully. It's just a matter of . . . "

A door opened and a trooper walked in with an AK-47. He sat in what looked like a sawed-down version of a lifeguard bench, the kind you see with the "Lifeguard on Duty" sign attached to it on almost every beach. Doc Walters signaled to one of the long white-coated orderlies who left and came back through the door with six soldiers, the same National Guard types that were out front and manning the perimeter and monitoring the halls. They were in their boxers and T's.

The orderly told them, "Pick your mate, boys. You've got sixty seconds."

The men wandered quickly through the grid of beds, some looking at faces, some squeezing breasts and thighs, a few looking under the sheets.

"Make it snappy," shouted the Doc, making me nearly jump to the ceiling.

"Calm down, Kent," he said. "This is just part of life. We're making life here. This is where the human race will begin again. I've even thought of calling this hospital 'The Eden Institute.' Get it? This is the new Garden of Eden and while we have a number of Adams and a great many Eves, it's basically the same thing. Don't you see?'

Tim coughed one of those coughs that actually says, "Bullshit!" but the Doc, he was too into the glory of this mess to notice the comment. I scowled at Tim with that same look your mother gave you when you were in church and you farted and giggled. You know, the look that says, "Make another sound, Junior, and you'll be pushin' up daisies."

Eventually the guys all chose the girls they wanted and stood at attention. The guard with the AK-47 tightened his grip on the gun and with a signal to an orderly, the lights went on half power which, if you know anything about fluorescent lighting, makes some of them flicker on and off like a coming electrical storm.

"This is part of the mood we like to establish," said Doc Walters. "We're not animals here."

The guys undraped the women who were still tied down. The girls were unbelievably beautiful—at least from the neck down. They were chronologically college girls, 18 to 21 or 22. But their skin was even younger. They had rejuvenated to the extreme. Perfect skin as if it had never been touched. I guess it hadn't except in the herding process. Each man approached the task at hand in a different way, each slathering his hard-on with a dollop of jelly. But in no time, the guys were on top of them or yanking them awkwardly up so their knees were pointed upward, oozing black where the straps dug in. Something inside me was completely revolted. I've been to frat house parties that were certainly as close to a Roman orgy as you could imagine. But this was sick. Real sick and I did not want to watch anymore. Tim stared dumbfounded. But the Doc, he was taking notes and periodically checking his watch. The girls were moaning or squeaking and the ones who were present but not involved picked up the sound until the room was filled with a drone like a humongous beehive. I put my hand over my ears but it didn't help. I started to leave and Doc said, "Want a turn? It's not bad, you know. It's a cold cunt, but I remember in my youth that I would gladly have taken . . . And think of it, you'll be contributing to humanity. Maybe a session in the prep room would help. Eh?"

"What's the prep room?" I ask.

"Just a TV and some porn vids. Nothing outrageous. Believe me, just about everyone here has had a go. It's for the good of mankind. Even myself. Nothing personal. Just science in its most forgiving manner."

"I think you're a sick fuck, Doc," said Tim.

"Are you a homosexual, Tim?"

"How about you go fuck yourself," said Tim.

"Listen, chill, Tim. I'm sorry, Doc. We've been through a lot. Tim's not himself. I think your work is important but we've got other fish to fry, you know. But don't think we don't appreciate . . . "

"You fucking bitch!" one of the soldiers shouted. He was on top of her and she was twisting so hard and giving out the raspy voice; she managed to spit on his face and hiss like an alley cat. He punched the girl in the face and she screamed, a shrill "nooooooooooooo" that made my blood run cold. The black ooze spilled from her mouth and from her nose and dripped to the floor like tar, teeth floating in it.

The guard in the lifeguard chair aimed and fired a stuttering volley of lead that blew the soldier right off of her. This set the other women screeching and snorting; the room was like the monkey cage in a zoo. Half the guy's arm and shoulder got blown away and landed on one of the unchosen girls who started chewing at it ferociously. Part of his head and brain sprayed all over one soldier who was orgasming in a woman while she licked the blood and brain that had landed on her face. He was cumming and vomiting at the same time. Put that on "Maury" and see how the fucking audience likes it.

"Everyone out!" shouted Doc Walters. "Every one of you, out of here! Get them out of here, Ted. Now!! Right now!! Do you hear me?"

"Yes, Dr. Walters, immediately. You, there, pack it in. We'll resume later if you've not finished." Ted was the lab coat guy but he sounded like this hairdresser that Jen took me to last year. He led the soldiers out like they were naked school kids that got caught by Sister Mary Patricia in a circle jerk. The attendants and orderlies rushed around dabbing here, picking up there, calming the screams and being careful not to get near the gaping chomping mouths. The lights came up. It was a slaughter-fuckhouse in hell. There's really no way I can describe it any more. And if I could, I don't want to. Maybe some things are better left unsaid. Unseen. Undone.

Tim and I left and sat in the lobby of that hospital and couldn't say a word. All I remembered was Mrs. Walters coming into my room the night before. I thought she wanted to get laid. She crept in—must have been 3 A.M. "What do you want, Mrs. Walters?" I asked." I'm engaged to be married and you're already marr . . . ."

"I don't want to sleep with you, you idiot. Listen. Don't go to the hospital with Paul. Don't. Please. They do things there. You won't want to see them. You're a nice boy, Kent. And Tim too. This world is gone. It's over. God has judged us and it's the End of Days. Save your souls and don't go."

"Sure. Of course. Whatever you say." I lied to her. She made me want to see it even more. Man, that was some mistake. Don't know if I can forgive myself. But if I don't, who will?

CHAPTER 14

"I could use a joint," said Tim. "Laced with PCP."

"Don't let it in," I said. "Let's just play this game and move on."

The Doc came out of the ward and said, "I'm a little disappointed in you boys. We need all the help we can get. A lot of these fellas here are shooting blanks, as they say, and some of them are . . . well, you might say genetically defective. I'm going for something big, you know, something that will serve and save mankind."

"I get it, Doc," I said.

"I don't think you do, my boy."

"We do," said Tim.

"What you two boys do not know is that on the current course of the disease and the attrition rate of human males, the species homo sapiens will be off this planet in about twenty years by the Pentagon's best guess."

"Yeah, that's a bunch of fucking geniuses," said Tim. "They're always right, aren't they?"

"Well, perhaps I can invite you boys to stay and help out as any patriotic American would feel compelled to do without needing a great deal of convincing. After all, we owe our country a debt of gratitude. Come this way."

He took us to a door that had his name on it and under his name it said "Coroner." Now I'm getting the picture. The door leads to a down stairway. It's the morgue. You know, with all the stainless steel doors and cabinets, the cabinets fitted with long drawers to hold the stiffs. Only the stiffs ain't stiff anymore. They are quite pliable and running around like the crazies instead of behaving and staying in the deep cooler. Naughty bitches, I'm thinking. Dead is dead, now girls, isn't it? Come, come now! Back in your nice sanitary if somewhat chilly drawers. You'll get a spanking and won't have any pudding tonight. Then I think, I'm losing it. My mind has flown the coop.

In the center of the room, there are three gurneys, stainless steel jobbers that have those whirligig wheels. Each sits under a lamp hung from the ceiling, the kind that throws down a cone of light like over a pool table, only no one is shooting pool. On each table is a ReGen, strapped at the wrists and ankles like the lovelies in the ward. But that is where all similarities end and the Twilight Sick Zone begins.

"This ReGen here you see has been vivisected from pubis to tracheal bifurcation," Doc says —his way of saying cut from neck to cunt. "I've removed the inner organs, the lungs the heart the digestive vitria, what you might call the tummy and intestines. The liver and kidneys are gone along with the bladder, uterus and ovaries and vagina. While she is still animate, she has no hunger and no craving. Here, put this soup bone in her mouth," he says handing a cow leg bone to Tim.

"No thanks, Doc, this is your show and tell. Teach me, Mr. Rogers, teach me do," replies Tim in a voice almost as insane as the Doc's but I'm thinking, this is important shit I'm looking at. Words like insane or crazy or psycho don't apply anymore. When your pal thinks his girlfriend is possessed by the devil, he's a psycho; when you think *your* girlfriend is, you're a theologian. It's all a matter of perspective, only the looking glass has tilted and bent and we are all seeing a brave new fucked-up funhouse world. Minus the fun.

He takes the bone and puts it in her mouth. She had that vacant milky white-eyed look but stares dumbly up at the ceiling as if absorbed in the light bulb hanging over her. She does not bite down, but licks it gently with her black tongue.

"For those of the men who prefer oral sex, she has been a delight. I know you think this is some kind of hideous perversion. I'll admit, I thought so too. But science in its crawl forward has often had to go against the contemporary morality and what might seem perverse in one moment in time, be-

85

comes genius in another. Hildy here, as I have named her after the star of my favorite Ingmar Bergman film, is a reward to those men who are faithful, diligent and above all, successful performers in the ward. But enough of Hildy. There, there, dear, thank you again," he says, patting her thigh. Hildy does not say "You're welcome."

The middle gurney has a spectacular redhead splayed and vivisected in the same fashion as Hildy.

"Who's this?" I ask, with the same tone I'm thinking a man would use when he's strolling through an orphanage pondering which kid to adopt.

"Oh, this is Katrina. I've named her for that hurricane that devastated New Orleans. She has killed and eaten at least a hundred and twenty-odd men that we know of. Got into a men's dorm at Kansas State University a few days after the disease first appeared but before its severity became apparent. She was a Teaching Assistant in the English department. Had most of the fellows in that dorm as her students. I like to think she was rather fed up, if you'll pardon the pun, with their off-handed obnoxious sexist remarks which I am most certain they made and somewhere in her twisted second phase brain she sought out a bit of revenge along with a good high protein meal. Security cameras recorded her every bite and swallow. After killing at least fifty and castrating them and ingesting the bits, the police made the strange assumption she should be captured and imprisoned. Thought she was a whack job with loony bin written all over her. Some cops fancy themselves like that Clarice chick from the Hannibal Lector movies, want to capture the psychos, not kill 'em. Caught her in a net used to capture rabid dogs. When she got to the jail, she berserked again and killed I don't know how many officers of the law. She was crafty enough to wait for them to return from patrol duty. A great number just bled to death after the castration. She was well-disposed to eat only penis and testicles as long as the supply was undiminished. We've discovered that any other parts of the male anatomy are only eaten when the GaGas are famished or in a frenzy. Given time and opportunity, they are strictly genital eaters.

"Now Katrina here seems to have undergone the same treatment as Hildy but there is a vast difference. She still has her reproductive organs. Note these here," he says pointing at what I guess is a uterus. He puts his bare finger in her guts and rubs a thing that looks like a walnut wrapped in ten layers of kitchen wrap.

"This is one of her ovaries and I think the secret of the progression of the disease lies within these two female organs. Of course, this is just a guess, a well-educated guess, to be sure, but it's the only thing I've come up with so far."

I know Jen is already way past this. Her research team knew all this shit at the git-go but I'm not going to burst this weirdo's balloon. I'm going to play his game and move on. I hope Tim can keep it together, though. He worries me.

The third gurney also has a ReGen on it but she's covered up and there are straps that cross her body, not just the ones at the wrists and ankles.

"This is Mallory," he says proudly. "She is my pride and joy." He gently removed the sheet that was covering her. The ReGen seemed to be sleeping, something I had not seen and thought was impossible without wondering why it would be. She too was cut open cunt to neck but her organs were still intact, far as I could tell. Her uterus was huge and distended.

"She is carrying my child," said Doc. We could see the uterus, something looking like a roast beef blown full of air or stuffed with something to the bursting point and that something was slowly moving within turning, rotating, lazily squirming.

"It was a happy accident," he continued. "I was particularly fond of her. We had met a few years ago when I was speaking at a forensics convention at the Denver Hilton. She was a student. It was one of those love at first sight moments for me. Perhaps she as well. I like to think so. It would not be out of the question. After all I was a city coroner and that type of powerful position would impress any woman. I think she recognized me as an alpha male. I'm not talking over your heads, boys, am I? Well, let's say we had a meeting of the minds. She was very coy of course, avoiding eye contact, but I could tell how she pulled her sweater closed when I came near her that she was secretly giving me the signal to mate with her. I was married—but these are conventions that lie outside the natural rhythms of the universe." He stroked her leg and I could see her flesh rise in goose bumps. She was not asleep, but pretending to be. I nudged Tim back from the table.

"She is very beautiful, Doc," I said like a lame brain. "I can see the attraction. It's obvious."

"You're a thoughtful and considerate lad," he said. "If my son that is currently within her turns out like you, I'll be quite proud."

"Well, that gives me the warm fuzzies," said Tim. A greenish slime oozed from Mallory's nipples. Doc put his finger in it.

"Interestingly, this has more nutritive value than a human female's breast milk. We've not determined all the positive compounds in it—we're terribly understaffed here—most of these men have barely graduated from high school. That is, in fact, my greatest fear, that their genes are not . . . well, to be frank, up to snuff."

"Bummer," said Tim.

"Oh, it's a bummer all right," the Doc said. "That's why I was hoping Kent would stay here with us. You, too, Tim, if it would make a difference to Kent; help him to be persuaded to stay. I think you'll see there are unlimited possibilities for fun as well as work. Don't tell me now. Think on it. We've all the time in the world. Well, maybe a little less than that, but you get my drift. I've got one more thing to show you here before we move on. Step this way."

He led us up the main stairs from the lobby of the hospital. All those stupid posters were still up, asking people to donate blood for the Red Cross, safe sex, obesity, all the major defects of body and mind. What a bunch we were, I'm thinking. Maybe Old Lady Walters was right about the end of the world. I was beginning to not give a fuck.

At the end of a long hall on the first floor, a dark green double door with armed guards on both sides opened to another ward room like the one downstairs. Women were milling about behind a wire fence. Some were strapped to the walls. A sign said, BEWARE! ELECTRIC! with a yellow lightning bolt. The women were, of course, all victims of the virus, but they were all pregnant. The more advanced they were, it seemed, the more likely they would be strapped to the wall.

"I'll wait outside," said Tim. I could see that memory was overpowering him.

"Stay out of trouble, my boy. We're not patient with trouble makers," Doc said. He chuckled. "I've made rather a bad pun, haven't I?"

"Yeah, that's a funny one, Doc. Ha!" I responded. "Patient. Get it, Tim?"

Tim left without a word, went into the hallway.

"Don't worry about Tim," I said. "He's a good guy . . . just been through a lot, ya know."

Doc Walters stood there eyeing me like I was sitting at a poker table and just raised him twenty grand and he's thinking, "Is this donkey bluffing me or does he have the nuts?"

"These are the ReGens who have been successfully impregnated by our men. Each one of them receives the best care we can give which, admittedly, is not the best for obvious reasons. But they are fed and seen to. We clean them up periodically and check on their progress by anesthetizing them. It's a simple matter to release nitrous oxide into the ward and while they are under, we do our servicing. Very humane and very productive."

The ReGens were moaning and chittering—a sound like the clicking of teeth together. They began to gather at the electric fence and stare at us. Beautiful women with eyes the color of white house paint, hair long, unkempt, straight. They would gather and stare—not quite blankly but as if trying to understand. One of them looked at me and clenched her teeth, started to reach for the wire but was stopped by another. I thought for a moment it was a random act. I hoped it was. But were they regaining something lost. If they were regenerating their bodies, why not their minds as well? No way, I thought. No way.

Then I remembered those nuns. The way they were able to speak and coordinate an attack.

"Look, Doc, we got to get going," I said.

"Not yet, boys. I've asked you to stay and I think you should see all the work we're doing here. You can't judge a book by its cover, can you?"

Without waiting for us to respond or, more likely, not giving a shit, he walked down the hall holding me by my arm.

"Tim, my boy. Wait here for us a moment, won't you. Jack here will bring you to the reception area," Doc said. As if on cue, a tall, beefy orderly showed up. In felt tip pen his name "Jack" was written on his white shirt which was three sizes too small. His arms bulged like they had yams under the skin.

"No, I think I'll stay with you two," said Tim.

"Not this time, me boy," Doc responded. "Now don't fret yourself. Kent will be down in a minute. I just need to have a private chat with him. Jack, take Tim here down to reception. Get him a donut and coffee."

"We haven't had donuts in three months, Doc," said Jack through his teeth.

"Well then, get him some refreshments. Now."

Tim made a pretense of not going along with the Doc's plan, but Jack's iron grip was persuasive.

"I'll be right down, Tim. It'll be all right. We're among friends here. Right, Doc?" I said knowing full well that dividing the troops, even if there were only two of them, was not a good strategy. I had to bet that Doc Walters was not going to kill either one of us. Not yet anyway, and time was on our side. Even if we had to stay a while, we'd eventually get out of here.

Tim reluctantly went with Jack. The Doc took my arm again and led me to an adjacent ward. As he opened the door, a scream so shrill came from a room across the hall that for a moment I imagined that MG would be the only one to be able to hear it.

"Oh, this is wonderful," said the Doc. "Miss Wilkinson is giving birth. Come this way." I followed him through a red door with a hand-scrawled sign that said, "Delivery—No Admittance—-This means U!"

There was a gurney in the middle of the room under a huge flying saucer-shaped light that intermittently flickered between too bright and too dim. On the table with her feet strapped into stainless steel stirrups was a totally naked Miss Wilkinson, a zombie bitch if there ever was one. She was lanky as a beanpole, with flat tits that were both oozing the same green mucousy slime that we had seen before. She was tied to the table with bright orange bungee cords that looked fresh from Casey's Hardware down the street. Her body, despite its thin, emaciated appearance—she must have looked like a walking stick figure before the GaGa claimed her—was wiry tough but covered in that very pink, very healthy looking skin that I'd come to see as the distinguishing feature of the ReGens. Her face had teeth that were too big for her mouth, that gave her a skull-like look, and her mousey brown hair, the color of dust you find behind a five-year-old entertainment center in your den the day you move out, was tied with duct tape. The milky eyes were another reminder.

My first view of her was her wide open vagina, ringed by matted, dark brown hair. What looked like a coconut stuck between her pussy lips was the top of the head of a baby about to be born. Surrounding her were two dudes in white lab coats that looked like they had been on duty at a Chicago slaughterhouse. Just below her gaping snatch was a red plastic beach bucket. She raised her head and let out a banshee scream and two turds squeezed out of her ass and fell with a thick plop into the bucket. The room filled with a cesspool odor that would have made any mortal man vomit his last three meals. But men in the times of the GaGa have grown immune to such improprieties. And I learned that zombie bitches still had to shit, which meant she had been feeding, but on what or whom I had yet to discover. Another guy in a green operating room smock stood near her head, but clearly out of reach of her snapping jaws which were chattering and gnashing in between bouts of screaming and grunting, grunting that sounded like an empty rubber garbage can falling down cement steps.

"Come on, Laurie, now push. Be a good fucking girl and push goddamn it!" shouted the guy at her head. "Push you motherfucking cretin bitch!" He slapped her real hard on the side of her head. She turned to snap at him but bit into empty air coming away with nothing. His shredded shirt cuffs were proof positive that he had had some close calls in the delivery room in the past.

"You know her name?" I asked the Doc with a considerable tone of surprise. This was a first.

"Oh, yes. She was my receptionist. Lived with a man named Gaffney in unholy un-matrimony. She complained about him almost every day. He was very short and, shall we say, minutely endowed. She would call him 'DIY' because he refused to pay anyone to do anything. He'd rake the leaves, clean his own chimney, haul his own garbage—a cheapskate.

I suppose that's why they never married. He was a lucky one; he'd been a forest ranger when the disease struck this area, chasing around in some state park counting bear turds or some other important government funded project.

"He had impregnated her before one of his week long absences. She's the first case of a GaGa being pregnant during the course of the disease although there are a lot of rumors about that unfortunate situation; a good many in maternity wards all over the world were infected with disastrous results, of course. Most of them were killed as far as anyone knows, but little Laurie here was not. I saved her by putting her body in a locked morgue vault just when she died. You should have heard the racket when she woke up in a drawer with the body of a wino that the cops had found dead in a refrigerator box in Stanley Park downtown. She struggled for a good five days. Ate most of the wino. When the food ran out, she went into the hibernation state. How her unborn baby has survived is a miracle yet to be explained. But you're about to witness medical history right here, right now."

"Is her husband here? The forest ranger, I think you said," I asked.

"Oh no. Poor chap. They found him near his Ford pickup. Seems a troop of Girl Scouts were studying the great outdoors where Mr. Gaffney was working. They came across him deep in the woods but he almost made it out of there. Tracks of his were found leading to his vehicle. Unfortunately, the girls were hot on his trail. Troop 29 out of Forestdale. Seven little tykes and a troop leader named Mary Rose LaBossa. They got him just when he reached the truck. Yes, they did. Did quite a job on him. Ate all the good parts, left his intestine full of his previous night's dinner hanging in a pine tree. Took his head with them. Might have been a snack. Ate the thing clean; brains, eyeballs, tongue. The whole shootin' match, and dropped the skull from an overpass on I-767. Trucker ran over it. Authorities only found the jaw. Mr.

Gaffney was identified through his dental records. Of course, by the time all that happened, the world had pretty much gone to hell in a bitch's hand basket. Great detective work though. So, no, the little asshole won't be here to see his wifey give birth to . . . who knows what."

We both turned to watch the grim scene unfolding in the room. The bitch was grunting regularly, sounding like a race horse coming in toward the finish line. One of the orderlies was spreading her legs apart by pressing on her thighs, softly saying, "Come on, push, that's it, push." It would have been quite a regular scene, I imagined, that had played out for millennia, but this was different. The grunting in between the snapping, the smell from the bucket and a new peculiar odor—a smell of sweetness something like sweet and sour pork sauce was filling the already too hot, too humid and too stinking room.

The Doc went over and pushed the orderly out of the way.

"Let me take over," he said

"Be my guest, Doc. She's a tough one. Not like the others."

"You bet. This is medical history, boy, and we're making it." The orderly looked at him like he was nuts, which he most definitely was.

The Doc grabbed the baby's head and started turning it. Blood was oozing, the dark dead ones' blood, that I had gotten to see more times than anyone should have to. He was literally unscrewing the kid from the ReGen's vagina. The shoulders appeared and Laurie or whatever her fucking name was, gave a scream that could have curdled milk in every supermarket within a fifty mile radius. I put both hands over my ears to muffle the ungodly sound of it.

"Come on, you fucking bitch," the Doc shouted. He put his foot on the edge of the gurney and gave a final tug. The baby slipped out with a resounding floop sound like someone pulling his stuck boot out of three feet deep of mud. The force of the pull caused the Doc to lose his balance and he fell backward onto his ass, then flat on his back. The umbilical cord was stretched taut as a tightrope. The bitch screamed and oozed more blood from her snatch than I thought one undead woman could hold. The placenta plopped into the bucket on top of the turds and the new GaGa mother went silent emitting only a deep groan like the sound you make when you're trying to scare someone by making deep, bellowing sounds into a paper towel cardboard tube.

An orderly started for the Doc to help him up but the Doc started to holler almost as loud as the bitch. He stopped in his tracks.

"Get it off me! Get it off me!" Doc shouted. The baby, unfortunately for the Doc, was not a boy as he'd surmised. It was a girl. Born with a full set of teeth that were razor sharp. The baby bitch attacked the Doc and bit through his pants into his balls. She was a piranha, a very hungry eight pound, six ounce one and was feasting on the Doc. His blood was pouring out through the tears in his pants.

"Get her off me," he shouted, but it was too late. I reached down to pull the baby off of him, but her head had already made its way into his lower abdomen. He was grunting like someone who hadn't taken a crap in a year and was finally letting it go. Nothing I could do. I wasn't touching anything. I wanted out of this place fast.

An orderly shoved me out of the way, reached down and grabbed the gnashing undead baby by the feet and pulled. She came away with the Doc's intestine still in her maw, uncoiling like a garden hose from the hole that used to be his dick and balls.

The bitch on the gurney lifted her head and started to laugh. Not a Ha-Ha kind of laugh like you're doing when you've had a few drinks and some lame stand-up comic is making his jokes. It was a high-pitched hooting, almost a howl that got inside your spine and made you think, maybe we're all better off dead. Another lesson for today. GaGa bitches could laugh. And if they could laugh, they could reason. This was not good, not good on anyone's planet.

We heard shots being fired. Laurie continued squirming and hooting, kicking like mad and snapping her jaws frantically. The slop bucket got knocked over and one of the orderlies slipped in the spilled mess and fell onto the Doc's dead body. The guy in the green smock grabbed two scalpels, one in each hand, and came down on her abdomen, drove those things right through; I could hear the points hit the metal table top. She rasped and inhaled like a vacuum cleaner with a too-full bag and stopped her squirming. The other orderly who still held the newborn by the feet lifted her up as if to smash her head against the wall, when the door burst open and a guard rushed in.

"They've gotten out. The bitches are out. Save yourselves!" As he said this, a bitch flew through the door and attacked him from behind, biting the back of his neck. The two of them spun around and slipped in the slop shit on the floor. Two others rushed in and got the baby from the orderly and then attacked him, tearing his guts out and breaking his ribs by pulling them from the outside in. Yet another bitch entered and took the baby and ran out with it like a running back looking for the goal post. I ran into a closet which was not a closet at all but a small room that held the elevator running gear with a service door for the elevator itself. The shaft was wide open and when I looked over the edge, the elevator was sitting down below at the lobby level twenty feet away.

I had no choice. Either slide down or wait for the bitches to break in and gut me.

I shimmied down the greasy cable, made it most of the way before I lost my grip, and fell the last five feet. Found the hatch door and jumped through into the elevator. I could hear screaming and gunfire, but I thought it best to make a break for it. I guessed that the bitches were going to win this fracas and I was in no frame of mind to be lunch.

CHAPTER 15

The parking where we'd landed the balloon looked like a pond under the light of the half moon. Hadley held my hand tightly and the hairs on the back of my arms stood straight on end. I know it was a mistake to bring her. I don't know why I did. Funny her mother didn't complain. But she was, literally, a time bomb. I thought that I might be able to keep her from contamination. It was just a matter of thought and planning. She needed to stay in the gondola no matter what and to never be indoors where GaGas had been within the previous twenty-four hours, which was the rumored incubation period. It was, under those circumstances, not impossible. Maybe I was just thinking of myself as some sort of hero. It never entered my mind before. I don't do heroic things and I don't believe in risk. I never skied or bungee jumped and I was not even the type that wanted to ride a roller coaster. I had been cautious all my life—even in relationships. Why engage in an activity for fun if there is even a remote possibility that you could get seriously injured or killed? I lived in ski country, had visited the slopes many times, even took a lesson one season with a girl named Sue. Even the bunny rabbit hill was evidence to me that I could mangle my ankles or smash a femur. For what? To slide down a fucking hill that I had to pay to go up? Surely you jest.

My uncle who was a car salesman at the local Caddy dealership once told me, "there was an ass for every seat." Watching people rocket down those slopes while I sat in the lodge looking at tit-filled sweaters and newly plastered casts, I told myself, "there is an asshole for every sport." Give me a pool cue and that's as risky as I'm going to be. You do it. Enjoy. I'll watch and then fuck your girlfriend while you're in the recovery room. 'There, there now sweetie cakes; he'll be okay. Just don't be alone for the first night; it's a real downer. Come up to my place. We can watch old movies and you won't be lonely.' It never failed.

But Hadley was different. I could not leave her back there. Even if she was doomed to turn into a GaGa bitch, it would not be because I didn't try to stop it. Fuck heroism; I did what I needed to do. No moralizing. The world is too far gone for that.

Tim didn't look happy about Hadley either and maybe didn't feel that putting his neck on the line literally for a future monster who might now be a sweet little girl was worth it. I used MG's collar and created a makeshift bell to attach to it. I could hear Tim's argument already:

Listen, Kent. I'm conceding that you're brain damaged, bringing this kid along, but you got to make this concession: she wears this ding-a-ling collar at all times, twenty-four-seven or I'm outta here. I may end up dead somewhere in the woods or on the road, but it will be through no fault of my own. The kid is dangerous, way dangerous. If she turns while I'm sleeping and I wake up dead, it will be my fault mainly because I let you talk me into it and then not taking a precaution. I agreed to do it. A deal's a deal for now. And I owe you. But I . . .

She didn't mind after I told her that: one, the collar was so we wouldn't lose her in the dark and two, it was a way cool fashion statement. Hadley became a jingler—that's what I called her. Hopefully, I wouldn't be dreaming of Santa and Rudolph when she came near.

I tell Hadley that I'm going to scout for food.

"Don't wake Tim up. Let him sleep. I'll be back before morning," I tell her. She hugs me around the waist.

"Don't do anything crazy. Please, Kent. Tell me you'll be extra careful. Please. Promise."

"I promise," I say meaning it. I'm actually feeling like I need to live not for my sake but for hers. It's not a feeling I'm used to or comfortable with. I leave her by the campfire and go to the river. The boat is waiting for me. I get in and start paddling.

CHAPTER 16

My boat was drifting with the uncertain currents through the night, clouds obscuring the moon and stars as if a moldy quilt had been cast over the world by a careless innkeeper not realizing I was adrift and alone at the whim of the inky river. Black froth licked at the prow and pregnant thuds knocked at the hull as the boat glided, circling over submerged stones, the forgotten eggs of long-dead sea monsters. I held tightly to the sodden seat, looking up and praying to any god that might listen to the prayers of anyone left in this hideous world. My clothes were ragged and the only thing I owned untouched by the world's nefarious tricks were the beautiful bullhide boots that I had stolen awhile back, back before the balloon, from some damnable itinerant preacher. I regretted having to kill him, but he awoke just as I had snatched the boots from his bedside. What sin this might have been, seemed nothing to me compared to the sin that God had committed in sentencing me to a life like this.

I hadn't thought of that moment for a while. Killing a man. A man who wanted to kill me. The world is changed now, but I assure you it doesn't make taking a life easier. I chose not to think of it anymore.

The river calmed after a time and I could make out the silhouettes of reeds and cattails along the edge, black as if poisoned by the darkness and bent and broken like a giant had stumbled in the dark, his oafish hands breaking his fall near the shore. The slim current led me toward the bank and I leaned over and started paddling, feeling the nibbles of invisible fish on my hands. After a time, about a hundred yards downstream, I saw a fire glowing through the reeds, a cyclops eye of orange and red with jellyfish tendrils of smoke escaping to the sky. Three men sat near the fire, one standing and holding a rifle. I called out for help. They turned in unison toward me and immediately I had regretted my outburst. One called out to me and I thought I heard another say, "should I shoot him now?" but my mind was playing tricks on me, I was sure. A rope was tossed out and I thought for a moment to forgo its welcoming hand, but I was near starved and shivering uncontrollably. I grabbed it and was pulled to shore, fending my way through the brittle grasses that felt like skeleton arms and legs, sere and stiff, the smell of dead things in the air.

"Thank you," I said. "My name is Walter," I lied. "Yours?"

"We have no names here. To name something is to control it. And, anyway, what's it to you?" the tall one said. He was clearly the oldest, the other two looking no more than in their teens, but drawn and sallow, the dim light of the fire swallowed by the dark sockets of their sunken eyes. One of them held the rifle, his thumb caressing the stock rhythmically.

"Nothing really. Just being friendly."

"There ain't no friends out here either. What are you doing on the river in such a state?"

"I was upstream a few days' ride back when a storm hit. Lost my oars in the rapids from the cloudburst and had my rudder crushed on the rocks. Lucky I'm alive."

"Lucky, yeah." The tall man spoke like a Southerner, the others were voiceless but all three were thin as wraiths. The youngest had on a tattered shirt with sleeves unevenly short as if something had been chewing on them.

"Might I sit by the fire a spell. I'm soaked through to the core."

"Sure. Sit."

I sat uneasily feeling the warmth of the fire immediately. A light rain began to fall and spatter on the coals. A large skillet was balanced on a few rocks and in it were a few lumps of meat, black and dry, an indeterminate feast.

"Have a piece of meat. Hand him a plate," said the tall man to the boy standing to my left. "You could probably use something to eat if what you say is true."

"Well, thank you."

The boy, whose hair I could now see was a knotted mass of red, went to the fire and with a long thin knife, stabbed a chunk of the flesh and placed it in a tin plate with a thud.

"It ain't pork," said the tall man.

"Beef then?" I said.

"No," he replied.

I tore off a piece and chewed its tasteless fibres, thick and dusty dry, my teeth gnashing it as best I could, flavorless, foreign, cooked through like a stone. One boy stood behind me, the other squatting, the rifle butt on the ground, the barrel held so that he could lean his face against it.

"Them is nice boots you got there," the tall man said. "Where'd you get 'em?"

"They were a gift. From my father," I said looking down.

"I don't think that's true," he said.

"I don't care what you think."

I looked at his boots and saw they were torn and held together with bits of string and bailing wire, a dirty toe peeking out between the two lips of a split in the leather.

"Them boots look like they too big for you," he said.

"I like 'em that way. Room to grow," I smiled without a response from any of the three who were quiet as pallbearers, the light tapping of the rain a somber drone.

"Where was you headin'?" he asked.

" 'Cross the river to Mecklenburg."

"What for?"

"My family is there. My father."

"The same what give you them boots, huh?"

"Listen," I said. "I appreciate your kindness, but I got to get going. Does that road lead back up north?"

"That road goes to hell, boy. Have some more meat. We're all done with her."

"No thanks. I am thankful to you, though."

After a time, he started removing his boots and when he had finished, he signaled to the boy behind me who took off his and put the man's on. The boy's boots were more tattered than the tall man's and a rank odor seeped out the top of them.

"Now you take those boots, mister, hear? And gimme your gun there."

Outnumbered, I took off my boots and placed them neatly in front of me, handed over my pistol. The boy took the boots and handed them to the tall man who slipped them on. He stomped a few times, did a quick jig and said, "These is fine, right fine. I thank you."

I put on the boy's boots without saying a word, the boy with the rifle standing suddenly and looking shiftily between the tall man and me.

"Should I shoot 'im, Pa?"

"No, I don't think so. He seems tame enough. Let's get goin'."

"But what about . . . ?" the boy with the rifle said.

"I told you that fire would work. I don't need to wait no more. We done good enough. Pack up."

One boy picked up the dishes and the skillet, dumping the lump of meat into the dying fire where it caused a shower of sparks to fly up through the damp air. The rain had stopped. The boy behind me stroked the back of my head. "He's a pretty one, Pa," he said.

"Not tonight, boy. Best we get goin'."

The three of them slipped off into the darkness as if they were made of it, the night closing behind them. At my back, the dim edge of the sun peered beneath the cauldron lid of the sky.

I had two choices and when I thought about it, they were reduced to one. I had to follow those guys. They had guns and ammunition and while they did not have any food that I could discern—the meat in the fire had charred to a black rock—the guns were at least a way of safely searching.

I gave them a ten minute head start. The sun was rising but a thick cloud cover kept the darkness as my ally. They had taken a narrow dirt path through the reeds by the water—could've been a boat landing for local fisherman—to a small roughly paved street that ran east. It was away from Tim and Hadley but I needed to accomplish something and besides, the old fucker had my boots.

CHAPTER 17

I kept to the brush beside the road and I could see the men a few hundred yards distant also keeping as much out of sight as possible. The new reality had scared even these thieving assholes. On the other hand, they could've killed me. Whatever was keeping them in hiding—the bitches of course—was also creating some sort of brotherhood between dick swingers. It wasn't much of a trade-off, but it was better than nothing. I felt that I needed to steal the guns and my boots back. I would return the favor by sparing them, if I could.

After about a half hour of hide and seek, they paused near a small house about a hundred yards off the road. It had a bunch of pick-up trucks parked all around it, but they were old and dilapidated; looked like they were the family's fifty year supply. A newish one was at the side door near a shed. If there was someone in there, they were acting like no one was home.

The three men hid by a stand of live oak that clustered at the mouth of the dirt driveway. The grass all around was tall enough to cover most of the parked trucks, all of them, I now noticed, various shades of red depending on how old they were and how much damage the weather had inflicted.

They waited a few minutes and with hand signals moved slowly up the drive, crouched and tightly sprung as if they were ready to pounce on something or away from it. I could go back now but I'd be empty-handed and worse off than when I left. When the men were fifty feet from the house, I climbed the stiff limbs of a live oak and hid in the dense browning foliage. Whatever they were going to do to whoever was inside was not my problem; for all I knew the inhabitants might have been worse than these guys. There could even be bitches holed up inside. A window was open and a ragged white curtain hung out, rubbing the grey shingles like a ghost's hand stroking a corpse. I'd have to wait either way.

They sidled up the driveway and hand-signaled each other to separate. The young boy sneaked up to a window and peeked inside. He raised his hand, got the others' attention and nodded his head in the negative; he could see no one inside. The elder son circled around back and, out of sight from my perch, apparently signaled the same way. The old man, now clearly visible as the noon sun peered through the cloud cover, walked stealthily toward the back door. I could see my boots on the old prick. He put his back against the left wall surrounding the door which had a window in it, like he'd probably seen the cops do on the three million TV shows that feature police. He peeked in through the glass, weaving his head like the snake he was. He signaled to the other two who quietly and carefully rounded the house and stood beside him. He reached for the door knob and turned. Whether it was my imagination of not, I heard the squeak of the knob and saw the door open ever so gently.

The wind blew steadily and its waves were reflected by the tall, reedy grass of the surrounding lawn. A few grasshoppers took off and followed the wind to the house where they collided with it with a tick, tick sound. It was then I saw the first glint of red hair in the tall grass. At first, it looked like some sort of huge wildflower, a Texas rose or a Japanese peony. I rubbed my eyes. It was still there but it was not a flower. And if it was, it wasn't the only one. It was a woman and before long I could make out other heads hidden in the grass; brunettes, blondes, even a few grays. From where I sat in my tree, I could count fifty or so. Two were behind a '54 Chevy pick-up that had two rusted banged-up oil drums in its bed. Behind the drums, two girls peered out, frizzy-haired kids that were maybe ten or eleven years old. Could've been twins.

One of the gray heads lifted itself to a full standing position and I could see it was a bitch. She walked steadily toward the door of the farmhouse like grandma coming home from a church social. She raised her arm when she was but three or four feet away and as she did this, a shotgun blast cracked the air and grandma's head burst into a million shards of brain skull and blood. The body collapsed like a deflated balloon, but the signal had been given.

The grass was swarming with zombie bitches. The fifty I saw was just the tip of the proverbial iceberg. There must have been three hundred. They were chittering and shrieking like a biblical plague from hell. The guns started firing and bitches were blown to pieces. Shotguns loaded with rifled slugs that could bring down a grizzly made holes the size of bowling balls. Heads were shattered, limbs lopped off, legs left dangling by stringy sinews. But they kept coming on. They surrounded the house and started scratching and tearing at the door. The idiots inside fired through the door which only helped the bitches' cause, because the door flew open with one shotgun blast and knocked four bitches to the ground. They got up, and with huge splinters of wood from the shattered door sticking in their faces and tits and bellies, they still came on.

I could here the men inside shouting and calling to each other. These undead gals were piling up at the open door as the men inside fired and the old bastard that took my boots stuck his head out of a second story window and fired down at them. He fired both rounds of his double barrel shotgun and the awkward angle made the butt jump up and hit him in the face. He fell forward and was dangling just out of reach of the zombies but one of them climbed on the accumulating heap of bodies and reached his hair and yanked him down just as one of his sons grabbed for his foot which had hung up on the window sash.

The tug from below was just too strong. The boy looking out the window yelled "Pa! Pa! They got Pa!" just as they covered the old fuck like locusts. They did not kill him, though.

They lifted him up screaming and kicking and dragged him toward a large tree that spread its limbs over the dirt drive. My God, I thought, they're so organized.

A gray-headed one indicated to one of the blondes with her hand and she returned from the shed with a coil of rope. They tied him to the tree and stood there looking at him, smelling the air but mainly just staring at him as he struggled and screamed.

Meanwhile, other women crowded through the door and shouts, screams and long howls of pain mixed with sporadic gunshots escaped from the windows and mingled with the locusts clacking and the distant caws of crows from beyond the woods. In a few minutes, the sounds ceased and zombies quietly and slowly exited the house each with a bounty of limbs, muscle tissue, inner organs and genitals. Most of the undead were covered in blood as if they had been washing their hands in it. They joined the others surrounding the still kicking and screaming old man and shared the bounty with them. All of them now patiently watch the old man writhe.

With a signal from the gray bitch, two of the younger ones start stripping the old guy down in a very orderly fashion. They remove his—my—boots and toss them far, as if to keep him from using them ever again. They land in the tall grass about thirty feet from where I'm hiding. I slip off the stinkers they traded with me in preparation for a pick up and getaway. But I continue to watch. This must be the fourth-stage development of the bitches. Some form of intelligence returns; communication through grunts, chittering and hand signals. This is at least good enough to organize, launch an attack and a whole bunch of other maneuvering which to me means the end of the world as we know it and forever into the future. This ain't Earth anymore. It's the Planet of Bitches.

In short order he is stripped naked. He is struggling and cursing, but the more he does the more they stare and tighten his bindings. They look at him as if he is some weird specimen never before encountered. Many of them who do not participate in the stripping have a weird way of tilting their heads, like dogs that are hearing a strange but appealing sound. The ragged clothing is passed around to the onlookers who sniff it, examine it and lick at it, particularly the crotch of his pants and the armpits of the shirts. Two of them have a tug of war over his stained boxer shorts but a scowl from one of the grays puts a quick end to that and the red-headed victor stuffs the shorts in her mouth and stands there with a vacant, serene expression like she's tasting caviar for the first time. I nearly puke from the thought of those asshole smelly, scorch-marked rags that fucker has wrapped his putrid crotch in without a washing for maybe a year or more. Reminds me once of a college girl I knew back in the good old days. She's driving this Mazda convertible into the service department on a hot Denver afternoon with the top down and she's wearing tight jeans and a sports bra top. I volunteered to follow her to give her a lift back to the dorm while her car gets its oil changed and other shit like that, which now seems so trivial and unimportant and fucking dumb that I cannot believe anyone ever cared about that kind of stuff now that the world has gone so far down the toilet. But it was good, those days, and I would trade both nuts to go back there and do nothing but give lifts to girls and guys and anyone who needed them just so that I don't have to be here and now today.

So, she gets out of the car and goes to the service writer's desk and he's all flirty and bullshit and she says, "See you later," and turns and walks back to where I'm waiting and the service dude and a mechanic type rush over to her car, open the door and sniff the seat where her sweaty beautiful crotch was just sitting. They guffaw at each other and the mechanic idiot gets in, starts it up and drives back into the cave-like service department. Probably jerked off to that smell. I'm thinking, guys do that shit. They sniff shit, sniff dirty panties and dirty socks and other wacky crap and get off on it but girls never do that shit. Never. Until now.

So the old dude on the tree stops the cursing and shouting and squirming and sort of hangs there limp and given up. But he starts pleading and tears are running down his face and he's saying things like he had two daughters who he loved and maybe they could help him find them and his wife also who was sick with the gout and breast cancer and how terrible it is that women get breast cancer and that they should be able get cured and it's not too late to stop all this killing and murdering and eating and maybe he could get the women to a hospital where they could be treated for whatever it is that has made them so . . .

But he is interrupted by a tall brunette who stares him in the face, races up and gently takes his face in her two hands and seems to want to pity-kiss him as if to say, "You're right. This is all so crazy. We should help each other, not kill each other." So she moves in for what looks like a giant French kiss and she instead digs in with her teeth through his lips and comes away with his tongue. Blood spurts from his mouth and he's gurgling shouting; piss squirts out his dick and another bitch runs toward him and drinks it right from his limp worm like it's a lawn spigot. She gets pushed away and another bitch finishes the drink then bites the dick clean off as if her teeth were bolt cutters. The gray pushes her out of the way and slits open his nut sack with a blade that appears from nowhere—might have been in her hair—and pulls the testicles out, holds them up for the group to see. The collective moaning and humming is deafening. She then swallows them whole as if they were oysters from a half-shell. His screaming is more a squealing as he continues to jerk hard at the ropes till they rope burn their way into his flesh and he's cross-crossed with bleeding slits from where the bindings hold him to the tree.

The gray head turns back to him holding what looks like a sharpened rib bone. She turns to the assembled bitches who make a groaning, humming sound that would be enough to drive any sane person completely schizo—but in this world, nightmares are the rule, not the exception. She raises the bone, turns to the tied-up geezer and chitters her teeth. He looks up, blood oozing from his gaping maw. With a quick downward slash she cuts through the layers of skin and muscle just below his ribcage. He screams through the blood which spurts on the bitch. She raises the bone again and makes another slit on his abdomen creating a triangular flap that she peels downward to reveal the dude's liver. She reaches for it and tugs out one of the lobes, deep reddish brown and glistening, like an udder on a cow. The other bitches kneel down and crawl to the guy whose head is swaying back and forth, eyes closed like he's praying which, would not be a bad idea at this point because it's as useless as anything else the old bastard might try. But I am pitying him, forgetting what he did and what he likely has done since civilization vanished from this fucked up planet.

The old gray is milking the liver the way you'd wring out a sponge one-handed and the other zombies are kneeling and drinking sips like it's communion wine. I can see the bony knuckles on her hand covered in blood as she squeezes and squeezes. When it's wrung dry, she pulls out some more liver and finally the dude seems dead or collapsed anyway from shock and blood loss.

When there is no more to drink, the gray one lets out a shriek which defies all description and the other undead femme fatales descend on the guy and eat away, the way I've seen so many times in the past. He's not dead, but twitching, his face contorted and jerking as the chewing, grinding and tearing finally releases him from his agony. The thighs have been stripped to the bone, his calves looking like corndogs on a stick with the feet at the bottom. Eventually, the carcass falls from the tree in pieces and the girls go at the rest of the meat. The head, as usual, is carried off. Most of the bitches leave but some younger ones, maybe twelve or thirteen years old are sitting picking at the bones and gristle, chewing toes and fingers, squeezing the colon until the shit is out of it then chomping on it like it's a rope of salt water taffy.

I count four girls; the oldest is maybe fourteen. Their backs are to me and clearly the pack has left making a wide swath through the cornfield. I'm thinking this is my time to make a break for it. I can see where my boots have landed and I creep on hands and knees to where they are. I'm in the tall grass covered from view when I hear a wheezing sound, maybe more of a whistle like you make when your nose is full of snot but louder. One of the pubescent bitches has sensed me somehow. I can see through the grass that they are on their feet quick as cats that have spotted a mouse.

I stand and start to run but have not planned this part of it. The house is no man's land so I head toward this ramshackle old barn, gray wood with faded blotches of red paint and a sign that says MURPHY'S OIL SOAP in big white letters that are also very faded and worn. I'm running toward the barn although why, I don't know. One of the little girls tackles my legs like a defensive back and I fall flat on my face, my mouth full of dust. She starts tearing at my calves with her teeth and I turn and kick her with the heel of my boot and strike her full in the mouth knocking out all her front teeth. She doesn't make a sound, just goes down again for another chomp but it's nothing. Feels more like a pinch so I kick her again this time connecting with her eye which caves in along with the side of her face. She yelps. I see others coming on slowly but steadily. I try to get up but the little one has a death grip on my leg. I kick at her maybe three or four more times until my heels have made a meatloaf out of her once cute as apple pie fucking face. Now others are standing over me watching and drooling, inhaling deeply as if smelling me before the eats.

A shot rings out and one of the bitch's heads explodes

leaving a stump and a piece of jaw with nice white teeth. Guess Mommy took her to the dentist; the braces are very shiny and clean except where a tatter of the old dude's meat is stuck and hanging. She drops. Another shot and the second bitch goes down, a huge hole where her little sweet tummy used to be. Two more fall flat as their heads bloom open. One is still over me, and too many more to count at the tree. I see Tim running over with his rifle but the thing is jammed and he's running and cursing and yanking on the bolt action but it is stuck.

The last one sees this, looks at me stuck on the ground with my legs under the first bitch, looks at Tim and charges him. He sees her coming, raises the rifle butt to smash her goddamned head in but misses and she leaps through the air, pushes him down, crouches ready for the chomp at his neck. He's screaming, "Get the fuck off of me!" when an arrow from out of nowhere whizzes through the air and goes right through her head from ear to ear like one of those dumbass fake arrows with the wire hoop that used to make people laugh but now it's just stupid, plain stupid. She topples over; Tim raises the butt again and smashes her face in, her teeth stick to the butt.

Tim says, "Hey, little girl, I like your scrunchies," and then smashes her head in some more. She quivers and then stops. The silence is very cool.

I turn to the direction of where the arrow came from and I see an old dude with a fat belly and white whiskers up in the hayloft. He's holding a bow and signaling for us to come over. It's either Robin Hood or Santa Claus. Either way, I'm a believer.

CHAPTER 18

In the loft of the barn we found a group of old guys. Well, it was a group only in the loosest sense of the word. It was four geezers who had hidden in the barn and then discovered they could survive on a stash of canned goods that had been put in the barn by its previous and now almost fully digested owner. They were armed with a pitchfork, a garden rake, two shovels and the bow and arrows that had saved Tim. All in all, it was an interesting crew of geezers that had saved the day.

"Come on up," said a plump red-faced geezer to us pointing at the handmade ladder that was used to access the loft. "I'm Artie." Artie looked like he had drunk most of the scotch in Scotland and had been on his way to Ireland when the plague had interrupted him. His thick skin literally glowed in the dark, pocked and pimply the way only the most seasoned drunk could get it to be. His hair was white and he had a two month's growth of beard. He had long johns on that sagged where they're supposed to be tight and tight where they're supposed to sag. They were irregularly yellow and stained, especially on the top of his bulging paunch. He had a Santa Claus twinkle in his eye; a Santa Claus that lived in the dry-out tank at the local jail.

Outside, the zombie bitches were now moving off, somehow befuddled by our escape. Before we closed the loft doors I saw the hick who'd stolen my boots was gone from the tree. They'd torn him limb from limb and left nothing to stay tied up. The two hick boys were gone as well. Like ghosts, the undead women sank back into the tall grasses and corn fields till I could see nothing of where they'd gone.

"Pleased to meet you, Artie," Tim said in an uncharacteristically friendly way. I realized that Artie was still holding the bow which had saved Tim's life. No wonder he was being friendly.

We carefully made our way up the ladder. The loft was quite large and well stocked with bales of hay which the geezers used to craft a make-shift fort. What good it would have done had the bitches found them up there, I couldn't say. But I'm guessing that geezers this age think a whole lot like kids, and a fort . . . well, where could you be safer than in a fort if you have a brain like a six-year-old?

They had undone a bunch of bales and had made some very cushy-looking beds. A hole in the floor in a corner, surrounded by bales was a latrine. They simply sat over or stood over the whole and it dropped down to the floor below. Someone had emptied out a few bags of lime and turds and pissed just plopped right into the lime. Sanitary, easy and not bad for a bunch of oldsters, the youngest of which, now that Tim and I were upstairs with them, could not have been a week under seventy.

Artie introduced us to his band before even learning our names.

"This is Jerry," he said pointing with an open hand to guy with dyed hair that had grey roots about half-way up the length of it. He had one ear pierced and had a hoop earring in it; he wore two shirts, both collared with a dinner jacket that looked like it fell off a scarecrow.

"Welcome, gentlemen," he said, shifting his pitchfork back and forth between his hands. "Well, aren't you the cutest things that the cat dragged in." This was followed with a wink and a smile that revealed a straight row of deep yellow teeth. "I'd offer you a cigarette and a martini, if I could. But no smoking allowed up here." He giggled. "Artie would have a conniption. Hee-hee. May I do the further honors, Artie, Sir?"

"Jerry, not now. Aren't you supposed to be on guard duty? Go to your post."

"Aye, aye, Captain Meany," Jerry replied with a mock salute and off he went to sit by the hayloft door which was half opened and had a panoramic view of the fields below and beyond. Jerry was mumbling something under his breath.

"Don't mind him," said Artie. "He's a good guy at heart. Had a tough life. Queers didn't do so well when he was out cruisin' for trouser trout. Got beat up more times than Cassius Clay's sparring partner. Oh, I mean Mr. Mohammed Ali, that uppity, good for nothin' draft dodgin' . . . "

"I'm Chaz," said a crusty old salt who sat on a bale with a long piece of straw dangling from his lips. His head was mostly bald and he, too, was flushed a sickly pink. I'm thinking there's a stash of booze around here somewhere and these old fucks are partying while the world is sliding down a giant toilet. Maybe they got it right. Chaz is wearing a black t-shirt, with what looks like snot stains on the front of it. The shirt says "Viagra" across the front. "Used to in the insurance business. I'm also a prize fighter so if you're thinking of fucking with me, you better not. I will fuck you up, both of you."

"Now, is that any way to talk to our guests, Chaz," said Artie. "These are fine young boys in the same pickle . . . "

"Fuck 'em," says Chaz. "If they think they can share our food, I say fuck 'em." Chaz takes out a notebook and starts writing, turns his back and stays hunched over, writing.

"Chaz is our historian," Artie explains. "Actually," he says under his breath, "Chaz thinks he's a novelist. Gonna write the next great American novel. Thinks this will all be over one day and people will say, 'Have you read the latest Chaz Bennett masterpiece?' Oh, did I tell you his name is Bennett, Charles Bennett. But everyone calls him Chaz. Makes him sound less the mick than he really is. He still takes Viagra, carried a hundred pill plastic jar with him in his supply pack. Was quite the ladies' man, he says. Talks about it every night . . . and every day. Got a new girlie story for every day of the week and two on Sunday. Every now and then he punches out little queer Jerry over there. Jerry doesn't seem to mind. Chaz doesn't hit very hard. Did you notice his sparring gloves? Still wears them even though no one thinks he ever set foot in a real boxing ring. Knocked a psychologist out cold at the home, flat on her ass. Beat the shit out of a few lady nurses, too. We were all there, in the same home, that is, Easy Glades near Scranton PA. A shithole of a town if there ever was one, but, yes, we're all from there. Exceptin' Big Fat Dick Gumbert over there," he says pointing to a huge fat guy in denim coveralls, stroking the handle of a garden rake and looking at us like we're duck souffle.

Jerry is watching from his post and says, "Yeah, Dick, tell them how you were a famous book collector. Dick there collected some very important books or so he says."

"How about you go fuck yourself," replies Dick. Turning to me he says, "It is true. I had a fine shop, specialized in Americana. Old American books and letters. I had a letter penned by Thomas Jefferson to Aaron Burr. Sold it to the Smithsonian. And I had a first edition of the *Book of Common Prayer*, one of the first books printed in the New World in English. Yes, and a copy of . . . "

"Figures the first thing those fucking Puritans would do would be to print a dumbass prayer book. The dumb fucks. Instead of telling people how to get along and be tolerant and work with the Indians they lord it over everybody with a goddamned prayer book. No wonder they had their glued-tight assholes kicked out of England. Too bad they didn't string them up by their holy balls," said Chaz. I had to agree with him but I was in no mood to discuss religion or politics.

"You tell him, Chazzy, boy," said Jerry, walking over. "It is definitely, certainly true. If the French had founded this country or, better yet, some yummy Italians, we'd have had a great old time. Those people knew how to live!"

"Speaking of living, can we get some grub?" said Tim.

"Good timing," said Artie, giving a dirty look to all his cohorts something like an old school marm. "Today, it's tuna and sauerkraut," he added, rubbing his hands together as if he was about to serve a banquet.

"Fucking great," said Chaz. "Stink 'n zinc. Just what the doctor ordered before we . . . "

"Now, Chaz, let's not get too familiar with our guests. Jerry, do set the table."

"Aye, aye, Cap'n," he replied.

While the geezers fussed about getting the food together, Tim and I stood by the hayloft door, peeked through a knot hole in one of the slats. The leaves on the trees far off on the surrounding hillsides had turned and stood frozen under the slate sky. The corn, trampled through like cow paths where the bitches had come and gone, was a glorious pale gold, dried and papery in spots.

"Well, here's another fine mess you've gotten me into," Tim said.

"Make the best of it. I'm pretty sure they're harmless and we can bed down here and clear out tomorrow."

"I wish I could tell Hadley, but she knows the score. She'll hold up in that pump house for ten years if she can. Her and MG making a stand till the end. It'll be all right."

My phone buzzed its sad buzz and I looked at the dim screen. Jen had texted me again, "HURRY HURRY." What a fucking torture, I thought. Almost better if she did nothing, said nothing. I texted back, "soon." Wishful thinking. But it's all I had.

By the time everything was set up, the sun had peered below the pot lid of the sky and filled the loft with a dim orange light. Dust and gadflies floated or darted in the air. The geezers sat around the makeshift table sitting on hay bales, the aroma of tuna and sauerkraut filled the air. Not disgusting at all, I thought. Looked like a Dutch masters painting. Old dudes sitting at a table, maybe farmers on the Zuyder Zee, pooped after a long day growing tulips or whatever those boring fuckers did three hundred years ago in Holland. Still, it wasn't bad. Not bad at all. I looked over at Tim and he looked at me. Thinking the same shit.

"Chow time," he said. "Let's dig in."

After dinner, the guys took turns at the watch. The rest of us sat and talked about the good old days which, for these geezers, is so far back I couldn't give a shit.

Jerry and Artie started a game of chess and Tim somehow developed an interest in Big Dick's stories about American history.

"Yepper," says Dick. "I had a plan to cure every major ill this great nation of ours ever had. It's democracy that stands in the way. You know, too many dumbasses with too many stupid opinions. It's all politics and back slappin' and blow jobs. We needed a dictator to pick up the USA out of the shit hole it was in and drag it screaming and kicking into the new century."

"Like a Hitler type?" asks Tim.

"Here, let me show you something I wrote. It's a way of getting people interested in new ideas. I call it a 'Memoir of an American Dictator.' It's a short chapter. I got the whole thing written and then this disease hits all the women and now instead of heading up a new political party, I'm holed up in a goddamned hayloft with a bunch of old farts."

Dick shuffles through a mass of yellowed typed pages and picks a few. I lean back on a hay bale and listen.

"January 20, 2109: My name is Big Dick Gumbert and I was the first American 'dictator.' After winning election as President for the maximum 2 terms allowed by law, a popular referendum enabled me not only to be elected to a third term but that this term should run 'until [my] resignation or death.' I served as President for nearly 43 years. I want these memoirs to be published after my death as an example of what one man chosen by destiny can accomplish if fate and God is truly on his side. There were times, I will admit, when I had to do things I would not ordinarily do. But isn't that how we Americans define a "hero"? With the Constitution in one hand and the Bible in the other, I managed to make our nation great again. It was my life's work and I did it because someone needed to.

"I saw drugs as one of the greatest ills of our country. Not only were they rotting the brains of our youth, but they were filling the coffers of foreign hostile governments, foreign illicit cartels and forcing, through the power of addiction, our own citizens to rob each other, often with mortal consequences. Our prisons were filled to overflowing with users and dealers alike. The Drug Act of 2088 in my second term made marijuana legal and gave a monopoly to tobacco companies to grow and sell it in exchange for their ceasing the production of tobacco products which became illegal by the same Act. To discourage the use of 'hard' drugs such as heroin and cocaine, I had the Army and Navy Joint Task Force intercept large shipments. These stores were poisoned (what we called, 'deleterious amendment') and the drugs replaced in the usual course of the illicit trade. Initially, tens of thousands of addicts died. After a time, as the interceptions and poisonings increased, those hopelessly addicted died and those who were not simply stopped. While only 5% of all drugs were actually 'amended,' no one could tell which 'hit' might be his last. Those addicts who preferred a sober life to a drug-addled death sought out effective recovery programs. Younger people who toyed with the idea of 'experimenting' sensibly decided not to bother. In less that 18 months, import and sale of those drugs came to a virtual halt, all convicts doing time for drug sale/use offenses were released and only small amounts of "amended" drugs were distributed. Robberies, burglaries and other street crimes of an economic nature dropped 94.6 percent.

"Terrorist organizations which were funded by the illegal trade found themselves without capital and nearly every country in the Western world followed suit by using the same procedures and laws. And without money, terror can be neither organized nor effective. Funds generated from the opium trade in the Middle East, were no longer available as reward money to suicide bombers' families. Despite the notion that suicide bombers act as a matter of faith, something I will not deny, the lack of funding to enable them to purchase materials and to ensure the economic safety of their families after their death simply brought terrorism to a halt. I will discuss in later entries other methods I used. People who produced hard drugs in local 'factories' for personal use or sales to locals were summarily executed shortly after arrest and conviction in 'Drug Abuse Tribunals' established by the Act. There was no right of appeal from these convictions. After less than a year, the DATs had so few cases to try that only one full time court was set up in Oklahoma City to handle the caseload of the entire nation. My greatest satisfaction came when my grandson, Carlton III said, 'Thanks, Grampa, for making my future safe. I don't just have to say 'No;' no one even asks!'"

Another senile motherfucker, I'm thinking. Maybe the bitches aren't such a bad idea after all. Hey, God, did you do this on purpose? Or are you as senile as these old farts? All due respect, sir.

So here I am stuck in this shithole farmhouse with Tim, and a bunch of retirement home rejects—one a Rocky Balboa wannabe who wants to kick my ass, and outside a boatload of screaming women who want to eat me and jump my bones—and not in a good way!

It didn't seem like only a few hours ago when all hell broke loose, and now here we are holed up with the "Gray Berets". It looks to me like this Artie is the de facto leader of the bunch. But I think his hold over this rag-tag band is tenuous at best. Jerry the queen, is his puppy dog, he'll do what ever Artie asks, I'm sure. Chaz there is another story, all latent hostility, wrapped in a veneer of bravado. He could step up, or just as easily cut and run to save his own tail. And the Big Guy in the corner, I just can't seem to get a read on him at all yet. He's a mystery, and I don't like mysteries. If things get dicey and I am sure they will, things can get ugly in here, fast. I need to figure him out, and quickly. He's a random element, and random elements can get you killed. As Sun Tzu said in the Art of War—*"Know yourself and know your enemy, and you need not fear the battle." That, and always be able to withdraw to a defensible position!*

"Thanks for the shot back there, Hawkeye." I said to Artie. "But I don't think you and these geriatric jokers have any idea what you're up against. We need to fortify this place—now."

"And just who the fuck put you in charge, Priss," said Chaz, brandishing his shovel.

"Look, Rambo 27, I saw a bunch of those harpies tear apart a bar full of dudes half your ages—if those bitches get in here you and the Geritol Brigade are toast!"

"Why you little pissant!" - and he swung the shovel at me, but before I could react, it stopped just before my face—held fast in an enormous hammy fist. The Big Guy pulled it from Chaz's hands, nearly lifting him off the ground in the process.

"He's right", he said, in a rumbling voice that was somewhere between Darth Vader's and my aunt Gladys' who smoked four packs a day.

"Thanks," I said

"Name's Dick, as you know, but my friends call me 'Tiny', he said, and tossed me the shovel.

"Tiny", I said raising an eyebrow. "Say, wait a minute—I know you, you're 'Tiny the Terrible'. Shit, when I was a kid I used to watch you every Saturday afternoon on Wrestling Roundup with my Pop and brothers!" So the brooder just became an asset. With a little luck we may just survive the night, but I still wasn't quite sure what we had to fear more, those things outside or each other. "That was a long time ago, kid, come on I saw some two by fours back over this way, help me find some nails—and let's see what we can do about boardin' this place up."

Chaz hocked up a big wad of phlegm, and spat on the floor. "Watch your back, you little Fucker."

"All right that's enough, Chaz, why don't you make yourself useful and try to find a hammer or some other tools we can use", said Artie.

"Why don't you get stuffed", Chaz replied.

"Fuck him, he's useless—I'll go", said Tim.

Tim was a modern day hippie. Wore his hair long in a ponytail, scruffy beard, Birkenstocks, Tie-dye, Greenpeace stickers on his Prius, the whole works, but he was an all right guy, and a good friend.

Artie turned to me and said, "Why don't you go see if you can help your friend find some of the boards and things we need—I'll see what I can do to unruffle Chaz's feathers; he's really not such a bad guy, once you get to know him." I nodded and walked off after Tim.

"You know, Chaz," Artie said, you really aren't making this any easier."

"Look all I know is, we were doing a lot better off until you started taking in all these strays—first the big guy, but him, he didn't bother me much, he just kept to himself, but these two—they are going to be trouble, mark my words. We were doing just fine when it was just you, me, and Jerry cooped up in here. Even them things out there didn't seem to care a lick about us—now since they chased those two here they, got all riled up, and suddenly we have to worry about boarding the place up and all. Like I said, things were just fine around here till they to showed up. And you just let 'em waltz right in."

"And what would have had me do, Chaz? Just leave them out there, to be torn apart, left to die?"

"You mean like we was all left to die at Easy Glades? Seems to me the world out there don't much give a shit about guys like us, Artie. To them, we are just yesterday's news. Lock 'em up, shut 'em up, drug 'em up - forget about 'em and worry about your own.

He poked his finger hard into Artie's chest, "and maybe its time you started thinking the same way—if you wanna live."

Artie could see the anxiety in Chaz's eyes. It was starting. Artie knew the signs of group cohesion breaking down all too well. Everything seemed fine, harmonious, but that's only on the surface. It seemed a lifetime ago that he was holed up with another group of guys—solated, cut off, like this. An experiment they called it. But that was in the Air Force—before he washed out of astronaut training, before they said he was unfit for space duty, before he began drinking . . . he shut off the *memory.*

"You guys look like you had some luck, let me see what you got there," Artie said to us as Tim and I returned from our rounds with our stash. Dick was still out scrounging. We had found the 2 x 4's Dick mentioned, along with a few boxes of nails, a couple of hammers, a pick axe, and a machete. We took the boards, and hammers and nails and started reinforcing every possible ingress to the barn. Artie coughed, as the sound of our efforts reverberated, and raised plums of dust. Chaz just stood in a corner—refusing to help, leaning on a shovel.

"Oh boys—boys, come here you have just got to see this!" It was Jerry, who was on watch. We all went to where he was looking out of the opening in the loft he was guarding. There, fifty yards in front of the barn was a girl, she couldn't have been more than 19 or so. But too far away to tell if she was a zombie bitch. What we could see was that she was gorgeous, dressed in very tight orange shorts, and a T-shirt with the name of some bar on it—which she was very playfully lifting up and down to reveal nearly perfect breasts. She twirled and gyrated to some un-seen beat, now taking off the T-shirt entirely exposing her well-tanned breasts, which she caressed lovingly, as she slowly licked her ruby lips.

"Whoa! Would you look at those puppies!" said Chaz, "I am sure glad I saved a few of these", he said as he unscrewed a pill holder he had on a gold chain around his neck and popped a little blue pill. "Hold on there, sweetcheeks, I'll be out in a minute or two."

The girl continued to dance; she now wriggled out of the little orange shorts and was completely naked, the sun glistening on her increasingly sweaty body. She got down on the grass, would roll back and forth a few times, stop on her back and arch upward - then rhythmically move her hips up and down, up and down.

We were all enjoying the show, with the possible exception of Jerry, who maintained his vigil, shovel held at the ready, when Chaz tried to push past him, "Let me go," he said.

I guess even old guys, stuck in one place who haven't had it in while, still think with the wrong head!

"You big horny idiot, you can't go out there." The girl was now on the ground touching herself, writhing back and forth. Intermittently she

would stop and lick her own fingers.

"Look, faggot—I've been stuck in here with you all too long, I know what she wants, and I don't think I'm ever getting another chance like this." Before any of us could stop him, Chaz pushed past Jerry and towards the nubile young incubus. She was still rocking back and forth on the ground as he reached her, and stood over her. We could see from the barn as she slowly climbed up his legs, and undid his pants, and they dropped around Chaz's ankles. We saw his hips rock forward and his head arch back in pleasure as she took him in her mouth.

Chaz's scream was deafening as we could see her head quickly withdraw from his crotch, blood trailing in a spattering arc along with it. With a shriek two more bitches bolted from the brush on either side of the shocked Chaz, gripping him by the arms and pulling - his arms ripping free as if they had just made a wish.

Dick, barreled out of the barn like a 400-pound juggernaut, rusted, metal rake held high. The rake tore into the back of one of the bitches and he pulled her off of what was left of Chaz, like a sanitation worker would spear and pick up a candy wrapper from the ground in the park. The second girl challenged Dick with a hiss and she caught the back end of the rake, shoved so far down her throat that it came through the back of her neck. The original dancer got up, and started to run, trying to flee, but Dick brought the rake down hard on her head and through her skull, and it wedged there. The momentum of her body carried it forward as the head stayed imbedded on the rake, her once pretty face nearly split in two.

Dick, breathing heavily, made his way back to the entrance of the barn. As he pushed the head of the dead girl off of the rake with his thick-soled shoe, I could see she had something jammed in her mouth— it was Chaz's still erect penis, but I guess he no longer had to "seek medical attention for an erection lasting more than four hours."

Jerry opened the door and stepped out to let the big man back in, when suddenly one of the women Dick thought he had killed, her back ravaged and spine exposed by the rake, clawed her way forward, and bit Jerry on the calf. He howled as I thrust my shovel down, severing her head at the neck like a guillotine. Dick dove inside the barn carrying the screaming Jerry along with him.

Put him down here, quick, quick."Iit was Artie. Jerry was scream-ing. Blood from his leg was mingling with the hay on the barn floor mak-ing a thick trail behind him. "You," Artie turned to Tim. "Over there by my bunk, there's a first aid kit. Bring it here, hurry, now!" Tim obeyed. Artie tore open a few 4x4 gauze pads and put them immediately over the gaping wound on the back of Jerry's calf.

"Here" he said to me, "Keep pressure here," and he had me squeeze tightly over the gauze, which was rapidly becoming soaked in blood. With his mouth, Artie tore open a roll of tape and started taping around the gauze. Jerry was still screaming and crying in agony. Artie took a small metal flask out of one of the pockets of his vest. "Here, old buddy, drink some of this." Jerry gulped down the booze.

"Holy Shit!" said Tim. "Did you see that, did you see all that!" Jerry's screams had died down to whimpers now, as he continued to take long draughts from of Artie's flask. I felt like I could use one myself. Eventually, Jerry drifted off into unconsciousness.

"Is he going to be all right?" I said to Artie.

"Well I've got the blood flow staunched," he said taking a long swig from the flask himself now, before returning it to his breast pocket, the deep red stains of Jerry's blood now commingled with the others of his ridiculous long underwear. "The thing is I don't know anything about that bite. At the very least, it could get infected, gangrenous—Jerry's a diabetic after all, at the worst..."

Dick interrupted, "At the worst—go ahead and say it, man, we all know what you are thinking. He's infected with whatever this shit is that's making them all go crazy—and if he is he can't stay in here, you got to get rid of him."

"Wait a minute, you don't know that," said Artie, "Besides only ones I ever saw get nuts like that are women."

"Yeah, but just cause we never saw anyone but women affected by The Plague, that doesn't mean it only affects women," countered Dick, "And Jerry practically was a woman"

"All right that's enough!" said Artie—"another crack like that, smartass, and it's you I'll be getting rid of. Now me and Jerry go way

back" —he lifted his bow, arrow cocked and pointed it at Dick— "so you just back off and shut up."

Dick stepped forward, pulling himself up to his full height. "Okay, Artie, settle down." He put his big hand on the bow and gently made Artie lower it down. In the corner Jerry started to thrash about still unconscious, he was sweating profusely. Artie went to him. "He's burning up,, he said.

"Look at his leg," I said. At the wound, just above the bandage, black lines like tendrils were reaching out, up Jerry's leg, already almost past his knee.

"You!" Artie shouted at me, "Give me your belt." I did, and he took it and strapped it tight around Jerry's thigh just above his knee.

"You think that will stop it?"

"I can't be sure," said Artie, "I'm no doctor."

Dick's large shadow slowly passed over Jerry and the two of us kneeled beside him. In his deep baritone he said, "There is only one way to be sure." And that was when I noticed the machete in his hand.

We moved Jerry up onto a table the oldsters had been using to play bridge, we laid him right on top of the cards. "Okay, okay", Artie said to me," you hold him down at the shoulders, keep him from squirming too much, here pour some more of this down his throat." He passed me the flask, Jerry coughed as I did as Artie asked. "Now, do it right here, just above where the belt is serving as a tourniquet. Try to make it one quick blow," he said to Dick, who was poised above Tim brandishing the machete. Tim was holding a makeshift torch made from some old rags we found around the barn, which he'd lit with a Zippo lighter lying on the table. He handed it to me and I pocketed it. Black, acrid smoke from it swirled toward the ceiling in a macabre dance. A bucket of water was at his feet. "Now, Tim, very important, as soon as I pull the leg clear, you have to press that torch quickly and firmly against the stump to cauterize the wound. And then douse it immediately in that water—if you drop it, or ignite any of this hay around here, it won't matter if this works or not."

"Okay, let's go." I took a deep breath, and said a little prayer as Dick raised the machete over Jerry's leg. Jerry groaned and let out a little whimper as I pressed down harder on his shoulders, but he remained barely conscious. The Machete came down with a sickening thunk, passing through Jerry's leg and into the table below as easily as Abe Lincoln splitting a rail. Jerry began screaming, but I shoved a "bite stick" from the First Aid kit between his teeth, forced his jaw shut, and held it fast.

"Tim, the torch, now!" shouted Artie. Tim, did what he was told, and the cloying smell of roasting flesh filled the air. I could feel Jerry slip back into unconsciousness as I heard the hiss of Tim's torch being extinguished in the water. That was followed by the clatter of the machete hitting the barn floor, Dick's broad back turned to me in disgust as he walked away in silence. "I need some air." I knew he shouldn't go outside, but I was not going to argue with the big man.

Artie took Jerry's amputated leg, wrapped it in some rags, and carried it over to the latrine hole in the floor, and let it drop through, it landed in the lye pile with a soft ploomf and puff of white powdery smoke.

Dick had been gone about fifteen minutes when I heard a strange sound.

"You hear that?" There was drone that was soon recognizable as a car engine, growing louder and louder. We all ran to the opening of the hayloft, just in time to see a black sedan barreling toward the farmhouse, running over and through the creatures—tossing them aside like rag dolls, beating out a concerto of bone cracking thumps. Then, the car took off like a rocket, hit an old tree stump, rolled over and over, finally coming to a stop just feet before the entrance to the barn. I could see the driver was still alive inside. He was trying to crawl out, toward the entrance, but was held by his seatbelt "Cover me," I shouted to Artie, as I grabbed the machete and charged through the entrance and out into the madness just in time to bury it deep in the face of the first creature that was about to pounce on the drivers back. The machete came free with a slurp, and she slumped to the floor. I barely heard Artie's arrow whiz by my cheek as it took down the second squarely between the eyes. Another came scrambling over the bottom of the overturned car, leaping, only to find herself impaled on my machete; it protruded out of her back, a limp and deflated silicon implant dangling from the tip. With a twist I removed the long blade, which slid back out through her once ample chest, covered in gore. I used the machete to cut the seatbelt that held the driver in the car, and dragged him back inside the barn, just as Artie got the barn doors shut.

"Are you crazy!" shouted Tim. "You could have been killed. If those things got in here we all could have been killed!" Whatever Tim was going to say next, it was cut off by a high-pitched blood-curdling scream. Jerry had picked that moment to regain consciousness, and was screaming, having noticed his missing leg. "My leg, what did you to my leg, my beautiful legs!" Artie went to kneel down next to him.

"It's okay, it's okay Jerry, you are going to be alright," and he cradled Jerry's head in his arms. Jerry's screams slowly subsided, but he continued to cry and whimper. He was muttering something about now he'll never dance with Liza Minnelli, as Artie passed him the metal flask from which he continued to drink deeply.

Tim, on the other hand, was really losing it—I had never seen him like this. His eyes darted from me, to Jerry, to Artie, back to the door.

"This is crazy, Man. Captain Viagra gets torn apart, the queen is screaming, the big guy's nowhere to be found, and there are more and more of those things trying to claw their way in here now, and you go and open the doors just to let another poor bastard in here."

"Hey, Tim—think! Use your head. If Artie there didn't open up and let us in here, we'd already be Purina Zombie Chow!"

"Better all calm down" It was the guy we just brought in. He was seated against the back wall, his head bowed between his knees.

"What?" said Artie. He still cradled Jerry's head in his lap, who had mercifully fallen back into unconsciousness.

The stranger in the corner lifted his head slowly; "I said you all have to take it down a notch."

"Hey, Mister, you just got here—you have no idea what we been through," said Tim

"And you have no idea what all your anger, aggression and macho bullshit is going to do to those things out there. You guys keep going at it, loose control, get the adrenaline pumping, and the testosterone flowing and those things are going to be drawn to this place like a pack of *hungry dogs to a butcher shop."*

"They must know we're in here now," I said.

Artie was hopeful. Poor guy. "Maybe they didn't see. We've been up here for a while without much incident."

"You're wrong," the stranger said.

"How do you know that?" said Artie.

"Because that's what it was designed to do. I'm David Keilar, and I am, or was Chief Science Officer of Vivax Pharmaceuticals. You ever heard of Oxytocin?"

Tim said, "You mean the painkillers that Rush Limbaugh was addicted to?"

"No you idiot," said Artie, "that was Oxycontin, Oxytocin is some kind of 'love hormone' isn't it? Supposed to be a human pheromone."

Keilar and the rest of us looked at Artie in surprise. He gave a look back that said, "Told you I'm not just a stupid old drunk."

Keilar nodded and said, "Yeah, but the stuff we came up with was hundreds of times stronger. We were trying to develop something that would make men," and he looked right at Tim, "any man, incredibly attractive, irresistible not only to women, but to everyone around him. Call it a kind of charisma in a bottle, but no matter what you called it, it would spell power to the user. But something went wrong. Horribly wrong, a few women in the trials . . . they died, but that wasn't the worst of it. They didn't stay dead, they came back as those things out there. Strong, fast, aggressive, you've all seen that, but they also seem to actually feed on testosterone, need it to survive like a mosquito needs blood. They can 'smell'" it, and it whips them into a feeding frenzy, the results of which you've all seen. Then somehow which we still don't understand, it started to spread to people that never even took the drug."

Wait a minute, are you telling me you're the bastard that caused this mess? Tim's voice rose, becoming shriller. "I mean, I thought, who knows maybe The Plague was just nature getting back at us, an Act of God, weird mutant virus like AIDS, or whatever. I should have known some suits were behind it." Tim started pacing, and circling like a rabid dog. "Shit, my girlfriend Christina became one of those things, and I watched her tear apart my little brother right in front of me." Tears were welling up in Tim's eyes, and something else; he picked up a bloody shovel off of the floor. "You God damn bastards, you knew, you all fuckin' knew..."

"Wait!" Keilar shouted. I could see the fear in his eyes, the veins pumping in his neck, his body entering fight or flight mode. "We didn't mean for this to happen, we didn't know. How could we?"

Tim started screaming at the top of his lungs. "Yeah, that's how it always is with you types. 'We didn't know there was melamine in the milk, Mad Cow in the meat, lead in the fucking toys'. You don't give a shit about people, man." And he raised the shovel over his head. I was the first to grab him. Then Artie. Tim was swinging the shovel around wildly, we spun and spun trying to get it away from him, he just kept shouting crazily, and he knocked me to the floor. Artie was still on him. Keilar had curled up into a ball in the corner.

"They did it man, they fucking did it—they went and killed us all."

Somehow Artie, with a strength that belied his slight frame, slipped his arms up and around Tim like an aging python, and he got him in a kind of a headlock.

"Tim, please," he said between panting breaths and through gritted yellow teeth. "You heard what the guy said. Please, settle down! You're gonna get us all killed!"

But Tim kept screaming and straining against Artie's grip. He still grasped the shovel and was swinging wildly. I couldn't get near to help.

BLAM!

There was a thunderous boom. And there stood Dick, coveralls soaked in blood, a shotgun in his hand. "Hey look what I found." There was the sound of the weapon being cocked again. He leveled it at Tim. "Now, drop the shovel, Tim, and step away, slowly from Artie." Tim looked like he wasn't going to comply for a moment, I saw Dick's finger tense on the trigger. And suddenly Tim just collapsed in heap, whimpering at Artie's feet, the shovel falling loose from his hands. There was sunlight streaming in, illuminating a pillar of dust in front of him from a gaping hole the shotgun had blasted in the roof of the barn. With that shaft of light before him and his long hair plastered on his face by *sweat and tears, Tim looked almost like Christ in a Raphael painting.*

Tim just curled up in a fetal position on the floor rocking back and forth. The guy from the pharmaceutical company, Keilar, wasn't doing much better. "Isolation Madness" is what Artie called it. I remembered seeing a show on 60 Minutes *about what was happening to prisoners in America's Supermax facilities and they said that prisoners who are isolated for prolonged periods of time have been known to experience depression, despair, anxiety, rage, claustrophobia, hallucinations, problems with impulse control, and an impaired ability to think and concentrate— add a few Zombies outside the walls and I guess it doesn't take long to go through all of the above.*

Dick lowered the shotgun. I had to admit I was glad to see the big fellow. "Found these too. Made my way over to the main house. You're pretty good with that bow, old man, but why don't you try something with a little more firepower." He unslung a deer rifle from his shoulder and passed it with a box of cartridges to Artie. From a deep pocket in his overalls he produced a .38 revolver, turning to me he said, "You ever use one of these, Kid?"

"Only in the Arcade, but it can't be that different," I said accepting the pistol and ammunition.

Artie cocked the bolt on the 30-30, and sighted down it like a pro. Again we looked at him incredulously. "Two tours in Korea. You hear that?" said Artie.

"Hear what?" I said. "I don't hear anything."

"That's my point, boy... the things out there, they been moaning and groaning and tearing at those boards since you all came in here. Now I don't hear a thing."

There was a thump on the roof, and then another, followed by a loud crash. With all the fury of a howling banshee one of the wild women tore through the hole Dick's shotgun had made in the roof. She leapt down and was on Tim's quivering form in an instant.

Tim was being shredded faster than a stack of documents at Goldman-Sachs. Dick let go with both barrels and the thing on top of Tim exploded in a hail of red mist. Behind her, another, dressed in a cheerleader outfit, dropped to the ground, landing lithely. She cartwheeled over to a panic stricken Kielar, and sunk her teeth deep into his neck. I heard the crack of the deer rifle as her head burst open in a shower of blood and brain matter.

Two, three, four—I lost count—dropped down after her. I took out the gal in the Armani business suit and the biker chick with the revolver. Artie nailed the jogger, the cop, and the girl in the Starbucks uniform, who I could swear had made me a double espresso Latte with no whip just a few days ago. The bodies of crazed women were stacking up like so much cordwood, when Dick yelled, "We gotta get that hole closed! I'll get them to chase me, you two seal the roof!" He started running. "Hey, over here, you psycho bitches, come and get three hundred pounds of one hundred percent pure Grade A dark meat!" He took off, at least half a dozen or more of the hells belles behind him. But for the moment, the onslaught had stopped.

Looking for something we could use to seal the breach, my eyes fell on the table where Jerry had lain unconscious through the melee. It was empty except for his sequined dinner jacket covered in entrails. Feeling the bile rise in my throat, I swept what was left of Jerry off of the table. "Come on," I said to Artie, whose skin had gone as white as his hair. "You couldn't have done anything more for him, now help me with this table."

Artie and I had just managed to secure the roof with the tabletop, when I felt searing hot pain as nails raked through my back, the force of the creature's blow throwing me forward like a rag doll, and right through the hole in the loft floor that was the make shift latrine. I landed unceremoniously in a pile of piss and crap, next to Jerry's severed leg! I heard Artie's screams above, and then a wet thud as Artie's head landed in the sludge next to me, his blind bloodshot eyes staring upward. I starred back at those blank dead eyes, transfixed, unable to move. My reverie was broken by the loud crash of the heavy barn doors bursting open. Dozens of the deranged women burst in. I still had the revolver and started firing wildly. As each harpy I hit fell, those behind her just trampled over it like a stampede of horny fourteen year olds at a Jonas Brothers concert, trampling it into pulp. The barn floor ran thick with ooze.

I tried to run but my feet could not find purchase in the slick cover-

ing of gore and waste, and the first bitch grabbed me, sinking her teeth deep into my belly. She tore free with a sickening rip, threw her head back and hungrily gulped down a huge wad of my flesh and insides like a penguin swallowing a herring. Holding my torn guts with one hand, I fired point blank through her left eye, tearing off half of her head in the process.

I half slid, half ran to the furthest reaches of the barn, back down a long corridor of unused animal stalls, firing blindly behind me. I reached a back wall, and stopped slumped against it, practically spent. I knew the ravenous pack would soon be upon me. The revolver was empty. I groped around in the dark and prayed for something that could help me make my last stand. Pay dirt! You know the old saying about no atheists in foxholes!

As the first of the horde reached me, the roar of the chainsaw I had stumbled upon was deafening as I cleaved her in two at the waste. Blood and body parts spattered everywhere as I dealt similarly with her sisters.

I crawled back along the waste-covered floor of the barn, covered in blood, no way to tell how much of it was mine, when my foot caught in something—a loop of rope in the floor. "Root cellar", something in my mind hazily recognized. I felt back along my leg and slipped my foot out of the rope, and sure enough it was attached to a trap door in the floor. It took just about all my strength to open it. It closed with a loud thump above me as I painfully crawled down. I was in total darkness. The floor of the root cellar was damp and spongy. It smelled like wet dog. I fumbled in my pocket for the Zippo; it sparked a few times till it lit.

"You look like shit." I said the figure before me. It was Dick. He was sitting propped up against a support beam, breathing hard dripping gore, a stark white bone protruding from his thigh.

"You don't look so good yourself."

"Any rounds left?"

The moans and shrieks of the ghouls and the shuffling footsteps in the barn above grew louder and steadier.

"Nope."

"Can you fight?"

"Barely lift my arms, think my leg's broke...you?"

"Out of ammo, no more gas in the chainsaw, couldn't find any other weapons. I'm pretty sure I left a good part of my guts all over the floor up there."

"You've been bit?"

"Several places. You?"

"Yep."

"I did find this though." And I passed him Artie's bloodstained flask. I was feeling really dizzy. Dick's face was fading in and out, and his voice sounding more distant. "You sure only women turn into those things?"

"Can't say I'm sure 'bout anything any more... I never did get your name, kid."

"George—it's George." My lying continues.

"Well! Here's to you, George..."

"And to you, Old Timer..."

Dick raises an ax over my head and brings it down.

I awake with a jump that makes everyone look at me.

"Hey," said Tim. "You okay?"

I looked at him and the quiet group of men who were sitting at the table playing cards.

"You okay?" he repeated.

"Yeah. I'm okay. Just a dream."

"Dreams are good for you," said Jerry. "They get rid of your fears and anxieties. One time I dreamed I was on a motorcycle with James Dean. I was holding on real tight and he made this turn, but the road was near a cliff and . . . "

"Whatever," said Artie. "Jerry, no one wants to hear your fairy godmother stories tonight. Let's turn in. It's late."

I go down the ladder and stand outside the door breathing the clean country air real deep. The corn stalk are still, no women in sight. Maybe they moved on. Who knows. Then, my eyes spot something heading my way and my heart kicks into overdrive but not out of fear. Hadley is walking toward me in her little pink shirt and jeans with a kitten patch sewn on one of the pockets.

"Hadley, honey, how'd you find us?"

"I just followed the trail. You know I was a Brownie for six years, now I'm a Girl Scout. We can do things like follow trails. I had two merit badges for woodland survival."

"That's cool. But didn't Tim tell you to stay with the balloon?

"No."

"Oh, I thought he told me that. Come on in. Let's get some sleep."

She followed me up the ladder and I tucked her in on top of some loose hay, sifting some stalks out of her hair. I didn't alert the others. I didn't want them to know a female was in the barn. I'd deal with it in the morning, after both me and Tim had a good night's rest. She closed her eyes and fell asleep in thirty seconds. I still couldn't believe she'd made it here without incident. She was tougher than I'd pegged her.

"Poor kid," I said under my breath.

I rolled over and pretended to sleep but just waited for the hours to pass, listening to grunts, groans and farts until the sun crept up the side of the barn and made bright stripes on everything. When I went to where Hadley had bedded down, she was gone.

CHAPTER 19

We said goodbye to the geezers, who wished us luck and let us take a few supplies, but not much. It took Tim and me a while to get back to the balloon but we made it without any problems. We even snatched some of those guns the Deliverance Family had dropped. The bitches were either hibernating or had moved on looking for more populated areas.

We found Hadley there and I wanted to ask her why she'd come back during the night by herself but the more I thought about it the more I figured she'd never been to the barn in the first place. That barn was just too full of bad mojo affecting my inner eye and my gut told me I'd hallucinated her arrival. Either way, she was safe and hugging MG so I let my confusion go. By nightfall we were aloft once again. It was good to be back up above the ground, looking down on all the destruction below. I counted the fires dotting the landscape like flickering jewels to pass the time. And it sure passed as slowly as an ornery kidney stone.

"We're almost out of fuel," Tim said later. I think he said it, I was so zoned out I couldn't be sure.

At some point I came out of my haze and I could just make out the New York City skyline. The sun was behind us and the golden light caught the windows of the Empire State Building just above a thin layer of clouds that hovered over the city. Stinking New Jersey sat below us, thick with industrial buildings, squalid with refinery stacks and the huge cannon-like incinerator stacks. Newark Airport, one of the busiest in the country, was lit by the oblique rays of the setting sun. Birds circled the control tower and tall grass had conquered the expansion joints on the runway. From this altitude, about 1,600 feet by the altimeter, the runways looked like the handprint of a gigantic robot that had decided to do a one hand handstand. Docked airplanes sat in corners and against terminal buildings like they were hiding from the robot. "Terminal buildings." Good choice of words.

The Meadowlands, a huge tract of some of the most polluted swamp land on planet Earth, stretched its hairy footprint north and east. It's the stink appetizer in New Jersey just across the river from the Big Apple. As we floated by, I could see the bitch paths worn through the tall reeds and cat-tails, the telltale signs that bitches were on the prowl in sufficient numbers to keep the weeds flattened down. Several trails ended at the Hudson River but others connected warehouses north and south as if they had been busily visiting each other.

The Reynolds Building in Passaic had what looked like a fire glowing in one of its windows, the penthouse office complex. As we passed a mere hundred feet or so to the north, we saw it was no fire at all but a cluster of red lights.

Tim pointed. "Look at that. There's a cross in the middle of those lights." Through the binoculars, I could see a cross made from fresh lumber probably looted from one of the many supply stores that hovered here just in handy-dandy reach of New Yorkers yearning to renovate their thousand-dollar-a-square-foot apartments.

In heaps around the lights were human skeletons arranged in an orderly fashion, all sitting and looking at the cross. On the cross, a blonde zombie bitch was nailed through the head, abdomen and feet. Her arms were tied with cable; a noose tugged taut around her neck. Her hair was down to her ass.

"Check it out," I told Tim, handing him the binocs.

"Man . . . " he said as he looked through.

A sudden updraft caught us and shifted us toward the building. Tim ran to the jet control and full-blasted it, but it was too late. The gondola slammed into the side of the air conditioning apparatus on the roof, the whole gondola tipping hard to the side. Hadley was knocked out and over. I reached for her arm as she went by but I grabbed nothing and she fell to the roof below, about twenty feet.

The gondola dropped and hit the roof, the balloon cables snagged on a cellphone tower. Tim tried to lift up but the force of the propane blast made the tower creak and moan, so he shut the gas down. Too late. We were tethered to the building. Tim had blood coming from his right ear where he'd smashed into the gondola rail. My wrist felt like a gorilla used it as a back-scratcher.

"Hadley!" I yelled, hoping to God I got a response. She was rolling around in pain, her lungs knocked clear of air. I start freaking out big time, reach one foot tentatively onto the rooftop, sliding from the basket warily as I quickly assume a defensive position on the tar. She looks up and coughs once, then gets up and takes my hand. I lead her back to the gondola and tell her to stay put. She wraps her arms around MG and lets the dog lick her face.

The pistol in my hand is cold, blue steel while the rifle on my back is light and sleek, to say nothing of the knife strapped to my left ankle. My eyes scout every nook and cranny on the deserted rooftop, looking for any signs of life or, for that matter, afterlife.

I hear Tim's familiar boots crunching on the rooftop gravel behind me, his breath sour and stale from another meal of Slim Jims and stale fruit roll-ups from our dwindling food stash.

"That's it, Kent," he breathes on my neck. "This is home until we find some gas and refuel."

"Spot any undead?" I ask, craning left and right and seeing none myself.

We climb the six short steps down from the ledge to the roof proper, leaning as far as we dare over the side to peer down twenty stories below. My stomach lurches to see the sight of a well-organized bitch horde patrolling the perimeter.

"What do you think?" I ask Tim. "Two hundred or so?"
"From the looks of it," he sighs, wiping his hair before putting on his backward baseball cap. "I hate it when they get organized like that."

I watch half the horde pace patiently to the left, the other half to the right.

"Get used to it," I say, turning around to avoid the depressing sight. "It's like they get smarter with each passing day."

"Not smart enough to talk, though," Tim points out with a grin. "At least not more than grunts."

Good old Tim; it all comes down to good guys and bad guys with him, even now.

We scout the perimeter of the rooftop, every inch of it, just in case. It takes a while and by the time we're done my legs are sore. Floating over New Jersey looking for fuel has left me feeling out of shape and lazy.

I wipe my brow with a handkerchief from my back pocket and rest on the bottom step of the roof. Tim leans against the railing behind him, tall and wiry with eyes that don't miss a trick.

Tim clears his throat to get my attention and says, "Sun's getting low, Kent."

I swallow and think, God, I hate the night.

"Right," I say out loud. "Let's see what treats this building has in store for us."

He helps me to my aching feet as we approach the metal door leading down from the roof. I can tell from the swollen bolts and scarred lock that it's been barricaded, but by now what hasn't been?

Months of straight-up zombie sieges have left every building in every city a fortress, though by now most of them have been deserted—or overrun.

"Looks recent," Tim says, running his fingers over the swollen seam between the door and the rooftop.

141

A familiar ripple of anxiety passes through my stomach as I inch back up to the balloon to retrieve our tools from the back storage compartment.

"How recent?" I ask, returning with two crowbars; one for work—one for what possibly waits on the other side of the door.

Tim takes his rifle and we both wedge the bars into the seam.

"On three, Kent," he grunts, digging his deep.

"One," I count, digging even deeper, "two . . . three."

The lock gives an inch or two as the door buckles in the middle but the door itself holds fast, even as Tim begins searching the seams for additional locks.

I hear rustling inside and crouch, wedging my crowbar against a bolt soldered near the bottom corner of the rusty door. He finds a similar bolt at the top and, after five minutes, the door gives a few more inches with a yawning sigh, its seal finally breaking to reveal, through the crack, a dark and dingy stairwell just on the other side.

"Smell that?" Tim asks knowingly, taking huge, gulping whiffs.

I nod; the overpowering smell of stale sweat and canned food and the slightest trace of urine is unmistakable.

"This building's occupied," I gasp, just as the door bursts fully open.

I find a pistol pointed at my face, the hand holding it delicate but unwavering as I back up a quick two paces until the heel of my hiking boots hit the bottom rung of the landing pad stairs.

The shooter has dark hair swept back in a thick, unkempt ponytail and quick, brown eyes that stare at me, unblinking.

"What the fuck do you think you're doing?" she spits and I avoid giving Tim a quick "eyes right" as she covers him just to the side of the open stairwell door.

"It personally took me two weeks to seal that door shut,"

she hisses, a tendril of black hair moving back and forth in front of her lips as she berates me. "Do you know how hard it is to spot weld without the proper equipment!"

"I'm sorry," I sputter, holding my gun up and out in a non-threatening gesture. "I didn't think the building was occupied."

She finally blinks, if only to help her focus on the balloon tangled in the tower at my back.

It should have been a quicker revelation for me. This bitch is a breathing, living, pussy-juiced, firm-titted human female.

"Is that what I think it is?" she asks, gun never moving from the point where my heart lies buried somewhere between my pit-stained, army green T-shirt.

"Don't get excited, honey," drawls Tim, kicking the door shut and slamming it into her wrist. "She's not going anywhere until we get some gas in her."

I assume he doesn't want to say anything about our asses being tangled and if we had all the propane in the world, we could not get outta here without some ingenuity.

She curses as her pistol clatters to the rooftop with a marvelous thud.

I pick it up and pocket it quickly, aiming my pistol at the heart now beating slightly more rapidly beneath a yellowed blouse with one sleeve missing.

"Shit," she says, more to herself than either of us. "That really hurt, you asshole."

Tim says, "One way to avoid getting a broken wrist is to stop pointing pistols at my buddy Kent here."

She rotates her wrist a few more times, making sure nothing's broken, before extending her hand in Tim's direction. I'm thinking that this girl has not been infected. No way. How is this possible?

"That's Kent," she says, still a little huffy, "I'm Molly and you are . . . ?"

"Tim," he says, not offering his hand.

"Before answering any more friendly questions, how about explaining why you're not trying to eat my dick and balls or anything else you could get your teeth into?" I ask.

"You're not my type?" she says with a smirk. Tim puts his gun to her head.

"You're not my type either, you fucking bitch. Now tell me why I shouldn't blow your zombie-prone brains out right now," he eloquently states.

She cuts him a pissy look that indicates it'll be "Timothy" for the duration.

"My gun?" she asks me.

"Answer first," I say.

"I don't have an explanation. I was in the secretarial pool when the shit hit the fan. Every female in the building turned just like it said on TV and . . . I know you know how it all goes down. But I didn't get the disease. I can't explain it."

"Maybe you're a genetic freak," says Tim.

"I wish it was that easy. But it's not. These guys have kept me alive here for the sake of the future. They're assuming that someday I'll be valuable to science."

"I imagine you're valuable for some other stuff as well," Tim says.

"Fuck you, you low-life hick," she says.

"I'm a low-life but only my father was a hick." He shoves her and she cuts her hand on the bent door.

"Fuck you!" she shouts rubbing the wound.

"There's got to be more to your story. Tell it," I say.

"Okay, okay. I'm a carrier. I don't get the disease, but I can pass it on to other females. As far as anyone knows, which is not very far, I'm the only known specimen. So the guys here figure something in my genes or immune system is unique and if there's any chance of curing this plague or whatever it is, I'm it. Though my guess is their motives are more financial than humanitarian."

"Why do they let you out of their sight then?"

"Where am I gonna go? Down there with the undead? It's safer here, sadly. So I wouldn't be abusing the last best hope of humanity if I were you because the two of you are not worth the lint in my navel compared to me. Get it, fuckers? Now give me my gun back and let's cut the palaver or whatever you assholes call conversation. I'm in no mood."

I glance at Tim, who shrugs; I give it back.

She pockets it in an ill-fitting holster around her narrow waist; it clashes with her gray tweed skirt, which might have been longer once upon a time but now rests just above her knees and looks torn rather than hemmed

She wears black sneakers with no socks, making her legs look even longer and more shapely than they might have in heels. This is sick, I think.

Her face has the same hungry look we all have now; lean and tight, wary and unamused. Her lips are full without makeup, her eyes tired but luminous as she once again eyes the balloon on the roof.

"She's really out of gas?" she asks.

As I pray Hadley and MG stay quiet and ducked out of sight (they'll be alright for a bit in the balloon), I notice the slightest hint of Jersey upbringing in this girl's accent.

"Why do you think we crashed your little party here, sweetheart?" Tim asks, doing that cocky, creepy thing he always does when he's in on a joke.

Tim was married once and I'm sensing that the sudden confrontation with a "normal" woman is bringing back painful memories

"It is a private party, isn't it, sweetheart?" he goads her, inching closer.

She stands her ground and, with a simple eye roll brings Tim back to earth. "You wish, Romeo. There's about nineteen more of us just down that flight of stairs, and they're not going to be very happy knowing you landed here with no

145

fuel in your ride."

"What choice did we have?" I ask, admiring the steel in Molly's jaw.

"None, I suppose," she sighs, leaning back against the railing behind her. "Still, it's not the friendliest bunch, if you know what I mean."

"If you're the welcoming committee," Tim quips, "We know exactly what you mean."

Molly finally snorts, but only once she's got the butt of her pistol familiarly in the palm of her hand.

After re-barricading the door with one of our crowbars wedged into the gap, we follow her down the stairs. The smells of habitation get stronger with each step, but even given Molly's expensive clothes and obvious pedigree, she doesn't seem to notice—or mind—the stale frat house scent of moldy food cans and human waste.

A fire flickers near an open window, the flames rising from the charred metal body of a reconditioned photocopier. It illuminates a handful of assorted shapes who linger on its fringes. Like all survivors they are pale and wan, hungry and distrustful. They eye us warily as we pass, making no move to follow us or, for that matter, fear us.

They eye Molly with a look of either reverence or distrust. I can't tell.

Several more survivors line the other office windows, the rifles slung over their backs prominent in profile as they perform obvious sentry duty. The windows are mostly closed, the shades mostly open, giving the barren floor a spooky end of the world feel as the last of the day's light bathes all in a savage orange glow.

Molly gives us a quick tour, showing us the various cubicles in the back where the office dwellers have set up makeshift bunks, with curtains for comforters and rolled up motivational T-shirts from some long ago corporate pep rally serving as pillows.

Along the wide windowsills sit solar lamps of various sizes, gradually growing brighter as the orange sky outside the towering plate glass windows eases from orange to a stunning gray.

We hear male voices, loud ones, as Molly inches toward a hallway lined with metal shelves heaped with canned food and bottled water. I give Tim a wide-eyed look and she catches it, smirking as she warns, "Hands off, boys; unless you want to leave without 'em, that is."

Our pace slows as we face two armed guards, burly but surprisingly clean-shaven, standing on either side of a conference room door. Through the open blinds I can see three men sitting inside, not big but clearly powerful, smoking cigars and sipping carefully from rationed drabs off a scotch bottle encased in a locked box.

Molly nods to the guards, who frisk us thoroughly. By the time they're through, eight lethal weapons lie on a fold-up picnic table to their right. I sigh for show, but am secretly grateful that Tim is acting the gung ho. Thankfully they've missed a few surprises we've carefully hidden on ourselves.

To diffuse the guards' suspicions, Tim makes a big show of staring at the pile of weapons. "We'll get them back, right?" he asks one of the guards.

They just chuckle, while Molly stares at her feet a little guiltily.

The air inside the inner sanctum is electric and intense; Tim eyes me cautiously as we both try to look aloof and un-alarmed, not so easy to do when you're unarmed, surrounded by strangers and your fucking balloon is stuck on the roof.

The three men inside are clean and well-fed, unlike most of the office drones we've seen so far and, for that matter, Molly. They're far from heavy, but they look fleshy and alive, unlike the rest of us walking skeletons who've been subsisting on starvation rations for at least the last few months. Each has a shiny new sidearm around his ample waist, each eyes us with suspicion bordering on distrust.

Molly clears her throat and says to the blond man in the middle, "Ed, these two just landed on the roof; in a balloon!"

Ed, a jowly type in rolled up work sleeves and a straining belt, grunts.

"Interesting," he says without regarding the men on either side of him, who glower at us a little less strongly with the news that we've brought a potential ticket out of their sanctuary. "Where do you two hail from?"

Tim starts to open his mouth and I cut him off quickly; the less these guys know, the better. "Here and there," I say cryptically.

Next to me, Tim hazards a smile, then quickly buries it in his face.

Ed's not so forgiving. "I asked you a question," he barks.

"I gave you an answer," I say.

Ed nods, fleshy face beet red, and slides the pistol from its holster.

Tim flinches, but stands tall, hands still on his hips, close enough to his belt buckle knife to use it if need be, but not obvious enough about the subtle movement to rouse the suspicion of the three men at the table.

"Let me tell you how it works," Ed explains, placing the gun on the table in front of him. "This isn't a democracy. I'm in charge; Bill here is my second in command, and Frank is my other second in command. You know how we got into this room?"

I'm figuring it's a rhetorical question, but Ed is one of those self-important guys who actually expects an answer.

Tim is only too happy to oblige: "While everyone else was sleeping?"

Ed's face glows another wave of crimson as his two lackeys slide their pistols on the table as well.

Molly unsuccessfully tries to hide a snort.

"We got here," Ed glowers, "because we're the fittest of

the fit. That floor out beyond this door? It's full of office drones with soft hands who haven't left this floor since the latest invasion six weeks ago. We're the ones who barricaded the door, who sealed off the elevator and who made it so those weaklings could survive."

As if to make up for the involuntary laugh at Tim's joke, Molly rushes in to add, "Ed alone has nearly a dozen zombie kills under his belt."

Tim and I give each other a weary look.

"Wow," Tim says, inching forward as the three men look at their guns. "Twelve zombies? Well, nearly twelve zombies? That's impressive. But I killed that many just trying to get to my dinner last night, and my partner killed that many just trying to eat his breakfast. So forgive us if we're not signing up to be a part of your little tribe here."

Ed's face is too red to blush any longer. He merely asks, "So if you don't want to join us, what are you doing here?"

"Our ride is almost out of gas and we're tangled in a cell tower," I interject. "Just a twist of fate, no pun intended. It's that simple. We broke in, Molly here caught us, and she brought us straight to you. All we ask is a good night's sleep and a point in the right direction to the nearest fuel supply. Some help with the tangle. After that, we'll be out of your way and you'll be free to rule over your little office fiefdom without any further threat."

At the mention of "fuel," the three men share knowing glances. I ignore them and focus on Molly instead, who looks away as quickly as our eyes make contact.

Tim gives me an arched eyebrow and says, "So, fellas, where is it?"

"Where's what?" asks Ed, muffling a smile.

I shake my head and take another step forward.

One of Ed's minions—Bill or Frank, they look a lot alike—reaches for his gun. Without blinking, I slide the recently-oiled blade from its buckle on Tim's waist and jam it into the soft web of flesh between the man's thumb and fore-finger.

He howls obscenities before yanking his hand away, leaving a few drops of blood. By the time the three men look up again Tim has grabbed all of their pistols and is holding two while I hold the third.

"Now, gentleman," I say. "You were going to tell us about that fuel source?"

I pick up the scotch, take a sip, which is warm on the back of my throat. The pistol is solid in my formerly empty holster. Tim puffs his new cigar eagerly while Molly offers us a tin of dried sardines and two packages of stale crackers, what amounts to a post-outbreak feast in this day and age.

The men eye our meal eagerly but, old hands at sharing, Tim and I make quick work of divvying it up and devouring it before there's so much as a drop of oil for them to consider. I want to eat it all but a little sharing might make the negotiations go smoother.

"The propane is in a storage tank downstairs," Ed is saying, still eyeing his gun almost as greedily as the empty sardine tin. As humbled as he is, Ed manages to give his henchman a knowing smile. "Of course, so is the toughest, most violent, most virulent horde of female zombies you've ever witnessed. And before you say you killed fifteen of them before breakfast this morning, let me assure you, this horde is smart."

I roll my eyes but Tim leans in and asks, "What makes you say that?" I know what he's thinking. While the bitches have certainly evolved they have grown in wisdom, leadership and violence.

I'd been hoping the office building was free of bitches. Now, to hear they're actually inside the building gives the mission a less than encouraging feel.

I look at Tim and his glowering eyes tell me he's feeling the same way.

"What's so fierce about this particular group of bitches?"

he asks.

Ed looks at him as if he's been waiting to tell this story all night.

"Let me tell you about our neighbors," he begins, but only gets that far.

"What, there are other survivors in this building?"

Ed waves a hand away, a big hand, soft and blustery like the rest of him.

I look to Molly in the awkward silence that follows. She confesses, "A group of cops found us not long after the outbreak. Their precinct had been run over, communication had been cut off, they figured Wall Street was still safe; they figured wrong. By the time they saw us, the horde had them cornered."

Her story, while finished, seems abbreviated. I push away my scotch and ask, "Cornered . . . where . . . exactly?"

Ed sits forward in his seat as she says, "Two floors below us."

Tim shakes his head. "You're kidding me. There's a unit of cops, two floors below? So, why aren't we talking to them? They can escort us to the fuel and, with enough of it, we can get out of here."

Molly shakes her head and starts to speak but Ed cuts her off with a bark. "We barricaded ourselves off from them when the horde caught up to them."

Tim opens his mouth to argue, but I nudge his foot. He quiets himself as I watch Molly biting her lip and eyeing her fingernails, already bitten to the nub.

I stand abruptly, Tim quickly following suit.

"Thanks for the grub, gentleman, but we've had a long day and it looks like we won't be getting fuel anytime soon."

The admission brings a smile to Ed's face. Instead of standing, he leans back in his chair. I smile and say, "Now, if Molly will be kind enough to show us to our quarters, we'll spend the night thinking of a Plan B."

Ed looks to his two partners before saying, "Good luck with that, Kent. We'll give you to the end of the week, and then I'm afraid we'll have to ask you to leave. Our resources are limited, obviously, and since we didn't invite you here, well . . . I'm sure you understand."

I smile and hold up his gun. "We'll give these back then," I grunt, sliding out between the two bodyguards without a backward glance.

I look for our weapons on the table outside but they're long gone.

I guess I shouldn't be surprised.

Tim cocks one eyebrow but makes no comment as Molly leads us slowly from the well-lit boardroom.

The rest of the floor is sunk in quiet darkness, the odd solar lantern lighting this random grouping of pale-faced office dwellers. We wind up in a corner cubicle, stripped bare but spacious, quiet and away from the rest of the group, who apparently prefer to keep their distance. The best part is it's facing the boardroom, so we can see while Ed and company plot against us.

There is a desk chair nearby and as Tim and I unroll our sleeping mats and settle in, Molly takes it with pinched lips and crossed legs.

"Tell us about the cops, Molly," I say quietly, reaching into my stained backpack for a little incentive.

"What about them?" she hedges, looking away, as if to see if anyone else is listening.

"Why aren't they up here, with you?" I ask, hands finding a dented metal tin full of little glass vials.

She avoids my eyes and says, "Like Ed said, guys, the horde caught up with them."

"You need to tell us about those cops," I say.

She sighs, uncrosses her legs, crosses them again and says, "Well, knowing you guys you were bound to find out anyway . . . listen, here's the deal. Most of the folks up here are brokers, or brokers' assistants, or secretaries, or secretaries' assistants. That means zero survival experience, period. When the last outbreak happened, everyone freaked. Most folks went home, but everyone up here stayed converting their money to gold and silver."

"Seriously?" Tim almost chuckles.

Molly gives a rare, wry smile. "Believe it or not, it seemed like a good idea at the time. You know, before the power went out and all the currency converters froze—forever. By that time the rest of the building, hell, the rest of Wall Street, was empty. We all went downstairs and were heading home when we saw the horde approaching.

"There were still a few security guards in the lobby at the time; they locked the doors, but not for long. Before the horde broke in, we raided the building's cafeteria for every possible food item we could carry; carted it all up here in big laundry baskets from the dry cleaners on the third floor. Anyway, once the horde broke in, we were trapped . . ."

I say, "Molly, I asked about the cops."

"The cops showed up just before the horde did. They tried to gain access through the lower floor, but by then we'd disabled the elevator and barricaded ourselves in up here."

"Why?" Tim asks.

"No, they weren't bad . . . yet. They just, well, by then Ed and the boys were running things and Ed made a pretty convincing argument that letting twenty-five more people onto the floor to share our food was a really bad idea."

"Let me get this straight?" I ask, struggling to keep the contempt out of my voice. "You barricaded twenty-five human beings out because you didn't want to go hungry?"

She merely nods, clutching the tin of worthless perfume samples as if they're protein bars.

"But they're cops, Molly, with guns and ammo and radios and training. They could have been powerful allies."

"Like I said, Kent," she says, "it seemed like a good idea

at the time."

I give Tim a hard look; he gives one back.

Then we give one to Molly; she caves.

"Okay, okay, so it was a dick move, I get it now. What can I say?"

"You can say 'I'm sorry'," Tim grins.

"To who?"

"To the cops," I say. "When you meet them later tonight "

The makeshift weapons shed is in the employee break room. Naturally, it's guarded by two security guards; the same two security guards who'd frisked us not-so-thoroughly before entering Ed's inner sanctum.

Most of the solar lanterns have been turned off for the night, and as we creep around a corner re-conning the guards, I ask Molly, "What's their story?"

"They were two of the security guards we rescued from the downstairs lobby," she whispers, her husky voice giving me shivers in the dark.

Tim says, "Oh, so you'll save two rent-a-cops, but not twenty-five *real* cops!"

"Well, we kind of needed their help hauling the food upstairs."

I shake my head and inch toward the first guard, my hands up, my face yawning as I explain, "Can you gents point me to the nearest restroom?"

The minute the first one points with his index finger, I slide a zip-tie from my cargo pants lining and yank it down to his wrist, spinning him around before sliding his other wrist through and sealing it tight.

By the time I've bound and gagged one guard, Tim has done the same with the second. Molly kneels between the fallen guards, rifling through their pockets and apologizing until she finds the keychain to the break room.

Inside are four vending machines, long-since emptied and replaced with an assortment of stun guns, pistols, mace, pocket knives, blackjacks and, more recently, the weapons taken off of Tim and I after our search. It's a sparse weaponry, but impressive for a bunch of fat cat brokers.

"Where'd these come from?" I ask gladly sliding my rifle back across my back and refilling my own personal armory.

"The guards had most of it, the rest was . . . personal."

When I arch one eyebrow Molly shrugs and says, "Hey, it's New York."

We fit her with a better gun belt, a bigger pistol and a machete; she doesn't flinch. I think to myself, who the hell had a machete on Wall Street? Talk about a cut throat broker firm.

"You're good with this?" I ask, sliding the last of the two security guards into the break room and locking the door behind us once we've gathered up as much weaponry as we can carry.

She looks around at a few flickering solar lanterns, grimaces at the sound of her former co-workers snoring and says, "I'd almost rather join the zombie horde than have to spend another night in this place."

Tim says, "You may have to before we're all through."

We tiptoe back across the office floor until we're at the entrance to the roof. At the helicopter, we're assaulted with the violent sounds of the horde on the ground below, their constant, collective mewling and gnashing of teeth audible even twenty stories off the ground. At least we think so.

"They're most active at night," Molly explains. "Before we barricaded the door, a few of us used to come up here and watch them at night; just to feel safe, I guess. It finally got too spooky."

Tim hands down the four five-gallon propane tanks from the balloon and we strap two each to our backs with bungee cords.

"Now, where is this side entrance you've been squawking

about all night?" Tim asks skeptically.

"It's for the maintenance workers," she explains, leading us behind the small metal tower that houses the barricaded door and the back of the roof. "Once we're two stories down, there's a small ledge, then . . . it's just a matter of getting the cops to let us inside and we can gain access to the basement through one of the stairwells."

"Oh, great," Tim says, testing the strength of the exterior stairwell and finding it sturdy enough to hold him. "We're depending on the two dozen cops you've shut out for two months to let us in?" She does not respond.

Molly looks uncomfortable as I set her on the top rung. At first I think it's just the fact that her butt is hanging out over a few hundred zombies down on the ground, but then she gives me a kind of apologetic look and I imagine it to be something else.

With all three of us risking our lives umpteen hundred feet up, the moment is quickly lost.

The rungs are rusty and coated with early morning dew, making the climb all the more treacherous. The weapons and awkward canisters don't help matters much, but I remain focused on getting Molly down safely and it manages to take my mind off the unbearable height, not to mention the hungry zombie horde down on the ground.

You'd think the balloon trip would cure a fear of heights. But here in the real world, it's another experience altogether. Tim stands on the narrow landing, squeezing against the rusty skin of a metal alcove to make room first for Molly, then me.

She looks relieved so I refrain from telling her that was the easy part. There is a single door and Tim makes short work of it with his crowbar. Inside, a silent hallway marked by metal frames and hanging wires; we don't smell the acrid aroma of human sweat and waste until about halfway in.

A second door shows weld spots around the frame, though the knob itself has been punched out. Inside the fist-sized hole that remains, a flame flickers, and I see movement.

I knock heavily on the door, a pistol in each hand. Still watching through the hole, the movement suddenly stops. Tim leans in next to me and I give him a good view while standing up and sliding Molly toward the farthest corner.

I hear a shotgun shell being racked into place, just before a hollow knock sounds on the other side of the door. Tim knocks back, and a gruff voice inside bellows, "Who goes there?" Tim bellows back, "Two civilians, we've just landed on your rooftop and need assistance finding fuel."

"Good luck," the voice inside says back, a little softer now. "We've got bigger fish to fry."

"Let us in," says Tim. "Maybe we can help."

Suddenly an eyeball fills the hole and bellows, "Stand back so I can see you. Hey, who's the chick? Are you nuts? "She's from upstairs," I explain warily. "She's the one that told us about you."

Empty laughter oozes from the hole. "Yeah, did she tell you she left us stranded with a dozen zombie broads trying to do us in?"

"Yes," Tim barks. "She'd like to apologize; in person."

"Nobody's coming in until you promise us safe passage out of this building."

"Promised," says Tim. "Hurry up."

There are scratching feet sounds on the other side of the door, whispering, cursing, and the slamming of bolts being driven out of place. When the door at last slides open, it does so to the side; they'd literally bolted it in place after yanking it off its old hinges.

A burly man in a yellowed undershirt stands at the forefront, while several thinner, younger men linger at his back, clamoring for a look at the newcomers.

The stench from inside is foul; like stepping into a dumpster that's been forgotten for a year. I see scattered cans and long-emptied water bottles. The men look hungry and battered, and eye Molly as if it's her personal fault.

I offer several protein bars yanked from the food supply as bribes, and while all the guys reach for it, the burly cop takes them and doles them out, saving the extra bar in his pants pocket for himself.

They eat hungrily, shamelessly, several men sitting down and savoring the calorie- and energy-rich meal bars.

"I'm Sergeant Dawkins," says the big man after he swallows the last of his bar. "These are my men."

"What?" I ask. "All of them?"

Molly says disappointedly, "But I thought there were more of you."

Dawkins looks at her with pure rage in his eyes. "Well, honey, after you and your fat cat friends upstairs blocked off the stairways, we were stuck down here on this utility floor, facing a mob of angry zombie bitches. One by one, they picked us off and fed on us as we've gone around looking for food these last few months. There might be more of us still alive if you'd let us in when we asked."

I shake my head. Tim looks worried. "I dunno," he says. "I was counting on at least two dozen men for help."

"Help for what?" barks Dawkins.

Tim yanks off the canisters and tosses them at Dawkins. "No one gets a free ride off this building, pal."

Dawkins' official police uniform is sooty and torn off at the sleeves, revealing his massive, tattooed arms as he loads his double-barrel shotgun and explains the hazards of the mission.

"The only way down is the east corridor stairwell," he says, sliding cartridges into the underside of his gun. "The west one we were planning on using it as an escape route a few months back, and started dropping bags of waste into to lure the horde in that direction. They patrol it daily now."

"Patrol it?" I ask.

"I'm telling you, Kent, this horde is militant. Whole mess of female zombies who act like some kind of modern army. They can't talk, yet, but they sure communicate. Somehow. You see 'em, it's like they're reading each other's minds. They work in teams, and by now they've probably figured out our little trick and are patrolling the east entrance as well."

"That's a risk we'll have to take if we want to get out of this building," I say.

He nods, a little suspiciously, like maybe I have no intention of flying him and his men anywhere. I nod back; nothing I can do to prove that until he's on the roof and I've got the fuel.

He leads us across a vast wasteland of empty cans and snack wrappers, overturned desks and broken chairs. Broken glass crunches underfoot and the rank smell of human urine comes from several overturned water cooler jugs near the broken open windows.

"Love what you've done with the place," Tim cracks as Dawkins gives him a scarred scowl in reply.

Molly hangs close, none too eager to fall behind and blend in with the cops, taking up the rear with their empty bellies and hungry eyes.

I can see remnants of the old sports company's logo on the walls, emblazoned on sports drinks and protein bars. I also notice empty bottles and sample wrappers on the floor.

"Is that how you survived?" I ask Dawkins as we near the barricaded door to the east stairwell.

He follows my finger to the wall poster of a young boy eating a protein bar at a soccer game and says, "Thank God the company had a store room full of samples or we'd never have made it this long."

He gives Molly a scathing look as we cluster near the dented metal door.

"Here's how it's going to work," he says as his men

quickly go to work sliding the bolts from the hinges. "This door's going to open, and we're going to run down the stairs without stopping. I don't care what those zombie bitches do, or who they get. If you can't keep up, you ain't makin' it. If you can't make it, we ain't slowin' down to help you. Got it?"

We all nod except Molly who, in pure pep rally mode, says "Got it" out loud.

She blushes as the last of the bolts clatters to the floor.

I hand Molly one of my pistols as we brace ourselves. Dawkins listens at the door, his face intent, the bald spot on the back of his graying head glistening with sweat.

Tim and I lean slightly forward, shoulders almost touching, Molly slightly at our back. She whispers, "Listen" and I do, but the sound isn't coming from the stairwell in front of us; it's coming from behind.

Suddenly a shot rings out, a slug burying itself in one of the nameless rookie's shoulders as blood splatters most of the group, including us. He goes down with a gush of air and a dull grunt as Dawkins rushes to his aid.

I turn just in time to see Ed barreling forth, firing away. Behind him are his two enforcers, plus the security guards we'd bound and gagged an hour earlier, as well as an assortment of stragglers from the brokerage office upstairs. All are armed with whatever we'd left behind, mostly a handful of small pistols and one rifle.

Tim and I crouch down to avoid the gunfire, dragging Molly behind a nearby pillar as drywall erupts in puffy white clouds just above our heads. Dawkins returns fire as well, as do his men, while the office dwellers from above advance with only minor injuries.

The floor is alive with the sounds of gunfire, the smell of cordite and gun smoke. Glass shatters, drywall crumbles showering plaster dust on everyone, giving us the look of frantic ghosts. Feet scrape and angry wounds sigh openly as blood spills onto the dry fancy carpeted floor.

The office dwellers are scattered now, as are the cops. Desks become barricades, chairs are tossed at vulnerable legs hiding behind bullet-riddled columns. It all happens in seconds before stretching into minutes.

"We've got to get down those stairs," Tim grunts impatiently, angling for a better look at the open stairwell.

"Ed will never follow us if we go now," Molly says, pistol raised.

"Well, that's good enough for me," I grunt, and run for the doorway, finding Dawkins pinned down behind an overturned metal desk.

"I can't believe we didn't seal that door after letting you assholes in!" he barks, tying off one of his officer's arms.

"Let's leave 'em in our dust," I say, handing him a flashlight.

He gets a gleam in his eye and smiles for the first time.

"Why didn't I think of that?"

Two of his men are still able-bodied and he shoves them toward the door, whether they're ready or not. Bullets still fly behind us as the first cop plunges through the doorway. Our flashlight beams fill the area with shadow and light.

The stairwell looks empty and, for the moment, safe. We cluster on the landing, hearing curses flood from the open doorway of the sports company's floor. A bullet rings out, ricocheting off one of the metal guardrails.

We curse and trample two flights down to avoid the erratic gunfire, huddling and out of breath.

"How many flights to the basement?" I ask, spying the number 17 stenciled onto the nearest wall.

"Didn't do too well in reading, eh?" says Dawkins as he hovers close to his point man, a young kid whose nametag reads FIZER. He has lean arms and a shaved head, with the nicks to prove he's been doing it himself since the outbreak.

His hands look steady on either side of his pistol as he crouches around the corner of the next landing; then we hear

161

the first shriek.

It's hideous, and all the more so because it's trapped in this stairwell, rippling off the concrete walls and bouncing off the metal steps. It's impossible to tell how near or far the zombie is, or if she has friends.

"Stand your ground," Dawkins barks, inching toward Fizer as the shrieking intensifies.

I feel pressure on my forearm and turn to find Molly's eyes wide with fear. Tim crouches in, looking high and low, his pistol at the ready. I swing my flashlight in Fizer's direction, we all do, just in time to catch a bitch yanking him straight down to the next landing.

Dawkins fires into the air, but the bitch shrieks back and begins gorging on Fizer's arm. She is voracious and violent, yanking out tendons like spaghetti and ignoring the young man's screams. Another wildly goes for his dick and balls, tearing through his pants like they are tissue paper. I wonder if my dream in the barn was a way of someone telling me something, that the bitches need the testosterone to survive.

The zombie's face has a wry smile on it as her teeth chatter and she dips her head into Fizer's belly and yanks out some inner organ with her broken, yellow teeth. It's his stomach and food, half-digested and yellowish, spills on the stairs and drips downward.

Dawkins fires at the zombie, missing her as she ducks to gnaw on Fizer's spine. One more shot lands in Fizer's thigh by mistake, but the boy barely moves. His face is ashen and pale, eyes vacant, already gone but for the routine of his gasping heartbeat.

Dawkins fires once more, this time hitting Fizer square in the forehead, splattering his brains across the pitted metal landing. One bitch licks up the brains, giving Dawkins a clear shot as he chambers another shell full of pellet and blows her head off with a straight, clean shot from less than five feet away.

The shrieking continues, louder now as the zombies smell blood. We retreat, scrambling up the stairs until the hollow sound of Ed's laughter fills the nearest stairwell and bullets from his security guards' guns ricochet off the stairwell. Tim and Dawkins find an open door just below them on the 19th Floor and shove through.

Molly and I follow, joined quickly by the two remaining rookies, out of breath and bare arms slick with sweat as they jostle against us to find room. We all hoist our backs against the door, keeping it shut as the horde of ravenous bitches bang against it. Their nails are sharp and scrape loudly on the other side, sending nasty vibrations right through the hollow steel door.

They shove and we buckle, but don't bend. Suddenly shots ring out, the shrieks intensify and the zombies clatter and crawl up the stairwell just outside. We can hear Ed and his crew shouting, shooting in a flurry of bullets that carom everywhere, even against the outside of our door, more screaming, and then the unmistakable sound of teeth on flesh and bone as the bitches find the 20th Floor vulnerable and full of live flesh.

The screaming stops as the feasting begins.

"Now," hisses Dawkins, looking to Tim and me for approval. "While they're occupied with your friends from upstairs."

I shake my head, then nod reluctantly as we lean away from the door, yank it open and leap into the stairwell, tumbling down two steps at a time and risking life and limb as we turn on every landing to see if the horde is following us.

They are not.

We fly from the 17th floor to the 16th, the 15th, zoom past the 12th, straight past the 10th, catch our breath on the 8th Floor, no bitches and we are nearly to the 6th floor before the shrieking cries begin once again.

The raspy screams are one thing, the claws are another;

they slither and scrape against every stair, scurrying across each landing, long and hard as steel and sharp as meat hooks, scuttling like giant crabs lurching forward inexorably, hungrily.

The 5th and 4th floor are a blur, the thundering of a dozen zombie feet echoing high above. Molly stays close, Tim angling for the rear with Molly's machete now, held high in one hand, the other clutching the railing as we hurtle toward the ground floor. Dawkins reaches it first, scrambling for the basement level and the fuel tank that hopefully awaits.

The basement is vast and ruled by great, giant condensers covered in shimmering metal foil. They stand six to a row, and each one is a perfect undead hiding place.

We search behind each one, the basement door barricaded by two huge computer clusters that take all of us to slide across the door and wedge tight. It holds against the first barrage of bitch bodies, but even while filling the gas tanks at the giant fuel reservoir in the depths of the basement proper, we can hear the linoleum floor being gouged by the bottoms of the computer towers as they give just an inch; then one inch more.

As I fill the last gas canister, I finger the nozzle shut, then watch as the door bows in a little more with every assault.

"Tim," I urge. "Give me your lighter."

"No," he barks back, even as he begins fumbling for it. "It's too dangerous."

"Yeah," says Molly, aiming her pistol at the clattering door. "As opposed to a half-dozen zombies trying to yank our brains out of our skulls any second now?"

"She's got a point," barks Dawkins as he turns to face the door.

"You and you," I say to Dawkins and Tim as I purge the fuel tank, sending a steady stream of liquid propane onto the floor at my feet. "Hide between the condensers on the right. Molly, you and I will take the left."

"Let's pray they break in before we're knee deep in—"

The door bursts open and from behind the condensers we can see four, five, six, then seven bitches slither in, all bony joints and rubber limbs, faces white from lack of sunlight and blood flow, eyes milky and blank.

They would normally sniff us out immediately, but the gas has us all in tears, and their senses—such as they are—in shambles. The splashing of the fuel from the gushing tank draws them in even as we begin inching from the room, first Dawkins, then Tim, then Molly, then myself.

We sneak back toward the door, routing through the condensers, staying low in the shadows. At the open doorway I gulp in fresh air from the stairwell, turn and flick the lighter; it flicks dry, with only a few sparks. The sound draws the interest of the zombies, who turn, still confused until they see me in the doorway, frantically flicking the lighter.

Their bare, hideous feet splash in the fuel, sending ripples my way as at last the lighter flickers to life and I drop it to the floor, sending a blue ripple of flame straight toward their clamoring limbs.

The fuel engulfs them, the fumes singeing them above the waist, the fire burning at their feet. The sound is horrendous as their screams fill the stairwell beneath as we spring upward toward the 5th, 6th and 7th floors, the smell even worse as burning flesh follows us toward the 9th and 10th. My shoulders ache form carrying the tanks up so many flights.

But it's more than just smoke wafting from the basement; the zombies, half of them anyway, are still in pursuit, slithering up the steps in slow motion even as the flesh falls from their bodies.

"God," Molly spits, out of breath and lagging behind. "Won't they ever stop?"

"They'll stop," barks Dawkins, panting rapidly as we crouch on the 18th floor. He takes one knee, a pistol from his shoulder holster, aims into the darkness below. "When we pick them off one by one."

I crouch next to him, inspired by the idea. He shoos me away, grabbing Tim instead.

"You get to your ride," he instructs, "and I'll keep pretty boy here as insurance."

Tim smirks and takes to one knee.

Molly and I turn hurriedly as I look over my shoulder, watching the flames follow the last remaining zombies up the stairwell as bullets begin to fly from Dawkins' and Tim's guns.

The 19th floor is full of corpses, both human and undead. Bullets riddle the walls while a zombie lies on the floor, cut in half and still crawling toward Ed's lifeless, gnawed on legs.

I silence her with a bullet to the back of the head as we crouch toward the outer stairwell. Molly grabs my arm and yanks me forward, dodging broken, bullet-ridden bodies until we are poised at the bottom of the stairwell on the exterior of the building.

"You first," I tell Molly, none too eager for her to be exposed at the bottom of the stairs should any flaming zombies make it through Dawkins and Tim.

"Can't we go together?" she asks, even as she grips the bottom rung with trembling hands.

"I don't think the laws of physics would allow it," I quip, inching up closely behind her just in case there's a bitch somehow waiting for us at the top.

Her skin is warm as I brush up against her calves while we pass the midway point up the ladder.

Her voice is trembling as she says, "God, I'm scared."

"Almost there," I urge, the gas canisters weighing me down as I lose a little steam.

She bridges the distance, moving forward as I struggle to keep up.

Behind me I hear tearing and look down to see a zombie, fresh and hungry, slicing at my calf. Her face animated and beautiful, her eyes empty and cold. I grip the rung with the crook of my elbow, none too eager to be yanked off the stairs and falling 20 floors only to be devoured by the hungry mob on the ground.

The zombie screams, dead blonde hair blowing in the wind. Her mouth is open and already full of gore, none of it mine. I imagine Tim and Dawkins already gone, but hear gunfire erupting from the stairwell inside and know that can't be the case. She must have been hiding on the next floor down.

Molly screams, and I tell her to "go on" but when I look up, that's not why she's screaming. I hear the chewing and feel fresh blood on my throat as a zombie stands, Molly in hand, chewing on her arm until it separates at the shoulder. Her body sails past me, face panicked as she screams the whole way down.

I kick violently, face drenched in blood, until the zombie's nose breaks, until the zombie's fingers break, until it too follows Molly into the gnarling, gathering mob on the street.

I scream, "no!" but there is nothing I can do. If Molly was any sort of hope for humanity at all, then humanity is well and truly screwed. But there is not time for remorse now, I have to keep going.

I inch forward, reaching for my gun until I'm just shy of the awaiting bitch, already licking her chops. Three rungs from the roof I aim and silence her with three bullets under her chin; she slumps, mostly headless, to the rooftop floor as I climb over her lifeless body and quickly pile both gas canisters into the balloon.

I head for the tangled lines and begin carefully working at them. The wind actually helps as it makes the balloon lurch backward and forward, alternately tightening and loosening the lines. I run to the gondola and uncoil a mooring line, grappling it to a drainpipe before completely untethering the gondola.

I jump in the gondola and fire up the burner. Hadley is curled up in a corner as if asleep. I chide myself for bringing her on this trip and leaving her alone, but she is still alive, and that is what matters. MG, looks up from where his head in on her lap and gives me a woof of recognition.

Thank God, I think. I stare at the roof door awaiting Tim's face, looking for movement, pistol aimed should the random bitch come flying at me.

Dawkins emerges first, turning quickly after a brief smile to reach for Tim's hand as he helps my partner up onto the roof. They sprint toward me, two bitches hot on their heels.

I aim for them as Tim reaches the gondola and tosses his full gas tanks on board. Dawkins turns to silence the zombies, riddling them with bullets until his pistol is empty. As he's reaching for the knife in his boot they reach him instead, my bullets splattering into their bodies but doing little to stop the carnage on the tarmac as they angrily devour Dawkins from the skull down.

Tim shakes his head, regret pooling beneath his pale blue eyes, and wedges himself next to me, unhooking the mooring rope. The zombies stand, Dawkins' gore hanging from their lips as they advance on the balloon.

I jam the burner to full and the balloon lurches up as if a giant hand has grabbed it and us. The bitches leap for the gondola. One is hanging on and using her talon-like nails to easily climb the basket, the tips of her claws penetrating the weave. The balloon rises at a furious pace. Tim turns his rifle around and swings the butt of it like it's a baseball bat just as the bitch's head clears the rim of the gondola. She looks at me and rasps, sounds like she says, "waiting for you," though I'm sure it's just gurgled nonsense, then Tim bashes her skull and she falls almost in slow motion as we watch downward, her flailing doll-like body hitting the ledge of a skyscraper and dropping into the dark void between buildings.

CHAPTER 20

"I'm going to try the radio," said Tim.

"I don't think you should. It's a long shot that anyone is going to be listening and it may be one of those jerk-off military groups. They see this rig we're in and they'll take it. Maybe kill us, make us slaves. Who knows? It's not worth it, Tim, not worth it," I said.

Tim was in no mood for my same old, same old. Couldn't blame him. Maybe he was finally believing what I'd been thinking since Denver: it's all a dead end. Why drag it out? Is life so important that we should hold on even if it's a living torture?

"Fuck it all," I said. "Use it. I don't give a shit any more than you do."

"You're lying," he said. "But maybe it's a gamble we can't not take. Nothing to lose . . . nothing to lose."

He pressed the transmit button and said, "Mayday, Mayday," just like in the movies. I looked over the gondola side; Hadley was standing next to me. She held my hand. Maybe I was supposed to care for her. Maybe she was my responsibility now and I couldn't decide just for me or let Tim decide just for him. But what was her future? If we landed even in a safe haven—something we didn't even know existed—she could still turn. Maybe Jen had a vaccine. Maybe it was bullshit and she only thought she had one.

"Mayday, Mayday."

"Mayday. Respond." A voice leaped from the speaker, full of static and so loud we all jumped.

"Mayday, respond," it repeated. "This is Berkshire Halo. Can you read me?"

"Fuck yes, we can read you. Berkshire Halo, what's your 1020?"

"We're at Crater Forge, fifty miles due west of Boston.

In the Berkshire Armory. Where are you at?"

"Just crossing the New York-Massachusetts border."

"You're crazy. That area is loaded with those things. They're controlling every road and pass. Now where the fuck are you?"

"Seriously, that's where we are. We're in a hot air balloon out of Denver."

The radio went silent.

"Hello? Hello? Mayday?" said Tim holding the mic to his mouth like he was kissing it.

"Shit, man, we thought that was a wacky rumor."

"What was?"

"That some dudes in a balloon were crossing from Denver. Had reports on and off about sightings but thought it was a gaff."

"Gaff?"

"Yeah, bullshit. But I guess not. You're the real thing. Can you target us on a GPS?"

"Give me your address."

He did. I logged it into the GPS and found that we were about 75 miles due west of the Armory, whatever that was.

"We're about three hours away from you. Any landing spots?"

"There's a helicopter pad in an open field just north of the Armory. Can't miss it. How many are traveling with you?"

Tim looked at me, curious about the question. Granny used to say, "Be careful what you wish for, you might get it." It just dawned on Tim that we were letting a bunch of dudes know where we were, who we were and that we were just two jerk-offs, a dog and a fucking kid in one of the most valuable things left on planet Earth.

"Respond please. How many are with you?"

Tim turned the radio off.

The moon was hidden that night and a crummy, drizzle fell. I could make out lightning behind us but it was so far away that the sound of thunder never made it to us; that one-one thousand, two-one thousand horse crap wasn't necessary. Glad of it, too. I didn't know how the balloon would take to lightning or it to the balloon and we had made it too far for me to not care.

"Uncle Kent?" asked Hadley. "I'm getting wet."

"Curl up over there. I'll cover you," I said. This uncle thing was giving me a peculiar slant on things. Tim just ignores it.

"Think we'll make it to the Cape by morning?" I asked Tim.

"No reason not to. A light tail wind and cover of darkness. Shouldn't be a problem," he said as the greenish light from the GPS lit up his face like a Halloween prank.

I cover Hadley up and say "Good night, sleep tight." I'm thinking how crazy this is but I could not leave her behind. No way.

We're sailing at a thousand feet or so. I can see the outlines of the Berkshire mountains like black clouds beneath us, thick forests covering the ground in every direction. I get lost in a daydream about *The Last of the Mohicans*—never read the book, but remember the movie real well—especially, I'm thinking about the part where Daniel Day whoever says to his little colonial hottie, "Stay alive. I will find you. No matter what." Or some such BS as that. But, you know, it's the way I feel about Jen. "Stay alive," I want to tell her. "No matter what. I will . . . "

The balloon lights up like midday. I think lightning has hit the goddamned thing. I'm blinded because the glare hits me full in the face. I jump back just as Tim says, "What the fuck?"

It's a search light. A voice blurts out of a bullhorn, "Land, good buddy, or I'll blast you out of the sky." It's the same voice that was on the radio. Tim reaches for the burn and sets it full blast. As he does this, a shot like a cannon explosion echoes through the hills. It could wake the dead, if they weren't already all up and at it.

"Do that again, boy, and the next shot will be right through you. Now land!"

Tim fires down and the balloon begins its slow descent. Hadley is up and clinging to me.

"Don't worry," I tell her, but I mean we need to worry. Big time.

As we drop out of the sky like a half-shot pheasant, we pass over a large compound lit up like a small town. It has a wire fence perimeter with watch towers like a POW camp. There's a large cleared area in the middle surrounded with tents and sheds. I can see maybe fifty or sixty guys scurrying about heading in the same direction as us. A Hummer in bright yellow cranks up and aims its roof lights at us as it follows our path downward to a clearing just past the camp to the east.

Tim does a great job bringing the balloon in and in a few seconds we're surrounded by a large group of guys that look paramilitary—cammy pants, t-shirts, shaved heads and guns, all of them shouting some shit, one of them waving a tattered American flag on a pole.

"Stay out of sight, Hadley," I warn her, as if she hasn't figured out the routine by now. She crouches at my feet with MG in her arms. The Hummer pulls up and a big dude gets out, one of those asshole professional wrestler types, big as an outhouse and looking like he's got the stink to match. He's the jerk-off with the bullhorn.

"Step out of the vehicle with your hands up," he says like this is a rerun of *Cops*.

"Sir," says Tim. "I can't put my hands up and climb out of this gondola at the same time."

A shot rings out whizzing past Tim's ear. "Give it a try," the bullhorn bleats. Tim and I do.

"Welcome to Camp Fuck You," he shouts. A sheep flock

of laughter rises from the crowd around us and drifts off into the woods.

With their guns aimed at us, we get frisked. Nothing, of course. Not even our balls.

"Welcome, men. This is one of the last holdouts of the white race in the great US of A. We are all one hunert percent American born and raised and don't countenance no Jews, niggers, nor your yellow people and especially no wetbacks. If they are out there, let the crazy bitches have at 'em. In here, we abide by the Golden Rule: I am the ruler!"

The crowd cheers this ignoramus.

"Now, y'all got that straight? You're good and white, I think. And I ain't seein' no Jew beaks. You ain't heebs, are ya'?"

"What's a heeb, your honor?" asks Tim.

"Why it's a goaddamned heathern Jew!"

"Well, then no your honor, we're Christians. And it's heathen, not heathern."

"You're lookin' like you might be a A-rab. You ain't no monkey-dicked-fuckin' A-rab, is you?"

"Your honor, my name is Tim Riley. This is Kent Zimmer. Do they sound like A-rab names? Meaning no disrespect, of course."

"Zimmer? That a Jew name?"

"My father's ancestors are German, sir," I reply. "Check this out." I whip out my dick which is as uncut as a newly purchased Halloween pumpkin. "Do you think either a Jew or a Muslim would have a pecker that looks like this?"

"No, I guess not. You're not queer, are ya'?

"I'd tell you to ask my wife, but I killed her when she ate my son. Is that sufficient, you dumb motherfucker?" Tim says. I put my dick away—the first time I needed it in months for anything other than pissing.

"I like your style boys," he replies. "But let's not get carried away. I'm Rex. This is my band of merry men and we're . . . "

"Hey, Rex, check this shit out," one of his henchman yells from the direction of the balloon. He's lifting Hadley out by the back of her jeans. She's kicking and screaming. MG is nowhere to be found. Damn dog probably jumped out and ran after a squirrel.

Rex walks over to the guy holding Hadley.

"Hey, you boys travel dangerously. This little cunt is murder on the hoof. Who is she?"

"She's my niece," I reply. "I've sworn an oath to protect her. She's clean. Look at her eyes."

Rex looks Hadley up and down.

"Put me down, you sonafabitch!" yells Hadley. "Put me down!"

"Hey, let her go. She's just a kid," I say.

"She's just a kid? Yeah, like a rag-head airline pilot is just a poor boy tryin' to make a livin'," says Rex.

The guy holding her let's her go. She hits the ground running toward me. A shot rings out and blows Hadley's chest out from the back. Her eyes catch a look at mine for a millisecond.

"No! Fuck no!" I shout as I run to her crumpled-up body. "She was just a kid, just a kid." For the first time since all this has started I break down and cry my eyes out.

"Too young for fun, boys, and too old not to be dangerous. She was gonna turn soon enough and she'd be eatin' your balls like Double Bubble bubble gum. That's what you needed? You two shits. I just did her and you both a favor."

I look up and he knows I'm going to rush him, rip his eyes out and drive my shoe so far up his ass my foot will come out his mouth, so he points his gun right at me. "I wouldn't. Not less you meanin' to disrespect my hospitality. This here is the way the world works now, boy."

Maybe he was right, I'm thinking. Nothing I can do now. I let her down, but what was the future? I go numb and put it behind me. Don't know what else to do.

"You'll thank me for this, boys," Rex says. "Jimbo, Arnie. Get these guys to the med tent. And bury that stinkin' kid."

"It's fresh," the man known only as "Rex" grunts. "No worries."

His voice is firm and tense, deep and guttural as if he's speaking to zombies, not survivors. Although, from the looks of his seedy, humorless crew, he might as well be most of the time. With glistening fingers the hulking figure bathed in firelight tears a juicy leg from one of the fresh chickens spread out on the table before us and shoves the fat end into his mouth, sucking at the tip greedily before yanking the bone, flesh-free, from his gaping maw; rotted but gargantuan teeth smile back, the wide gaps stuffed with flesh.

I look hesitantly toward Tim, licking his blistered lips next to me and already reaching for a wing. I don't want to partake of anything these jackoffs have provided, but I'm hungry and join him. The taste of hot, sizzling, juicy flesh assaults my taste buds, providing an almost painful sensation as my confused stomach threatens to send back the first fresh food it's tasted in, what . . . six weeks?

"Sure beats canned beans," Tim announces to the table full of healthy-looking men, all featuring shaved heads and distrustful glances and headstone-sized teeth identical to Rex's.

They grunt appreciatively, watching us carefully as their large-knuckled fingers caress the butts of the shotguns propped casually on each knee.

Has it only been half-an-hour since we stumbled on their camp from the road, the smell of a roaring fire and the klieg lights surrounding the walled encampment beckoning us like moths to the flame?

A guard had frisked us, finding only two moldy backpacks full of stale candy bars and the last of our canned food, the remainder of a vending machine raid back a ways.

We were immediately strip-searched and deloused in a military style tent, shoved into sweatpants and flannel shirts and our old boots, and suddenly here we are: in Rex's private tent feasting on roasted chickens and grilled corn.

Southern fried rock wafts in from outside as a tent flap opens and a leggy young blond dressed in a cheerleading out-fit stumbles inside. The men at Rex's table gawk appreciatively at her long, slender legs, slender waist and generous breasts, barely concealed beneath the top half of her too-small cos-tume. Her mouth is tied with a gag and duct-taped for good measure.

Her hair is greasy and long, but her unkempt mane only adds to her evocative allure. Her eyes look haunted but fo-cused, grimly set on completing her task, that being setting another tray of cheap canned beer on top of the wooden pic-nic table next to the open bag of potato chips.

Rex grabs her wrist but the cheerleader barely flinches; only regards him with cold, dead eyes. Her skin has a grayish tinge and a marble texture, but even from across the room I can see the life in her eyes and the grim set of her jaw.

"Say hello to our new friends, Buffy," Rex says while lick-ing his lips. He regards us with empty, dark eyes and says, "Buffy's one of our prized possessions, fellas. Prime, grade-A tail from the local women's college about two clicks yonder. We ran across 'em on a hunting party a few months back, chowing down on their dean, the dumb motherfucker; twenty-eight sorority girls just itching for a little male com-panionship, right, Buffy?" The cheerleader regards Tim and me with contempt, but remains motionless, even as Rex crudely yanks up her blue and yellow skirt to reveal a daring pink thong beneath. It looks crooked and ill-fitting as if, like the rest of her costume, it was chosen for her rather than by her; as if she'd been dressed by another rather than allowed to dress herself.

I watch as Rex eyes her warily, a small silver taser near his hand on the roughhewn picnic table in the camp leader's expansive tent. Rex strikes me as a man afraid of nothing, not even a camp full of wiry, neo-Nazi thugs, but something in this woman's eyes has his fingers chained close to a few thousand volts of electricity.

She turns to leave. Rex lets his guard down and, immediately, the cheerleader turns and with a gnarled hand slices at his cheek with razor sharp nails.

Blood from a thin gash across his jaw line glistens in the firelight as he stands, stun gun at hand and shoves it deep into the wanton woman's neck; the sizzle of human flesh burning singes the air as she bucks with the current of electricity jarring her body.

When at last she is stunned and helpless he tosses the taser casually onto the table and with a dirty fist punches her once, twice, three times on the side of the head; along the way something cracks, but the woman shows no pain, only a dazed kind of patience as two of Rex's thuggish minions drag her, kicking and screaming, from the tent.

My stomach is nauseous with the strength behind Rex's punches, with the slickness of his greasy skin on the side of her head, with the gleam in his eyes as he held nothing back while unloading his massive strength directly at her face.

Tim swallows audibly and Rex zeroes in on it.

"You like her, pal?" Rex barks, dropping back into his seat with a healthy sheen of sweat glowing across the many skull and naked women tattoos covering his shoulders and arms.

I nudge Tim under the table, still uncertain as to whether we'll stay in the small, quasi-military camp, but he stoically nods.

Rex leans in conspiratorially and explains, "You can have her after dinner. One of the boys will show you to the Cat House on the edge of camp."

"You m-m-mean?" Tim stammers, no need to finish his

sentence as Rex nods. "B-b-but how do I pay for her? I ain't got no money, Rex." I can see that Tim is playing the game for higher stakes.

Rex fixes him with a steady eye, licking his lips as he rubs the swollen knuckle of one hand with the other.

"None of us do," he explains. "Labor is the only currency here in this camp. For a prime filly like Buffy there, you need to work two days."

"Sold," Tim blurts before Rex can finish, causing the table of greasy men with shaved heads to bray with laughter.

Tim, all 145-pounds of him, laughs back, aware they're bawling at him, not with him. I'd defend him but he's just my traveling partner, not my friend, as far as these idgits know—I got to play along. We ran into each other on a hunting party awhile back and since we were both headed the same direction decided to team up. That's the story for now. And we've probably said less than two dozen words to each other since. I figure if they think we're just two unrelated stragglers, they can't use one against the other. That's what I'm hoping. Tim looks sideways at me and I know we're in synch. Still, I think Tim is out of his depth here. If Rex can barely control Buffy with his massive fists and the use of a stun gun, what's Tim going to do?

"What about you, pretty boy?" Rex barks in my direction, his calculated leer sizing me up like the runt of the litter. "You willing to risk two days of hard labor on one of our work crews for an hour in heaven with the sorority girl of your dreams?" I shrug and say, "I don't know, Rex; I've never made it with a zombie before."

"Zombie?" Tim asks, looking at me as if I've just told him there's no such thing as Santa Claus. "What? You never said nothin' 'bout making it with no zombies, Rex!" Rex barely looks at him as he asks, "What'd you think she was? A debutante? You know any human women can take a beating like that and stay standing?"

Then he ignores him, looking at me with his dead, soulless eyes. "How'd you know, smart boy?" he asks, massive fists clenched atop the table.

Only then do I notice the rough, homemade letters tattooed between each knuckle of his massive, sausage like digits. On the fingers of his left hand is spelled out the word "W-H-I-T-E" while, on the left, the fingers spell out "P-O-W-E-R."

I shrug again and say, "I've seen that phenomenon on the road, Rex. For some reason the female zombies regenerate their form, even their warmth, allowing them to look beautiful even as they crave human flesh. I never imagined they were trainable, though."

I'm in this BS up to my nuts and sinking fast.

"Trainable and doable," Rex boasts, as if he himself is the cause for this medical mystery. "Plus they have a little extra talent in store for us after dinner, if y'all agree to stick around, that is."

"Extra . . . talent?" I ask of Rex and the rest of the chrome domes.

They murmur among themselves giddily, like drooling dogs around a bone, but Rex is thoughtfully quiet, his question still on the table as he continues to glower menacingly in our general direction.

The mood in the room is civil but cloyed, Rex's large eyes hooded but also masking a not-so-hidden undercurrent of violence and psychosis. I've seen his type before on the road in the good old days. Men who once were powerless, despite their massive size. Whose lack of education or formal breeding made them servants to smarter, wiser men; in many instances, men like myself.

But once the infestation started, once violence prowled our streets, ate our families and threatened life and limb, men like Rex—crazy, violent, scary, angry men like Rex—became leaders.

By now, after the bitch takeover, that power has gone to their heads, their every wish catered to by weaker, greedier men, their every desire fulfilled by the complete and utter breakdown in order, rules and laws. Now these men make the laws, enforce the laws, have become judge, jury and executioner. And men like me, to say nothing of men like Tim, are at their mercy; what's worse, they know it—and so does everyone else at this table.

Tim looks at me, and I see the decision already made in his eyes; so does Rex. The others look at me expectantly, hands on the butts of their sawed off shotguns, bellies full of fresh meat and vegetables, as if daring me to say "no."

I'm tired, I'm hungry, I'm weak and, frankly, I'm numb. Life after the outbreak has been brutal, unkind and bleak, and to say I'm not aroused by the bevy of beauties tending to Rex and his partners in crime, however crude, would be to lie openly—and loudly—to myself. Besides, I'm not sure Tim and I really had a choice the minute the lookout caught us in his sights less than an hour ago, stumbling and dirty from the road.

I nod quietly and Rex's graveyard smile of big, rotten teeth and dark, fleshy gaps barely manages to conceal his contempt at my presence. He may not be glad I'm here, but if I'm still alive, there must be a reason for it.

I only hope I can convince Tim to escape before I find out what that is.

From beyond the thick walls of the canvas tent an alarm sounds, one of those hand-wrung numbers with the tripod and the crank that sounds like an old air-raid siren from one of the first world wars; you know, the wars between humans.

The men of Camp Alpha stand abruptly, most slapping their hands together and wringing them excitedly as they stream through the canvas tent flap. Rex sits with us, the first sign of life springing into those dark, liquid eyes as his crooked smile splits over those hideous teeth to announce,

"Trust me, you boys are gonna be glad you decided to stay. Come on, let's check out the main event."

With that, he stands, knees hitting the edge of the table as he rises and pivots in one fluid motion. Tim follows quickly while I linger behind, stuffing a few stale rolls and snack cakes into the pockets of my pants.

Outside the tent the camp is in pandemonium, the sound of the siren wail ever present and mingling with the cries, grunts and curses of nearly a hundred men, most baring tattoos of swastikas on their arms, shoulders, some even at the back of their clean-shaven necks, grimy with dirt and sweat but clearly visible as they scream across the open area in the middle of the camp to a high, fenced wall at the far end.

Tim springs ahead, desperate to keep up with Rex who has all but forgotten us in his hurry to be the first inside the circular fencing.

I call out, "Tim," but he rushes forward intently, waving me forward without looking back.

I slow to a crawl as rough, sweaty bodies stream past, grunting impatiently as I move slightly to the side.

Left behind, ignored, I use the precious time to recon the encampment. It is bordered on all four sides by a high fence. The base of the fence is chain link, but it's been buttressed over with everything from road signs to car bumpers, from license plates to metal doors. Across the top runs several rings of rusty barbed wire, stopping only at the four rickety guard towers from which armed snipers aim klieg lights and rifles at rare passersby.

Even if the fence itself weren't impenetrable, the camp's inhabitants create an "inner wall" amongst themselves. It only took me a few seconds inside the high, patchwork wall to realize that the camp is full of white supremacists; neo-Nazis who used the outbreak as a platform to fuel their psychotic ideas about America's growing race war. As such they have taken natural selection to the extreme. Every man inside is white, although it's hard to tell from the filthy layers of sweat, dust and lust that cover every inch of their half-naked bodies. Their preferred form of dress is jeans or khaki cargo shorts and they all wear sweat-stained wife beaters, the better to show off their offensive tattoos and bulging muscles.

Taking up the rear, I give up on the idea of escaping tonight and follow Tim into the enclosed circular area, around which the grunts of the Camp have erected "bleachers" of a sort; six-feet wooden platforms on top of which the entire camp sits in a smattering of broken, leaning, rusty picnic chairs.

Most stand anyway, leaning against rickety metal railing as they look down into a sandy pit about as big as half a high school football field. I follow Tim up a warped flight of stairs to stand at the edge of one raised platform, watching as Rex wedges his way to the best seat in the house directly in the middle of the nearest platform.

The feeling in the air reminds me of a prize fight; men hungry, desperate even, for violence. So hungry they can't wait for the main event; mini-fights break out across the platform as burly Aryans tussle and scrap for the best remaining seats.

I steer clear of the maddening crowd, throat constricting with the threat of real violence erupting about me, on me, at any moment. Fires flicker above the grandstands as the smell of burning diesel oil fills the air with its pungent stench. Loud rock music bellows from old-fashioned speakers lashed to high beams along the length of the grandstands.

Tim nudges me and asks nervously, "Waddya think's going on?"

"I don't know, Tim," I mumble as the crowd around us grows more violent with each passing moment.

"Looks like some kind of show or something," he says.

Off to the side of the walkway, two guys with Confederate flags sewn onto the seats of their coveralls are lasciviously giggling and guffawing at someone tied to a picnic table in front of them.

"Let's check it out," says Tim.

"Oh, fuck it all, Tim. Can't we just figure what the hell this is all about and then get outta here?" I say.

But it's too much for Tim resist; he is a man with nothing to lose. We walk over to the table and there is the most beautiful zombie bitch we've ever seen. Naked as a jaybird as these fucking redneck hillbillies would say. She's dark haired with perfect, real tits. Of course, the eyes are that putrid milky white with the needle hole pupils but when she was alive, she was a show stopper. One of the grunts is pinching her nipple really hard and she's just staring at him, her mouth wide open with two rows of perfect teeth. She grunting and I notice a funky smell in the air. The other grunt is saying, "Looky here," to Tim as he points at her crotch. They've inserted a soldering iron in her snatch and the fucking thing is plugged in and smoke is coming out. For a minute I'm thinking this looks like a miniature forest fire for some kid's train set, but the smell is burning meat or over-cooked tuna casserole. Her pussy is literally sizzling and popping, pushing out puffs of dark smoke.

"Couldn't do ya when I knew ya, Suzie, baby. You was all high and mighty, wasn't' ya?" says a grunt. "Yer a hot one now! Ha!" They laugh till they can't stand it no more. Neither can I.

"Tim. If you don't walk away from this, you can stay here forever, for all the fuck I care," I say as I turn and weave my way through the crowd.

Tim catches up. "Sorry, Cap'n. Just checkin' on the sideshow," he says.

"This is going to be something fucked up," I tell him quietly. "Look at the door across the way. And the weapons leaning up against the walls down there. If I'm not mistaken, Tim, this looks like some kind of arena."

Tim winces, his pale green eyes losing themselves in folds

of wrinkled flesh as he peers closer at the garage-style door built into the ground floor. I point out the chainsaw, the axe handle and the ninja sword resting carefully along wooden pegs at shoulder-height above the ground.

"Arena?" Tim whispers, scratching his scruffy red beard. "What, you mean like some kind of Thunderdome or something?"

I look into his eyes and nod: "Exactly."

I drift closer to the railing, sliding in between two massive skinheads swilling stale beer out of dirty plastic cups. They barely notice me as I stand at the edge, peering down into the dirt field that lies at our feet.

There are several garage doors down there, now that I can see more clearly. I lift my feet up and tap gently on the wooden planks beneath my skuzzy work boots; the floor feels hollow and, if I'm not mistaken, we're standing above another garage door or two.

More weapons line the walls, from axes to spears to sledgehammers to butcher knives. Many are crusted with blood, as are the walls that surround the circular dirt field. I notice movement behind the homemade "window" carved into the nearest garage style door and see a dark, male face peering out; he looks petrified.

I swallow dryly and drift back to where Tim leans against the back railing. He looks at me with those fearful eyes, so uncertain, his skin sallow beneath his baggy shirt.

"I don't like the looks of this," he whines as I urge him with my eyes to keep his voice down. "What are they doin' down there?"

I open my mouth to answer when static interrupts the guitar solo of "Freebird" and Rex's voice barks out a healthy, "Welcome to the Fuck You Arena! Tonight we have two of our finest fighters, set to square off with the loveliest ladies in camp. But enough of this foreplay, fellas; let's get ready to rrrrruuuuuuuummmmmmmbbbbbbblllllle!"

184

Cheers of moronic macho delight fill the air as shit kicker rock continues to blare in the background. Rex steps onto a small wooden platform shaped like the bow of a ship, which dangles precariously over the dry, dusty ground under his massive weight.

"Our first contestant is last week's champion, our dark-complected friend known simply as Buckwheat!"

The crowd roars as Tim and I and the rest of the audience inch forward, crowding for space around the rusty, slimy railing. A garage door across the field cranks slowly up and two muscular skinheads yank a tall black man out from the darkened recesses under the walkway and throw him into the arena. They quickly retreat as he turns and bangs helplessly against the closing door.

The crowd taunts him now, openly harassing him and tossing plastic cups at his head. He avoids the walls, massive chest bare and clad only in too-tight cargo pants, no socks or shoes.

His hair is matted and his eyes furious as he reaches quickly for an axe handle and strides to the middle of the field. His chest is scarred with long, pale swatches of missing skin.

His eyes are wild with rage as the crowd taunts him with racial slurs; he flicks them off with his free hand while swinging the axe handle furiously with another. The vengeful act whips the crowd into a lather of crying, cursing, jaunts and jeers and applause as the crap music reaches its crescendo.

After a blistering guitar solo Rex breaks in and spits, "Now, welcome to the stage that feisty little beauty known as Bambi!"

I feel a mild vibration beneath my feet and the man known only as Buckwheat looks in our general direction; his eyes grow large and he backs away, hoisting the axe handle with both hands now as in a split-second a furious bitch launches herself at him, mid-field.

Bambi is lithe and limber and dressed in tight, clingy yoga pants that read "Juicy" over her ample backside. She's bare-chested, tits bouncing firmly with every jog step she takes. Her feet are encased in shiny pink running shoes, which kick up tiny puffs of dust as she races to attack Buckwheat.

She reaches Buckwheat in seconds, fearlessly launching herself at him with a speed that is nearly breathtaking, almost surreal. Buckwheat, big as he is, falls back, stumbling as she tears at his hair with bent fingers and fierce nails. Blood spurts onto the ground, making a long, wet streak as at last Buckwheat manages to slide his axe handle between him and Bambi. He literally has to pry her off and down onto the dirt.

He wastes no time, kicking her in the ribs and forcing her at least six feet across the grainy gray sand. She barely flinches, leaping up and flying at him again, claws outstretched, face a mask of rage and hunger, but he is already swinging the axe handle and it connects with her stomach, sending her reeling; but not for long.

They trade blows, but he is human—and flawed. He is strong but slow; she is maniacally rageful and so damn quick. Three minutes and his cargo shorts are in tatters and splattered with blood, all of it his own, and everywhere he steps blood falls onto the sand in thick, wet clumps.

Still he manages to hold her off with the bloody end of his axe handle and she circles him warily, looking to wear him down. The crowd grows restless, eager for a violent kill and Rex readily responds.

"That Buckwheat is too damn good!" he opines over the grainy loudspeaker, whipping the crowd into an instant lather. "Let's introduce some new blood! Gentleman, I give you Sushi-Boy, our newest fighter in Zombie Fight Night!"

The crowd roars as a medium-sized Asian man is forced from yet another grumbling garage door and into the bloody arena. Buckwheat barely turns but Bambi senses an opportunity and sprints for the new guy before he can reach for the nearest chainsaw.

He sees her, panics and runs. The crowd boos, pelting his half-naked body with plastic cups and cigarette butts and chicken legs as he stumbles but retains his balance as he finally reaches for an axe from the wall of weapons.

Bambi is right on his tail but out of nowhere Buckwheat tackles her with a mighty crunching sound, making the crowd go wild and relieving me as I watch Sushi-Boy scramble away to relative safety.

He catches his breath, axe handle in the dirt, hands on knees, before plodding back to help Buckwheat. By now Bambi is all over the larger man, tearing at his torn shoulders, yanking at his bloody biceps when Sushi-Boy approaches.

She senses fresh meat and springs from Buckwheat, leaving him sprawled in the dirt, grown muddy with blood as he shakes his head and struggles to his feet. Sushi-Boy approaches but is given pause by a ravenous Bambi, literally licking her lips of the bigger man's blood as Sushi-Boy stands, trembling, with the axe in hand.

The crowd stills, realizing what's about to happen. It's like every skinhead in the stands knows that Sushi-Boy is doomed, outmatched, even before he starts. The man is thin and obviously in shape, but his face is gentle and passive; he's no match for this warrior woman with the glazed eyes and bloody claws at the end of each finger.

It would be like me standing down there, holding an axe, wondering if I'm getting ready to use the right end. Some warriors are born, others are made; and some men are never meant to draw blood.

Bambi inches forward, fakes left to draw Sushi-Boy into committing with a massive swipe of his axe and, once she's free of it, she dips in right and slashes at his face, ripping off flesh down to the bone.

Sushi-Boy howls and drops to his knees, hands trembling and rushing to stem the tide of blood spurting from the exposed flesh just below his nose. Bambi gnaws on the thick flap of skin, licking her lips before crouching to bite into his neck, growing more rabid with each ounce of blood and tearing back and forth like a bulldog into a throw pillow; Sushi-Boy goes limp and pale, his body and the sand beneath him drenched with blood as Bambi rips him limb from limb.

Her tits are slick with blood, her neck awash in gore as she pauses to relieve Sushi-Boy of his lower jaw with a swift, sickening "thwock" sound, like your Uncle Mort stepping on Puddy Tat road kill.

She yanks down his pants and gobbles his dick and balls as the crowd cheers and whoops like a bunch of fucking rednecks, which they are, at a conservative republican rally, which they are not. She is so intent on devouring Sushi-Boy limb by limb that she ignores Buckwheat, who after creeping up on her finally has the drop until some skinhead on the audience screams, "Look out, you bitch!"

Bambi hears Buckwheat and ducks. Buckwheat swings and misses and is so intent he loses his balance, falling in the muddy dirt at Bambi's feet. She licks her lip as he writhes on the floor, desperate to rise from the muck and mud, hands gripping the soft, wet, bloody sand as Bambi launches herself at another tasty human morsel.

At the last minute his hand finds Sushi-Boy's fallen axe; he grabs it, whips it around and slams it into Bambi's neck. It sinks halfway in, giving her a crooked, bent expression as she lands with a shudder to the ground. Still writhing, she wails and scratches as Buckwheat stands, yanks out the axe and methodically chops her to bits.

The crowd roars, then boos, until at last Rex breathes heavily into the microphone and barks, "Sorry, Buckwheat; the crowd has spoken. Looks like one bitch isn't enough for you, so . . . let's double the fun!"

With that, two garage doors open, revealing two starving zombies fresh on the scent of drawn blood. Buckwheat wisely crouches near Sushi-Boy's body, standing behind the crumpled comrade as the zombies tear toward the living man only to be distracted by the bloody remains of poor Sushi-Boy.

As the zombies crouch to feast on fresh meat Buckwheat inches closer to the wall of weapons, grabbing the nearest chainsaw and clinging to a garage door as if for protection.

But it's not protection he seeks. Instead, Buckwheat ignores the feasting zombies, focusing instead on the nearest garage door. A whiff of apprehension flutters to the crowd and my gut feels funny.

Cheers turn to jeers as I yank Tim back away from the railing, our precious places quickly filled in by curious skinheads, all flinging cups down at Buckwheat. I drag Tim down the rickety steps and pass by just as the bloodied warrior jams the chainsaw blade into the garage door in a fire of sparks and slices through the lock.

Shots ring out, ricocheting off the flimsy tin door as it flies up to reveal a dozen hungry, ravenous zombies who don't rush toward Buckwheat, who don't mind the bullets whizzing past their heads, who don't rush the stands but who instinctively begin climbing the struts attached to the nearest gun tower directly above.

"What are they doin'?" Tim asks as we hit the ground running.

"I think they're trying to escape," I grunt, sprinting for Rex's tent where he'd casually tossed his taser after silencing Bambi less than an hour earlier. I grab it and crouch toward the main gate.

The siren is wailing again, shots ringing out, pandemonium raging as I crouch behind Rex's tent to watch six bitches storm and silence the two skinheads in the gun tower. Even from the ground I can see blood coat the struts holding it up, and then the excitement as the female zombies begin tossing body parts to their partners down below.

The stands are clearing now, skinheads racing around and

I spot Rex charging for his tent.

Tim opens his mouth to draw Rex's attention but I silence him, yanking him down behind an oil drum as the camp leader storms into his tent and emerges seconds later with a rifle in each hand.

His face is a hard mask, sweat beading at his temples, mottled blood still thick across the gash left by Bambi.

Another skinhead, one of the motley crew who'd dined with us earlier, storms up and Rex literally throws a rifle at him. "Stay close," Rex barks. "Those bitches have finally figured out how to get out of here—"

A loud smashing interrupts him as both men—plus Tim and I—turn to see the guard tower toppling beneath the weight of at least a dozen raging, smashing, slashing zombies.

"Shit," Rex barks. "Those bitches ain't trying to get out, they're letting more zombies in!"

A horde of bitches that have obviously been milling around outside the camp for God knows how long breach the gaping hole left by the toppled sentry tower. Rex's second in command unleashes a volley of gunfire at the streaming army as Tim stands, stumbling forward and calling out "Rex! Rex!" as if the skinhead leader can protect him.

Turning on his heel, Rex fires three slugs at Tim without flinching. I crouch behind the oil drum, staring in disbelief as Rex's beady eyes zero in on me. He grins, mouth agape and full of those rotten teeth, aiming at the top of my head when Buffy emerges from the maddening crowd, eyes red with rage and leaping toward his tattooed throat, tearing out a fist-size chunk and bathing in the stream of blood jutting from his jugular as if it were shower water.

While she's occupied I grab Rex's discarded rifle, climb into the oil drum and slide the top over. I crouch into a ball, clutching the gun, waiting for the cheerleader zombie to remember me, listening as feet stumble and fall, crack and bleed all around me, the sounds of the infestation brutal and damning.

I peer between the heavy lid of the drum and blink at the scope of the violence spread out before me; it's like mini-Armageddon, a hundred skinheads overrun by twice as many undead, all voracious in appetite and ruthless in their level of violence.

Skinheads scream like little girls as the bitches tear them apart, leaving the leftovers for their comrades, who shuffle along after the fact and gnaw the fleshy bones clean.

It takes less than an hour for the women to completely consume the skinhead camp. My feet bathed in heating oil, I am spared merely because the diesel fumes that threaten to overpower me also mask the sweat, the stench, the fear that would otherwise have drawn them straight to my hiding place like a hound dog to a escaped convict.

I don't know which is worse; the violence of the infestation or the eeriness of its aftermath. To watch these dead women, sated and fat, stumble around appreciatively, bumping into each other, licking their lips, already sniffing for the next meal, is to watch the planet's future dissolve like Alka-Seltzer in a glass of warm water. Plop plop fizz fizz, we're fucked.

The food supply exhausted, the bones clean, the skinheads decimated down to the last femur and knucklebone, the zombies begin shuffling off, one by one, led by two blondes in the direction of the next meal.

The Massachusetts Berkshire countryside provides them plenty of cover as they move westward from the camp, not so much growling as mewling.

It takes many more hours for the bitches to make their exit than it did to waste the entire camp, and only when it is dark and the grounds have been quiet for at least two hours do I dare slide off the top from the oil drum and slip silently out.

My legs are cramped and sore from the hours spent in such a small place, my boots drenched in diesel oil, my head pounding from the fumes that, quite certainly, saved my life.

I crouch toward the nearest tent, then one more, then another, staying close to cover lest a zombie with her keen eyes and even keener sense of smell sniff me out and snuff me out. I stumble on the orientation tent, where Tim and I had been deloused and redressed less than twelve hours earlier. I'm about to get showered and dressed in cleaner duds when I hear leaves rustling. Shit, I think, they're back. I hide stupidly behind a rack of clothing.

"Kent? Kent?"

It's Tim.

"Tim, what the . . . " I go out of the tent and Tim calls, "Up here." He's in a tree.

"Man, I thought you were dead."

"Me too, but that fucker missed me. Well, sorta, I got a gash in my arm, but it's nothing. I'm coming down." He climbs out of the tree. I go over to him. I hug him.

"Welcome back," I say.

I strip myself clean, showering for too long, using too much soap, too much shampoo, luxuriating in the lather and the normalcy of the act. I find clean clothes in a metal cabinet; fresh underwear, thick socks, cargo pants, undershirt, flannel shirt, ski cap, parka and an empty backpack.

"Your turn," I say to Tim.

"No thanks, Captain. I'm hearing too many noises out there in those woods. Let's just get outta here."

I grab a pair of boots, size 11, from a row by the door and put them on quietly before slipping into a nearby tent and finding a supply of canned food; tuna, sardines, ham, chicken, small tins of pure protein. I fill the backpack half-full then slip from the tent, crouching low to the ground as the fires still burning the arena platform to the ground illuminate my path.

My eyes land on a nickel-plated .38, lying close to the gnawed-on bones of a skinhead's hand. I grab it and slip it into a pocket before slinging a loaded rifle across my back and making for the shattered hole made by the zombies and finding it barren, littered with fresh bones.

"Let's get back to the balloon," I say.

If the bitches are heading west, which they are, to the land of blood and honey, we're going east to where the balloon set us down. I pry the bloody axe handle from Buckwheat's savaged paw, wrap the business end in a skinhead's discarded wife beater and dip it into the flames, lighting my path with my improvised torch.

Outside the gates I can breathe again, the copper stench of spilled blood dissipating from my assaulted nostrils, the mountain air crisp and clean as dawn approaches silently over the Berkshires to the west.

"Tim, let's say a prayer for Hadley," I say.

We both stop and bow our heads in silence. To whom or to what we are silently speaking, neither of us knows.

CHAPTER 21

We're about 200 miles from the Cape and there's been no contact from Jen, but I expect that. The sun set and we're floating over Massachusetts at about a thousand feet using the GPS and our eyeballs. The moon is bright and small silver gray clouds lie in the distance like the smoke from an old steam locomotive, thick, billowy and all in a row seemingly sticking together. They're a group of blind men holding hands as they follow a leader into territory unknown. Blind leading the blind. Don't they all end up in the ditch?

The yellow and red and brown trees all look gunmetal gray in the light of the rising sun. I was missing Hadley, remembering the good days when she played with MG near my feet. And Jen. I understood pilgrims, making long journeys through hostile territory for a spiritual union, for some experience of the great beyond. Maybe they were just fucked up and looking to get out of Dodge, to get away from a wife and some scraggly kids, a beat up old farm on a rocky hillside in France. Those Crusaders were looking to get somewhere or get away from somewhere. That was me. I was both getting away from a life that was a zero and going to a life . . . maybe one that was less than zero. I could cheeseball it as good as the next guy and imagine me and Jen with some kids in a three bedroom, two bath house in a neighborhood with cars in the driveways and loads of shit in the garages. A place with satellite dishes and people going to church on Sunday mornings and putting up Christmas lights on the roof in December and maybe not taking them down until March. That whole "Honey, I'm home," sorta bullshit life that maybe wasn't/isn't life at all but the habit of life, the notion of life, the shadow in Plato's Cave kind of life—just an image of what could be or what might be or what should be but you get so used to the humdrum of it, to the repetition that you don't know if it's life or maybe just breathing and doing all the supposed tos. Maybe this ramble is what I mean and it all is just a path from cradle to grave and no one knows whether it curves or bends or goes over bumps or you take a wrong turn and you're in a goddamned river up to your ass in drowning and when you say, "honey, I'm home," maybe no one is there to hear or care. I'm thinking I want someone to hear and to care and if that is not Jen then I can't ever face the breathing again.

I'm quiet, of course and Tim says, "I hope this wind stays steady. We're moving good and we got plenty of gas. Going to make it, I think, pal-o-mine. We're making it to Cape Cod, wherever and whatever the fuck that is."

My only thought is to get to Jen even though I have no idea what lies in wait for me, if anything. We're heading toward the coast and likely, the bitches are all heading into the heartland. Thank God for small favors and granting wishes that he probably has nothing to do with. Just an old-fashioned way of looking at things. I mourn silently but don't exactly miss the old days. Don't know why. Don't ask. My approach will take me away from humans, away from outposts and camps and fires and klieg lights and the danger posed by my fellow man.

We have enough food, if careful, to last a short while. I keep thinking maybe I should just settle in the woods below, a life of solitude, of getting the lay of the land, of putting the road behind me and life as a mountain man ahead of me. I sense Tim feels the same way. But who can read minds anymore? And what would the pages say? I know there are pockets of what used to be called humanity still out there. Christ, I'm heading toward one at the brink of this continent. Jen is hiding from something. Or someone.

I've tried the social route; it didn't work for me. Now maybe it's time to embrace the solitude of life on a desolate planet, of wariness and silence. Let the skinheads and religious fanatics inherit the earth; I'll settle for the mountains, the stars, the trees and the uncertain future.

CHAPTER 22

We had a tail wind of over 40mph so we dropped to five hundred feet. Off to the north, I could make out the hulking cubes of Boston as the sun setting behind us cast its long orange beams through the deserted metropolis. To the south, the ragged New England coastline hugged the gray Atlantic, white caps in neat rows marching out to sea, white mist from the off shore winds like witches' hair.

"We got to land, boss," said Tim. "This is the Cape. See that strip of highway? It goes mostly the whole way to Provincetown. But about forty miles out it makes a hard turn northward—it's the hook of the Cape. Where P-town sits."

I looked at the GPS map and saw that Cape Cod was like an arm raised into a fist aimed at Europe.

"Yeah," said Tim. "The Cape is shootin' the bird at the rest of the western world."

"Let's take it out as far as we can. We'll land, tie her up and make it on foot to P-Town. Maybe find a vehicle."

"You never know," he said.

It had been over a week since I heard from Jen. All I knew was that she's in the basement of a dinner theater on Baker Street. Shouldn't be hard to find. Even at the lowest safe altitude we could make, the wind would push us out to sea and we'd never get back.

A half hour later we saw the curve of the highway northward and Tim began the descent. Long rows of white houses fringed the coastline and made me think of summer days by the shore, sailboats, surfboards, swimming. Chicks in bikinis. Guys with Frisbees. Beach blankets. All gone. All fucking gone.

The gondola dragged its bottom for a few hundred feet along

the sand and came to a rest near a light house. The sun was nearly set behind us and the red brick glowed with the waning light. We jumped out and tied the gondola to the stakes as the balloon deflated. Tim folded it and we took some extra steps to secure it because we didn't know when or even if we'd be back to claim her. We buried the silk in about six inches of sand far enough above the high water mark to be certain it would be all right when we returned.

We walk over to the lighthouse, which is locked. Tim kicks in the door and we are out of the wind and weather for the first time in a long time.

"Let's head up," he says as he starts up the spiral stairway that looked like it could go to the moon.

"Not yet," I say. "There's probably a galley over here. Let's see if we can cook something up."

We walk over the creaking oak floorboards to a kitchen that looks like it sits on the edge of the world. The sea stretched out to a gunmetal horizon and whitecaps blow away from us from the strong off shore winds that had been so kind in getting the balloon this far east. It was a blessing of sorts, if you can count anything a blessing in the middle of the end of the world.

The refrigerator was full of moldy food and hadn't been running for months from the look of it.

Tim opens a pantry and there is a shitload of every kind of Campbell's soups known to man. Black bean, tomato, chicken noodle, pea, beef barley. It is heaven in tin, heaven in red and white.

"Man, this is great. Let's find the can opener. See if the burner on the stove works."

Tim turns the knob and the hiss and smell of propane, the gas that saved our asses, hits our nostrils like manna from heaven. He turns it off and finds a big box of old-fashioned wooden matches in a drawer. He strikes the match and the burner comes to life while I pour two cans of soup into a pot that was sitting on the drain board.

"Guess they left before the big hit," I say.

"Must've."

I find a box of Saltines that is sealed and still relatively fresh. We sit across from each other at a table that looks a hundred years old. Two old rain coats hang from hooks on the wall over two pair of high water boots. On a small table nearby are some hats and gloves. A barometer hangs on the wall near the window. As the light dwindles, Tim finds a kerosene lamp and lights it. The wind begins to howl and the waves march in like legions, white capped and relentless toward the rocks, smashing up against the base that this lighthouse sits on. I fell simultaneously safe and exposed, snug but vulnerable.

"This wouldn't be a bad place to stay, you know," I say.

"Maybe not. There's plenty of food. Probably plenty of propane. You can see for miles in every direction. My guess is you could fish off these rocks. It would be a waiting game but there are worse things to do."

"Yeah, and worse people to meet," I respond.

"You thinking about this as your last stand, Captain?"

"I don't think hanging onto this rock is the way to spend the rest of my life."

"Got a better way?"

I look at Tim maybe for the first time since this all started. Look into his eyes and I see him for the good man he is. It's not an adventure anymore, not a tale of true grit or a story of men against the odds. It's about two guys that are human trying to figure out what that means now that humanity doesn't count for much.

"I'm going up top to take a look out the glass," Tim says.

"Wait a sec," I say. I see that there's a hatch door in the floor of the kitchen. I open it and look down into a cellar that's pitch black.

"Hand me the lantern," I say. Tim hands it over.

I climb down a soft almost rotten wood stairway and the light casts its feeble beams into an earthen and rock basement, damp and smelling of the sea. There is row upon row of canned food of every type from beans to ham to canned fruit. On one row of metal shelves are six cases of beer.

"Shit. I knew it," I yell up to Tim.

I shoulder a case and head up the stairs, the light of the lantern casting a glow on Tim's worried face which begins to crack into a smile.

"I knew you were a Captain in another life," he says. "Maybe even an admiral."

The stairway to the light box is like a corkscrew. It is black wrought iron and quivers slightly with every step and our footfalls echo up the tube.

"Now you know how a wad of cum feels when you're about to shoot a load," Tim says. Maybe he's more of a dumbass than I just thought. On the other hand, maybe he's right.

We get to the top and the clouds are almost black, illuminated from behind probably by the moon and there's a strange luminescence over the water, a greenish glow like a trillion fireflies on a hot July night in the backyard.

"That's algae. That green light," Tim says.

The wind has died down some and we look at the mechanism of the light. It's a huge silver backed mirror like a bigger version of a flashlight you keep in the nightstand drawer knowing full well the minute you need it, the batteries will be dead. From up there we can see to the horizon which I've heard is only thirty something miles before the curvature of the Earth gets in the way. Landward we can see up the coast; small white houses, docks and boats moored, bobbing up and down, ghosts of another time. Nearby is a large fishing boat, decked out with all the bells and whistles, moored to the dock of a large white house squatting behind some short trees bent away from the sea like girls turning their backs to the wind.

"Now that's a ride," says Tim. "The masts must be fifty

feet tall."

Turning more toward the west as we walk the perimeter, the land looks completely empty, devoid of any life of any kind. Toward Provincetown to the north and west, there's a glow in the clouds but, again, it's probably a trick of Mother Nature.

"How far to P-Town?" I ask.

"I'm thinking fifteen miles. Could make it easy in a day . . . or a night. I'm not sure which is safer. Seems pretty dead around here, no pun intended. I mean you got to figure that the bitches have all headed toward food town which would be west of here no matter how you slice it. There are likely some guys holed up but from what we've seen, my Captain, they're no better than the bitches."

Of course, he's right. Hadn't thought of it quite that way. It's sort of like thinking your family is really a nice bunch of people but after a while you realize they're just as big and bad a bunch of assholes as anyone else only you're stuck with them because they came out of the same hole—no offense to my mamma or yours.

We can see some fishing gear tied up near the dock that's part of the lighthouse and a small cabin cruiser likely used to save people or some shit like that. There's also a small cabin about fifty yards off to the west.

"That's where they sleep," says Tim. "The lighthouse keeper and his wife and kids. Some life, huh?"

"I guess."

"Let's bed down up here. I ain't going exploring anymore tonight. And I don't know who or what is in that house. Fuck 'em for now. Let's go secure the door," he adds.

We wedge some two by fours against the door and it is solidly closed. I find some padded water tarps and life jackets and we use the coats for blankets. The temperature is dropping faster than Rhoda Schwartz's panties at the senior prom. We drag the stuff up to the light box and bed down, the wind and the waves lulling the world to sleep.

At about 2 AM, I awake and huddle under the covers. Tim's steady breathing is a reassuring sound, the wind hissing through the chinks in the glass. I get up and look out the glass. The clouds have scudded off the sky and a half moon sits near the horizon casting a milky silver light on the ocean that looks cheesy enough for a postcard, one of those "wish you were here" things your girlfriend sends you when she's off on spring break getting humped by some Mexican stud in Puerto Vallarta while you're whacking off to the latest porn vid from Netwank.

I imagine I can see dolphins breaking the surface of the water in schools, having a celebration now that all the fishing boats are docked and the fisherman have been eaten. Who'da thought? they must think, praying to their sea gods and saying thank yous galore, fucking each other and laughing with the tuna and cod. Fuck them, they're thinking. What goes around comes around. They know the whales are all hanging around Tokyo listening to the screams from those whaling bastards as the little geisha girls with their deformed feet and clown make-up chow down on those tiny dicks and hairless balls. Millions upon millions of eaters and eaten. "Hey, listen to that one howl," says one whale to the other. "Those fuckers have had it coming to them. Ain't it so?" I know it. And I never liked sushi, either, even though I pretended so people would think I was cool. I'd talk about China too, if I gave a shit. Talk about food. A billion motherfuckers all eating each other. Enough for the bitches to eat for years. Nothing like Chinaman liver with a nice bowl of rice. On the other hand, bitches, hold the rice. Go for the brains. They're on sale this week and extra small in bite-sized pieces. Just watch out for the lead and PCB content.

I lie down under the covers again and begin to doze off with visions of sugar plums dancing in my head when I hear a creaking hinge and footsteps on the iron stairwell.

"Tim," I whisper. But he doesn't hear me. "Tim . . . ." I figure if I'm quiet, it or he or she will get too tired to bother coming all the way up those goddamned stairs. How'd it get in?

It gets quiet. I reach for my pistol, but it's gone. Fuck. Where did I leave it? There's a shadow in the doorway. A short bitch that's moving real slow, like a cat creeping up on a mouse. I try to scream to wake Tim up but my voice is frozen. I'm fucked. That stupid sleeping sonofabitch Tim is next on the menu. What a way to go, I'm thinking, after all this bull-shit. What a way to go.

"Uncle Kent? It's me, Hadley," the shadow says.

I find my voice. "Hadley, baby, how'd you get in? Are you OK? I really missed you"

"I know, I know," she says softly. "I missed you, too. Can I stay with you? I'm so cold."

"Sure. Come under the covers," I say, lifting the tarp and raincoat. She crouches down and curls up next to me, colder than an icicle. "You'll warm up in a minute," I reassure her, putting my arm around her.

"I missed you, too," she repeats, shivering. "It's a long way from there to here. I'm so glad I found you. I couldn't bring MG, though. I'm sorry. I lost him in the fog."

"That's OK. He's a good dog. He can fend for himself. When I get out of here, I'll find him. Maybe you can help. Would you help me find him?"

"Sure I will," she says. "I gotta sleep now."

"Yeah, get some sleep, sweetie. We got a ton of food. I'll make you breakfast in the morning. OK?"

"Yeah," she says. "That would be great. I'm so hungry, Uncle Kent. So hungry and so tired."

My grandmother always made me say my prayers at bed-time. "Now I lay me down to sleep . . . ." Didn't like it then. Like it even less now.

■■■

I feel like I'm in a blast furnace when I wake up. The sun is hitting the reflector on the light housing and it's focused on me like ten million watts of tanning bed. I put my hand up to shield my face. "Fuck!" I say to the world.

"Top o' the mornin' to you, too, Cap'n," sings Tim.

"How about you go fu . . . ."

"Now Cap'n, is that anyway to talk to the galley slave what just made you some fresh canned peaches and cornflakes over easy with a fresh pot of instant coffee and home fries from real potatoes and thinly sliced canned ham?"

The smell of cooking had risen up that stairwell like it was a chimney. It did smell good. It was then I notice Hadley is gone.

"Where's Hadley?" I ask Tim. He looks at me and does-n't answer. Shakes his head annoyed. He always thought she was bad luck or something. That poor kid. Didn't stand a chance and when she got shot . . . . That's right, I think. She was shot. What am I thinking?

I look at the place in my makeshift bed where she was supposed to be sleeping. There's a small c-shaped indent in the water tarp. Or is it my imagination?

Tim is looking at me sideways as he pretends to look out at the risen sun. Gulls are circling the lighthouse and dropping clams on the rocks, diving to pick up the sweet innards.

"I'll be right down. Sorry I overslept. It wasn't a good night," I say.

"Any night we live till the morning is a good one, Mon Capitan," he responds. He heads down the stairs whistling some stupid '60s song. I'm hoping it's not "Up, Up and Away in my beautiful balloon."

I'm pulling up my pants when I see a red dot in the dis-tance. There's something coming up the road from the di-rection of P-Town.

"Tim," I yell down. "There's someone coming our way." I rub my eyes to make sure it's not a trick of the light or a floater in my vitreous humor. Go look it up if you don't know what I'm talking about. It could happen to you.

Tim comes running up the stairs like a gazelle.

"Where? Who? What?"

"Look there," I say pointing. It's clearly a red car of some sort. It's moving fast and birds that were sitting on the road are scattering out of the way and shredded bits of paper and leaves are flying up behind it.

"Get down," I say. We both crouch just peeking a bit over the edge. "They must have been by here or the place would have been emptied out, right?"

Not right. It's a red Jeep, one of those Wranglers with a black ragtop. There are three, no four, bitches in the fucking thing and they go racing by us and I'm thinking, holy shit-stains, they've remembered how to drive! Tim says, "That was a close one," but the brakes get slammed on and the backup lights brighten and the fucking thing backs up to the driveway of our lighthouse. It stops and I can see the bitches looking at us like we're hanging out on the roof.

"Fuck. Get the rifle," I tell Tim. He rushes down the stair-well and I hear him running back up, all out of breath and wheezing like he smoked eight packs a day all his life.

"Sorry, chief," he says. "It was the cooking. There's a small smokestack over the stove and I guess the smoke attracted the bitches."

He guessed right. He cocks the rifle and sits next to me. "Let them come for us. We can pick them off in the stair-well."

"Right," he says. "Maybe it would be better to pick them off from here. I got a clear line of fire."

"Wrongo," I say. "If they don't all get killed, they can race back to wherever they came from and bring a horde with them." I'm imagining us getting eaten in a lighthouse in Cape Cod. If somebody told me this shit on graduation day in high school I woulda said . . . . Fuck, what does it matter what I would've said? I was a bigger dumbass then than I am now, damn it all to hell.

Tim slides open one of the vent windows and pokes the muzzle out, takes a second, and fires at the driver of the Jeep. The window shatters and the bitch behind the wheel collapses, blood splattered everywhere. The doors open up and three bitches tumble out.

"Hey, you dumb motherfuckers, what are doin?" says one of them sounding very much a baritone. I peek out and see her legs belong to a running back. A blonde with shoulders bigger than a door, shakes her fist. "I'm going to beat the livin' crap outta you!"

Tim wisely fires another shot into the dirt and some pebbles and dust fly up. He turns to me and says, "Thems ain't zombies, Captain, thems is drag queens."."

"Listen, girls," I yell. "I'm sorry, but we thought you were women or, more accurately, zombies. You were very convincing. I'm sorry for your friend there but we didn't want to end up on a bitch-from-hell menu. I hope you understand."

"Understand? You shot Helen right through his head! I'll admit the make-up was good and he just waxed his beard, poor dear. But did you have to kill him?"

"Well, I guess you know what's been happening around the world. Can you blame us?" I say. "I mean, you're dressed like women. Think about it. Not like we feel good about it now."

They whisper to each other.

The brunette shouts, "Okay, dammit. It's a truce. Accidents happen and we can't blame you guys. Well, we could blame you. You shot a hole in her fucking head. But I might've done the same thing if I was in your shoes. Come on down."

Tim says to me, "What do you think?"

"I think we've got no options; no real options anyway. Let's go."

We pick up our stuff and fill our backpacks with food. I open the door and Ryan, as I learned his name to be is standing there. He says, "Don't need supplies. We're chock full for now but if it suits you to bring your own, be my guest."

Standing next to him is Greg, a tall lanky dude in a tight dress and yellow heels the size of banana boats. He puts out his hand all limp-wristed and says, "Pleased to meetcha."

"Likewise, I'm sure," says Tim getting into the routine. "I'm Tim. This is Kent."

"Hi guys," says Greg. "I'm Greg; this is Ryan. That's Darlene over there," pointing out the beefy brunette. "I mean AJ. But he prefers Darlene. You can call me whatever makes you happy." He winks.

Ryan, sounding suddenly masculine and in charge, says, "All right, girls. Let's get back to camp. Darlene, you stay here. I'll send Edna for you with a pick-up. We might as well get the stuff that's stored here now before it falls into the wrong hands. Be a dear and help clean up this mess that Annie Oakley just made in our limo."

Darlene says nothing in reply but shuffles over to the lighthouse in his chiffon gown and engineer boots. I know he's going to eat my breakfast.

"Guess he's gonna eat your chow, dearie," says Ryan as if reading my mind. "Your fire was a little smoky. And a lot careless. There are still undead whores running around. Not many, but a few. We go scouting every now and again just to see if maybe the military is back in control or something good is in the news department. We're pretty isolated out there in P-Town. Don't want to miss anything."

"We get it," says Tim.

"No, Miss Thing, I don't think you do. That cooking fire of yours could have brought all hell down on you. If you do that careless kind of shit at our camp, I'll shoot you myself."

Before we all get in the Jeep, Ryan announces he has to "take a leak." He pulls up his dress and unrolls his dick. It looks a foot long.

"Now you know why she's in charge," says Greg.

After Darlene and Tim clean the remains of Helen out of the car; they drag his body off behind one of the dunes. Everyone says a word or two and a silent prayer and we all pile into the Jeep. Death has become just a way of life now. Everyone moves on pretty quickly, though it doesn't make me feel better about accidentally shooting someone. Greg drives and makes a quick U-turn and we are on our way to P-Town. I certainly am not going to bring up Jen and I look at Tim sitting next to me in the back and he knows, as usual, what I am thinking.

"So where are you two from and what the hell are you doin' here?" asks Ryan.

"We're from Denver. Worked at a radio station. We figured the Cape was safe because it was isolated. Knew the plague was only hitting females and knew also that P-Town was more than likely to be safe," I responded.

"I don't believe that story really," says Ryan. "But whatever suits you. We're pretty harmless, all-in-all. But how did you get here from there?"

"In a balloon," I say quickly. Doesn't make a difference anymore. "It's buried back at the lighthouse. Won't do anybody any good anymore."

"Now that is a story," says Ryan. "Maybe I'm believing the whole thing. Like Dorothy and the Wizard. You're right about P-Town. It's all gay now for sure. We had our problems with a bunch of local dykes and some turista broads. A lot of bloodletting, if the truth be known. But about twenty seminary students from Boston showed up one day in a motor boat; they had just made it out of Bean Town before it was overrun by the horde and they arrived in the nick of time to save our ungodly asses."

"You mean a bunch of Catholic priests made it in a boat?" Tim asks.

"Not priests exactly. But on their way to being priests. Seminary of St. Jude. Nice bunch of guys. And don't start in about child molesting and all that shit. We're what's left in this part of the globe and, like it or not, we're the survivors. The only hope of mankind," says Ryan.

"God works in mysterious ways, my friends," says Tim. "Greg, what's your story?"

I look out the window of the Jeep at the dunes and saw grass, the shifting sands that have covered most of the road since there is no longer a highway department to clean up after Mother Nature's mischief. There are gray-shingled cottages with sand piled up against their sides as if trying to hide from the weather and the world. Abandoned cars, toppled lawn furniture, a deserted produce stand, tattered remnants of American and nautical flags on weathered flagpoles, the halyards clanking in the wind. Greg's voice breaks the reverie:

"I was a school teacher at P-Town Elementary. I'll never forget it, Mary, never, if I live to be a hundred—not that I would want to unless they can do something about wrinkles and age spots—no, honey, not me. Anyway, I'm teaching the little cuties about squares and circles and triangles and I've got their full attention, which is not easy, I might add. And I hear a shout from outside in the hallway. Help, Help! Someone is yelling and then screams. Well, I am thinking this is Columbine but for tots. And, no, it couldn't be; that was in Colorado which is full of bigot rednecks with pick-up trucks and gun racks. No this is P-Town the land of the free and the home of the homo. I don't even think the police have guns. Anyway, I look out in the hall in a very cautious fashion and, sure enough, Miss Watling, the assistant principal who is at least 350 pounds on a dry day, is purple and gushier than usual and she has Mr. Boyle on his back on the floor eating his— well, his private parts—and two male teachers, Mr. Conroy, the cutest math teacher you ever saw and Mr. DaBrama, a hunky Italian from Boston are pulling on her fat shoulders and shouting for someone to call 911 and then some new teacher named Mrs. Haversham looking like it was Halloween in May comes running down the hall with a man's arm in her mouth, jacket sleeve and all, and I nearly passed out and kept thinking of my old fucked up Christian grandma telling me about the end of days and the Crapture and all that Jesus-with-his-terrible-swift-sword bullshit and I say to myself, 'Honey, that old dried-up bitch was right! It *is* the end of the world and where am I going to be sentenced to?' Why just two nights before, I had a dildo up my ass the size of a Louisville slugger and Jimmy—he's my hunka-hunka burnin' love dish of the week—jerking off by my side. I'm hoping that Saint Agnes or the Holy Moly Mother of God or St. Peter, Paul and Almond Joy were not watching me in the privacy of my own home. After all, even queers have some constitutional rights, right? And I start praying out loud, 'Dear Jesus, I never sucked a dick or had one in my ass and I'll never do it again! I promise on the grave of my old fucking whore Bible thumpin' grandma, may she rot, I mean live, in heaven with you and those eye candy angels. Anyway, I slam the door shut and lock it and I turn to see all the little girls have collapsed on the floor and the little boys are standing there, some crying, some just dumbfounded and then, of course, there is fat little Jerry Koonders laughing and pointing at Emily Boyd's little panties full of scorch marks and I yell, 'All right, boys, back up to the black board. Give them some air,' but the little rascals all come running over to me because, of course, they are scared out of their little wits. And then the little girls get up and I figure that it must have been mass hysteria and I can hear police sirens outside and I am glad for the first time in my life that the cops are on the way and it's not to arrest me for public drunkenness which only happened once when I was in New York City at a club called Furnace and I did more ecstasy than was prudent, if you get my meaning, and the next thing I know this fat guy named Jeffrey is breathing on me while I'm passed out and saying, 'She's not dead, I think. Let her sit here for a while. She'll come to. I hope.' Well, I did but the place got raided and I got taken to a hospital and I would bet a thousand dollars that the ambulance guy had taken my shoes off and was smelling my feet and whacking off, but I couldn't swear to it because, well I was e'd out of my mind and I wouldn't have minded anyway; I love a man in a uniform. I was put in a room with this drag queen who was so ugly she reminded me of my dear old grandma who was dead and rotting in her grave. Well, back to the school, the tyke bitches get up and they do not look healthy and happy like little American girls should look, all sugar and spice and everything tuna. No, my friends, they are tottering tots from the land of the undead, oozing black shit from their mouths and like little monster wind-up American Girl dolls, they start attacking the little boys en masse and biting and tearing and it's not even lunch period yet, the little bitches. One of them goes for my balls, but I punch her on the top of her head and collapse her skull in because I'm scared outta my panties. I remember seeing those pigtails with the pink ribbons go straight up in the air covered in her brain matter. She collapses and I smashed her face in with my Prada boots which were never the same since, damn her. I know I'm not going to run into the hall, so I go to the window and try to lift some of the boys through. I get three or four out and tell them to run wee, wee, wee all the way home but I don't get a good feeling about that especially when that dyke gym teacher comes staggering out of the gymnasium and grabs one of them and tears his arms off and eats him, jeans and Ed Hardy t-shirt included. Just his little high tops were left. I climb out and the bitch starts chasing me, but I make it to the bike rack and jump on one of the bikes and pedal my ass off, tears in my eyes and racing through that parking lot like Glinda the Good Witch of the South going to save Dorothy but, fuck her, I got to save myself. It wasn't long before I found this bunch of queens hiding out in Pete's Peter, the gay bar that used to be a jail, and we are all safe. I think someday I'll write my life story. But I don't think there are many publishers left. Do you?"

"No, I don't think so," I answer. I'm out of breath just listening to this queen. But I can sense the terrified desperation behind the glib humor and the thick make-up. In not too long a time we make it to a barricade across the road. There are cars, buses, garbage dumpsters and miscellaneous vehicular detritus not only blocking the roadway but extending to and over the dunes in both directions from sea to shining sea. The blockade seals off the small tip of the Cape at its narrowest point. There are makeshift guard towers every fifty feet but they appear unoccupied. There are, however, four guys in military fatigues with Uzis. We're stopped at the entrance and two muzzles are pointed at us.

"It's us," says Ryan. "We lost one and found two."

"Get out of the car, all of you," barks one of the guards.

Greg says, "That's what used to be a seminarian. What a bitch. It's protocol. Don't worry, guys, it's okay."

The last time I heard that, it was most definitely not okay. We all get out. The car is looked over and under.

"Welcome back, Ryan. What happened to the other two you left with?" asks a guard.

"Helen had an accident. She's dead. Darlene is back at the Nauset Light collecting provisions. Send Anthony and Chuck out with a van. She's waiting."

"Sure," he responds. He raises his arm and gestures and a school bus that is part of the barricade backs out of the way and the road ahead is clear, a small street that leads to a cluster of perfect New England Victorian houses and cottages in various shades of white, yellow, gray, sea green and pink.

"How cheery and gay," says Tim.

"How unoriginal," says Greg. "Welcome to P-Town."

We sit down to a meal in a former restaurant that overlooks the water. The breeze is light, the sun strong for this time of year and gulls walk on sand with plovers and other small birds. There are rocks out about a hundred yards offshore with seals on them.

"This place really is beautiful," I say.

"Yeah. Used to be worth almost a thousand dollars a square foot for a house out here. Lots of Boston peeps and New Yorkers. A lot of queers have money. No kids to spend it on or save it for and almost every household with two earners. Those were good times. Not that we still don't throw a bash now and then," says Ryan. "There are about two hundred of us at 'Fort P-Town' now. Every now and then a few leave. A lot of guys want to find their parents or brothers and sisters or even old loves. It's not an easy adjustment. It's great here, don't get me wrong, considering I mean, but it's still a prison even if the bars are sand, surf and a pile of junk blocking the town line at the peninsula neck. Occasionally, a guy or two just vanish without so much as a 'see ya later' but I figure everyone has to deal with farewells in their own way."

"It's still way better than any place else we've seen. You wouldn't believe it," I say.

"We've heard some reports mostly over the radio and sometimes we'll catch something on a boat CB. We have a lot of boats docked here—moored I should say—we decided to destroy all the docks to make landing more difficult. We don't know how organized the zombies are."

"My guess is that they are evolving and from what we've seen crossing the country, it won't be long before they really organize," I respond. I continue with a brief description of what we've been through. Tim adds his comments and the table, which now has about twenty guys listening to us, is getting updates on the state of the union. It's not what they want to hear but when we're done, we get thanked and there's a lot of 'boys, you got balls' talk. Most of them have been living some kind of delusion about how serious it all is. The student priests especially have been talking a great deal about God's judgment and all that horseshit and they even convinced a bunch of the guys to attend church on Sundays. My own views I keep to myself but if they think God has figured out a way to help, I can't avoid thinking that maybe he should not have let the plague happen to begin with. Just me though and I guess it can't hurt if these guys find some solace in their prayers.

The meeting breaks up and Ryan tells a twenty-something named Terry to show us to our quarters. Terry was a Broadway dancer and he tells us about some of his adventures on the great white way. He tells us there is an old boarded-up dinner theater on the east side of town and he'd love to re-open it someday and start putting on shows.

"Where is the place?" I ask knowing or hoping or dreaming or wishing that that is where Jen is. How could she still be alive? I think.

"Let's get you two settled in and I'll take you over. Okay?"

Tim looks at me. "That would be fun," he says.

Terry waits outside while we unload our gear in an old motel that's in the middle of town. I would have preferred a water view but I think it's better to be in the middle of things on the theory that there is safety in numbers.

"Let's do the tour," I tell Tim.

"I know what you're thinking and I think I'll pass. I'm toured out, Captain and I think I'll settle in, maybe walk a little."

"Suit yourself," I say as Terry honks the horn. "I won't be long."

Terry heads north and there are people walking around

like everything is normal, like the good old days. No women of course, but the guys are in groups, smoking, standing around being social. Some are on porches, sitting on porch steps, candles, kerosene lanterns lighting the untended gardens and overlong grasses that smother the picket fences and stream up through cracks in the pavement. Terry pulls up to a very tall lighthouse at the northernmost point of the Cape and turns the lights of the Jeep off. We watch the waves roll in.

"Is the theater around here?" I ask.

"About two blocks away," he says. "I just want to sit a spell. I used to come here every summer. It was great. My parents had a cottage near here but one of those nor'easters tore the hell out of it and they ended up selling the land it used to sit on for like ten times the amount they paid for it. I guess they were motivated by watching me watching all the guys. It wasn't easy for them."

"Were you here when the plague hit?"

"You mean the GaGa, right? When you say plague to a queen, we usually think AIDS."

"Yeah, the GaGa."

"I remember the night I first heard of the virus scare. I didn't know quite what to do so I simply went to bed after locking and double locking the doors. Even that was not enough; I got up and nailed the windows shut. Almost broke a few but I was careful. Got back into bed and thought and rethought my life. My bedroom was dark, the ceiling the blue of dusk, the furniture deep gray. I had my headphones on and was listening to the love theme from *Terminator II*, my favorite part of the film. As the music rose and fell, I could envision the scene as clearly as if I were in the theater. Michael Biehn, the hero of the first *Terminator* movie, was bathing in a lake in the woods, his well-scarred body tan except for the cheeks of his rear end which were the color of mayonnaise. There was the Arnold Schwarzenegger Terminator hiding in the woods peeping through the limbs of some blue spruces, his red light eyes bright as Christmas ornaments on the Rockefeller Center tree. He watched Michael wash himself, particularly observing how the wan sunlight caught the peach fuzz coating on his ass, that beautiful double scoop, vanilla ice cream ass. Terminator's eyes narrowed and glowed fiercely staring at the twin hemispheres of masculinity. He could take it no longer but strode out through the trees and, as if to show his peaceful intent, raised his hands in the air and said, 'I come in peace, no pun intended.' Michael slowly turned and said, 'I knew you were there, big boy. What took you so long?' Here, the violins and oboes made a lilting crescendo as Terminator grabbed Michael and nibbled the back of his neck.

"It was only a minute before his hydraulic reproduction pod penetrated those buns and when he orgasmed his machine oil into Michael, he blew him up from the inside, showering the serene lake with bits of blood, colon and stool in a most egregious fashion, startling a pair of mallards into flight and making the fish jump for a hundred yards in every direction. It was such a sad ending for our hero, but Terminator learned the dangers of man-love and would never be a threat to humanity again, not if he had anything to say about it. As the oboes and piccolos danced their sad dance in my headphones, Terminator took what was left of Michael and carried him to an old well nearby, tossing him in as a tympani thrummed away and the music ended with three cymbals crashing as the lifeless body fell down the shaft and landed in an antique wheelbarrow that some wayward youths had dropped down a few years earlier as a prank on a local pig farmer. Surely, no cinematic scene could have been more profound. I dabbed at my tears with the brittle end of my pillowcase and cursed my mother for insisting on starching my bed linens. Jesus, they were stiff as a priest's collar and crunched all night long as I moved to the inner rhythms of my sleep. I wish real life was more like the movies.

"I had started seeing my ex-wife, Susan, again. Old loves die hard and while I had fallen in love with Robert, Sue never left my heart, my achy, breaky heart which creaked and groaned when I re-lived those moments with my childhood sweetheart. Unfortunately, Robert had discovered my liaisons with her by following me one day and seeing the two of us at a small café in the village. We were only talking, but it might as well have been a major doggie-style sex party on the sidewalk. Robert is one of those 'hold it in, then explode' types so I was not prepared when he cross-examined me that night as I lay in bed early complaining of a headache. He caught me in the lie and when I told him he should mind his own beeswax, he went temporarily insane. He smashed his fist down on a glass cocktail table that I had lovingly purchased at a designer close-out sale at Bloomies. The glass split into large triangular shards and he picked one up, entered the bedroom, and holding it like a dagger said, 'I'm gonna cut your fuckin' heart out if I catch you cheating on me. Do you understand?' Well, of course I understood. I held the sheets tightly under my chin as if that over-starched 400 count Egyptian cotton could offer any sort of protection against a shard-wielding queen on a jealous rampage. Even his slight lisp had vanished like a blackbird in the night. The moments he spent looming over my prostrate form seemed like hours. I'd thought he would never leave. But eventually, the door to our apartment closed and I knew he had gone for a walk to cool down and contemplate how he could make up to me for being so violent.

"As I thought about it, I felt every inch like Michael Biehn bathing in the lake. Robert was my Terminator and I was filled with romantic notions of man love and how truly repulsed I was when I saw Susan's breasts in her tight-fitting Gucci T-shirt. Those things are so gushy—yikes, nothing like a good hard set of pecks on a real man. Governor Arnold, where art thou? Art thou in the woods espying me? Robert? Robert, please return unto me.

"I'm just a die-hard romantic, I guess. I put on my head-phones again and longingly listened to the love theme from *Godzilla*. Oh sad Jurassic monster, come to me. Trumpet your tragic growls. I am here. Needless to say, I slept soundly as a log considering the world was coming to an end outside my window."

I'm thinking, what the fuck? when he says, "Let's walk to the theater. It isn't but a few hundred feet away. It's a beautiful night."

"Whatever you say."

He takes me over to the building that used to be one of the biggest attractions in P-Town, tells me how many Broad-way stars would do summer stock up here and on that stage. Next door is a shuttered ice cream stand with the sign hanging off at a forty-five degree angle. Uncle Benny's Luscious Cream Shop.

I walk back and forth in front of the theater. Looks completed deserted; boarded up real tight. I don't want to seem too curious.

"This place must've been something in the day," I say.

"Yeah, used to be great. Let's get going. I'm tuckered."

We get back in the Jeep and he drives me back to the motel.

"Don't suppose you need company tonight?" he asks.

"No. I'm pretty tired. It's been a long day."

"It's been a long year," he says.

"Thanks for the tour," I say.

"Anytime."

The Jeep disappears into the night and the lull of distant waves and the smell of salt air surround me.

CHAPTER 23

The moon hasn't risen yet and I'm thankful for small favors. I can easily remember where the Brookstone Dinner Theater is thanks to Terry's tour. I stick to alleys and dark corners, avoiding lighted windows. I can hear guys laughing as I pass a house and see candles on a table, shadows moving and some even dancing. Life goes on, I think to myself. The irony of these guys being some of the last men on Earth is not wasted on me. I hear the sound of a car behind me and duck behind a large stand of dune grass near a tattered picket fence. It's one of the jeeps on patrol with its top down and two men sitting in it armed with rifles. They have those over-top mounted searchlights and for a second I think I'm spotted as the light catches me but the grass is so thick and the breeze blowing it around is a perfect cover. It goes by and I can hear Bruce Springsteen music on the CD player as it passes. It turns at the next corner and the motor noise diminishes to a whisper and then silence again. I walk hurriedly, being extra careful to notice places I can quickly hide in.

The dead neon sign of the theater looms against the black sky, heightened by the fact that the building sits high on a sandy hill that drops off at a steep grade to the water. I go under it and walk around the back looking for a way to enter. Nothing. The backdoor is nailed shut with three pieces of weathered plywood. The same for all the windows. The place is tighter than a bank vault. If Jen was inside, she couldn't get out. If she had gotten out, she'd have been summarily shot; that was the rule, wasn't it? Ryan had made that amply clear. Any female seen on P-Town ground was to be exterminated. Whatever foolish hopes I had been holding onto all this time were for nothing. I sit up against the back of the building and watch the small waves lap at the shore, little furlings and un-furlings of black water against an empty beach. I should be thinking about what to do next. Stay? Keep moving? But to where and for what?

I start down the hill to the water and notice about halfway down that there is a large drainpipe that opens onto the hill. It's about four feet in diameter and looks like a storm drain. I'm thinking if any place needs storm drains, this is it. The whole town is only a few feet above sea level. But this drain does not lead toward a road but back to the theater. I take out my flashlight and shine it inside. It's dark as hell of course but there is nothing in there; no standing water, not flotsam. Nothing. Actually, it's so clean it looks new. Why haven't the P-Town residents blocked this off? Maybe they checked the building already and deemed it empty. Maybe they figured no one would bother wading up a drainage pipe. They must be getting more comfortable than they let on.

I crouch down and head into the pipe. The flashlight beam glistens off the aluminum sides but gets blurry straight ahead. Still, I continue and at the end the light catches a small doorway, more like a hatch. I pull on the handle and it slides open easily as if on well-oiled hinges. A smell of feces, garbage and an indeterminate odor of rotting flesh makes me close the door again. I turn and lean on it, rethinking things. Am I insane? What am I supposed to find in here? But the answer is made for me. The door is shoved open and two bitches leap out and grab me, drag me back in, their grip on my arms like vices. My voice is lost in the wind and the sand.

I'm dragged to what I am sure is my certain death. The odor is overwhelming; rot, putrifaction, shit, cess; every disgusting smell that humanity has ever encountered and a few more for good measure. Now I know why no one came up this way.

"Why don't you cunts get it over with and kill me?" I ask real dramatic and all when, in fact, I have let go a few ounces of piss into my pants. "Come'on, you fuckin' bitches!

Come'on!" I even sound ballsy to myself. But they are most definitely not impressed.

I'm pushed through a door of an oak-paneled saloon, something out of the roaring twenties or whatever they used to call it. There are bitches standing like department store mannequins all along the walls and some ten or so are sleeping in a heap in a corner like cats. Most are naked, but it's impossible to get any more detail because it is so dimly lit.

A tall, dark-haired one enters the room from an arched doorway. On either side of her are girls that stand at least six feet tall, straight-haired and milky-eyed. They chatter their teeth imperceptibly. The main bitch stops and the two side bitches approach and pat me down. I go to kick one of them but her hand grabs my leg feeling every bit as if a pit bull has clamped his jaws on my thigh.

They then get on either side of me and hold me by the arms and shoulders; feels like I'm tied to an oak tree.

"Kent," the head bitch says. "How nice to see you." Her voice is raspy like two pieces of sandpaper getting rubbed together.

"How do you know my name?" I ask. Then it dawns on me. Seconds pass. "Jen? Is that you?"

Tears run down my cheeks as I see the absence of human light in Jen's eyes. This whole trip has become meaningless, and yet I would have gone crazy not knowing her fate had I stayed back in Denver.

Jen is truly evolved, she's one of the talkers. She explains to me that the bitches are organized along the lines of beehives only there are more "queen bees" than a real hive, which has only one. She tells me that the hives are in communication with each other but does not explain how and that most of the zombies do not speak but respond to subtle non-verbal signals given by the queens. It becomes obvious, as if it wasn't obvious long ago, that the bitches are taking over the Earth, evolving into something powerful, albeit undead. I'm thinking this is not necessarily a bad thing. After all, guys did a way less than perfect job for the first ten thousand years or so.

"Jen, are you going to kill all the men?" I ask and then realize it sounds like I'm pleading for my life which at this point I don't give two shits about. At least I'm thinking that but you never know. People can bullshit themselves into temporarily believing anything.

"Do you still love me?" I ask her. Holy crap, I think, I never thought I'd ask such a lame question.

"Sure," she says trying to take the sandpaper edge off her voice and looking into my eyes. Those white, milky eyes don't say much but there is something there that ain't good. "Of course I do." I know for a fact that when you ask someone a question with a yes or no answer, the "of course" is bullshit, complete and total.

"Have the women taken over the whole Earth?" I ask.

She looks at me as if to say, what's it to you?

"Yes. We have left small islands for the men. We need them. When the time for the circle to close arrives, things will be different."

She explains their attempt to keep at least ten percent of the twenty to twenty-five year old bitches pregnant.

"But how do you get the guys . . . " I ask forgetting that most guys will fuck anything that moves. I had a friend named Andy from Iowa who did sheep. Lots of guys do their dogs. It's a sick world but I'm not the one to judge.

"Let me show you," she rasps. I follow her into what was obviously a storage area. There are three wooden tables dimly lit and on the tables are three guys each naked face down. They are guarded by six bitches, two for each guy. There are buckets full of stool and vomit at the edges of the room, a slop sink and a neat row of plastic cups on a shelf near a sink. Jen nods her head to one of the bitches who goes to the sink and lifts a long neck beer bottle out of it.

The bitch with the bottle grabs a cup and robotically goes to the guy on the left of the three. She signals one of his guards who takes the cup from her and kneels down beside the table and partly under it. I see then that the guy's dick is hanging through a hole in the table. She places the cup under his dick while the first one inserts the long neck into his ass. He groans but I can see he is too weak and too tied down with rope and duct tape to move. She inserts the neck straight down and then tilts it backward toward his feet slowly, working his prostate. I've heard of this technique of course, hear it makes it harder to resist if its worked the right way . The kneeling bitch starts pulling his dick like she's milking a cow and in maybe fifteen seconds she has milked him of his cum in small ropey squirts while he moans, perhaps a little more out of pain than ecstasy.

The cup is brought over to Jen, but as she begins to look at it, an explosion rocks the place. Dust falls from the ceiling. Then another. The bitches begin to run around madly, with their insane chittering teeth and grunting, a few vomiting the blackish ooze. Jen looks at me and slaps me so hard I fall to the floor almost unconscious.

"What the fuck," I say looking up at her as she raises her booted foot as if to crush my skull. I roll out of the way and it comes smashing down where my head used to be.

"Jen, it's me. I didn't do anything," I plead. Another explosion rocks the place and I can see search beams glistening through newly opened chinks in the walls and ceiling.

"I didn't do anything. I don't know what's going on. I swear," I say.

"You brought them here, you fucker. You brought them here."

"Believe me, I didn't."

She reaches for a piece of pipe that has fallen from the ceiling but I'm too fast. I leap for the hatch door that got me here and I'm running down the drain pipe as fast as I can crouched over. There are bitches ahead of me running in the same direction. A light is focused on the end of the drain; I can see it ahead. Bitches are running out and being mowed down by rapid arms fire. Fuck, I'm thinking. I turn around and Jen and two bitches are chasing me. If I run out, I'm dead. If I stay, I'm dead. Another explosion rocks the pipe and sand sifts through the seams like small water falls. I can hear distant gunfire, shouts, screams, the grunting of the killing zombie bitches, men calling to each other and the repetitive sounds of explosions.

I stop at the mouth of the drain pipe and turn around to face Jen.

"You gotta believe me," I yell at her. "I love you."

"Fuck you," she yells and runs at me faster than I've ever seen a zombie run. She has the pipe in her hand coming at me like a knight on a horse with a lance. Instead of backing away or running, which would take me into the fire storm outside, I crouch low as she takes a plunge at me and trip her up. The other bitches stop in their tracks as they see their queen go down. I get on top of her and pin her shoulders to the floor of the drain pipe.

"Fuck you and your kind to hell," she screams, spitting the black ooze onto my face and almost blinding me.

I look in her eyes, remember who she was, the times we had, wanting so much to kiss her and hold her, but knowing in my heart this is not that Jen. This thing is something using Jen's body and brain, but it sure as shit isn't my girl. "Sorry, you fucking zombie bitch from hell," I say as I yank the pipe from her hand, place it under her jaw. I guess you're just not into me anymore." I jam the pipe up through her lower jaw, teeth stuck in the black ooze seeping from her mouth. "It coulda been real nice." I press my knee against the bottom of the pipe and knee kick it as hard as I can. Her brain pops out the top of her head along with shards of her skull, her eyeballs getting sucked inwards as they are dragged out with her brain at the point of the pipe.

I suddenly feel the two bitches on my back, both biting into my shoulders going for my neck. With all my might, I leap out of the culvert into the glare of the search light.

"Don't shoot. Don't shoot!" It's Tim barking orders. "Kent, get out of the way."

I have no idea what he means but I just crouch down as the bitches have begun gnashing their teeth into my shoulder blades.

"Get these fuckers off me, for Christ's sake," I yell.

Before the words are even out, I can feel the thuds of clubs crushing the bitches' skulls, ooze and brain matter running down my face and neck. They are yanked off of me and riddled with machine gun fire. I look up and see Ryan and Tim standing together with Uzis smoking. "Welcome aboard, Captain," says Tim.

Bitches are leaping out of windows, through doors and out the drain pipe like cockroaches. There must be two hundred of them. Some guys armed only with baseball bats are jumped and have their throats torn out but instead of being eaten, they are left to die. Gunfire sputters incessantly, bitches heads being blown off in every direction. One of the guys has a girl on the ground and while his pal holds her down with a well-planted boot on her chest, smashing her face in, he puts the barrel of his shotgun in her crotch and explodes her from the inside out, covering his friend in zombie gore.

"Good shot, you crazy fucker," he says.

"Don't worry, it washes off." They both laugh and move on to more killing.

The bitches seem to outnumber the men and there are clearly some of them in charge. An old gray-haired hag screams something that I can't make out and six bitches charge at me where I lie on the ground. Tim and Ryan open fire and the zombies drop where they're hit, but one lands on top of me oozing stink and black blood, biting at me through my shirt.

"Oh fuck!" I yell. Tim pulls her off by the hair but not before she has latched on to my left nipple with her teeth and it comes away with her head and she's standing there chewing it like its bubble gum.

I grab my chest which is bleeding and lean forward.

"You didn't need that anyway, honey," says Ryan as he smashes the bitch in the face with the butt of his gun and caves her nose in like a rotten cabbage.

In a half hour, maybe less, the bitches lay dead and dying everywhere. We only lost about ten guys but I use the term "only" without fully realizing the tragedy of us losing anyone.

One of the guys is patching me up with a first aid kit. Ryan sits by me.

"We knew there were bitches hiding somewhere in town. We've actually searched that theater two or three times. Didn't know it had a 'speak-easy' room downstairs. Fred tells me that's what he thinks it was. Left over from prohibition days when a girl couldn't get a drink in a decent establishment. Guess the Brookstone family knew what they were doing. No wonder they bought up half the town back in the day."

"But what made you find it tonight," I say aware of the more-than-coincidence timing of the attack.

"You did," Ryan says. "I didn't believe your story about wandering across this whole fucked-up country to hang out in Provincetown with a bunch of sissies. You were after someone, likely a girl. That hangdog look I've seen when I was in the army. Every swinging dick with a girl back home had that same sappy look even in the middle of the action. We knew zombies were stealing guys here and there; that they were not just strolling off into the night. To what? The world gone mad? I don't think so. They were kidnapped and brought here. Some for food, some for milking. Can't believe they outsmarted us this long."

An explosion lights up the sky. The dinner theater has been doused with gasoline at the foundation and set ablaze, its weathered old siding like dried up kindling flash-firing, thick orange smoking billowing into the night air. We can hear screams inside.

"There were men in there," I say.

"We got them out. The screams are the pregnant bitches. If any of our guys were going to be daddys, it wasn't going to be like this."

Ryan heads over to a thirty-five-foot sail boat, docked at the only remaining dock in P-Town. The mast glows white against the darkening sky of evening but orange beams from the setting sun make the boat glow as it rocks slowly on the still sea. As we get closer, I see the name of the boat: "MG."

"The guy that owned this beauty collected antique sports cars," says Ryan. "He loved MGs. Had a red MG-TD. I think it was a 1952. Beautiful convertible with a black rag top and wire wheels. He owned the dinner theater. Left here when the disease first started. Think he had family in Boston. Haven't heard a word since, of course."

Steve, a man I'd only seen briefly at the restaurant, arrived with a few of the guys in a dune buggy. He had packed his bag and had sea charts rolled up in a leather strap.

"Seeing as Kent is the Captain, Father Steve, I guess you'll be the navigator," says Tim.

"Look, let's get this straight. I'm not a priest. I didn't even finish the first year of seminary. So please, do not call me 'Father' unless I am your father and if I am, your mother was my right palm and named Melanie after this girl I knew who waited tables at a diner near my house in Parsippany, New Jersey. Your mother named Melanie?"

"No, Father," says Tim. "I mean Steve. You're not planning on preaching to us are you?"

"You think you need it?" Steve says.

"Probably, but it wouldn't do any good," answers Tim.

"I didn't think so. So, no, I'll just stick to navigating, if that's all right with you," says Steve a broad smile on his face.

"I never got your last name, Steve," I say.

"Hadley, Stephen Hadley," he responds.

Most of the night we stock the boat with provisions, re-check our water supply and batteries.

The next morning the three of us board the MG and a few of the guys, mostly seminarians, are on the dock to say farewell. Ryan comes over to me and shakes my hand.

"Are you sure you want to leave us. This place is as safe as any, you know. And you're welcome here," he says.

"Like I said last night, Jen told me there are islands out there with guys on them. I gotta see if there is some way we can communicate with each other. At some point, the bitches will come for you guys. You're not going to stand a chance. I think you know that and don't take it personal."

"I don't," he says looking out at the horizon as if truth was rising instead of the sun.

"We'll radio back every day. It's a slim hope, I know, but there has to be some point in our surviving and the only way we can do it is to join forces with any men out there who have not already fallen off the deep end and try to end this thing for good. We'll sail down the coast and check out the barrier islands, then make our way to Puerto Rico, Cuba, the Caymans."

"Sounds like fun, Kent," he says. "Maybe God really is a guy and he'll keep an eye on you."

I look at him like I don't know what he means. But I do.

"Red sky at morning, sailor take warning; red sky at evening, sailor take warning," says Tim. Everyone looks at him.

"Say what?" asks Ryan.

"He's okay," I say. "Not the brightest bulb on the Rockefeller Center tree, but a good buddy."

The moon is a fingernail in the sky, the stars mute witnesses to our voyage. The wind has made us her sons and we are soaring through the sky reflected in the Atlantic, deeply black, glistening, vibrant. Beneath us, the sea teems with life; I imagine dolphins and Wright whales following us through schools of fish so huge they run to the horizon, dense enough to lift us out of the water and carry us on their backs. Tim is at the helm. Steve is reading his charts in the cabin, the soft glow of the desk lamp reflecting up onto his focused face. The wind slaps the sail and I see the North Star behind us, ducking under a stray cloud but ever present.

END

Zoot Campbell lives in Massachusetts with his wife and two children. He is busy writing *Zombie Bitches From Hell* part 2.

www.ingramcontent.com/pod-product-compliance
Lightning Source LLC
Chambersburg PA
CBHW031955240626
47153CB00003B/988